THE
HOUSE
 OF
MOUNTFATHOM

ALSO BY NIGEL MCDOWELL

TALL TALES FROM PITCH END

THE BLACK NORTH

THE
HOUSE
OF
MOUNTFATHOM

Nigel McDowell

With illustrations by Edward Carey

First published in Great Britain in 2017 by
HOT KEY BOOKS
80–81 Wimpole St, London W1G 9RE
www.hotkeybooks.com

A CIP catalogue record for this book is available from the British Library.

ISBN: 9781471404047
also available as an ebook

1

This book is typeset using Atomik ePublisher
Printed and bound by Clays Ltd, St Ives Plc

Hot Key Books is an imprint of Bonnier Zaffre Ltd,
a Bonnier Publishing company
www.bonnierpublishing.com

This story is for Chris: with love and thanks, for everything. For *always*…

I came on a great house in the middle of the night,
Its open lighted doorway and its windows all alight,
And all my friends were there and made me welcome too;
But I woke in an old ruin that the winds howled through . . .

'The Curse of Cromwell', W.B. Yeats

'You must face the Monster,' says father to son. 'You must know the Unknown.'

'How?' says the son. 'I will be alone.'

'No,' says his father. 'You are so very far from being alone.' Takes a breath, goes on. 'I want you to think of this: time can be likened to a well-thumbed book, can it not? It could feel akin to a familiar and much-read story?'

Son is unwilling to think, doesn't wish to theorise. But he nods.

His father says, 'So, does it not then stand to reason that with careful diligence and understanding of the story, you may learn to flick ahead or browse backwards? Does that not strike you as simply logical?'

'I suppose,' says the son. 'If I knew the story well enough?'

'Indeed!' says the father with sudden passion. 'This is the possibility! But as you say so rightly, if you do not know well the story, you risk losing your place. But more than this, you may risk losing your own self . . .'

Father settles back into bed.

Son sits silent beside, and wonders, What now or next? Where to journey in the dark? But it is late. Flames shrinking blue in the hearth, firewood snapping like stiff knuckles. And the rain – started hours earlier and hasn't eased, impatient fingertip-patter against panes.

The son says, 'Everything is failing now. So how can I know where to begin? If I have no destination, how can I be sure where the door will lead?'

'You cannot,' says his father, in a keen whisper. And manages to smile. 'You cannot know for certain what awaits in the dark. And is that not a great excitement? As with an unknown story on the shelf – where will you be taken? My advice is this: simply open the book, and trust. Turn the page, and so begin . . .'

PART ONE

THE CHILD

Lord & Lady Mountfathom request the
pleasure of your company at their home –
The House of Mountfathom
On Christmas Eve
To raise a toast to the joy of the Christmas season!
And also to celebrate the joyous
Naming of their son . . .
Festivities will commence at Seven o'clock
in *The World*
*** Please note – you are warmly
encouraged to Conduct ***

Directions?

There is a road. A narrow way that circles countryside in twist and hairpin and meander and whirlabout, but difficult to find – not a road that maps are keen to show. Stop and ask a local? 'Not just anyone can find that road,' they'd say. 'And even if you do, you'd never know where it might lead!'

If you are somehow fortunate enough to discover this road, follow it.

There is a wall: high and hemming in swarming forest. Visitors wonder, *Is it behind there?*

On one side, a lake, grey and cool and flat, split by a causeway of stone that stretches from stone shore to a small crannog and a stone tor. The surface of the lake slowly swells and subsides – some say it breathes.

Visitors ask, 'How do people ever find this House?'

Answer: to be led or allowed is the only way in – to have been invited.

And the road ends. And still only that swarm of forest before you . . . so where now? A blink and heartbeat and suddenly swarming forest is separated by a new road – shingle and broken shell. And so the visitor can proceed into a delicious dark.

Gentle progress, as though burrowing, as though being slowly swallowed. Forest stays close on either side.

A procession of limestone pillars next, each topped with a silvery limestone lion bearing a limestone shield engraved with a coat of arms; not for nothing is this called the King's Entrance. Holding their breath, guests pass beneath the watch of the lions and some tingle in the spine makes them feel as though they should look back – did that limestone lion open its mouth? Lift a left forepaw to rest on its limestone shield?

But too late to puzzle or ponder more – on and in and on . . . and suddenly out! From shadow into such a sight.

Christmas Eve

'They're here!'

They arrive. From everywhere and from dawn onwards! On motorcycle and horseback and in motorcar and pulled trap!

Up the front steps –
    fur-coat,
        top hat,
            tails going flap-flap!
                Boots black,
                    bags stacked,
                        heels clack!

Another hysterical cry from one of the Erranders: 'They're here! They're HERE!'

Slap across the back of the head from Clodagh (head housekeeper of Mountfathom) and, 'Compose yourself, you silly clot!'

In come Earl and Duchess, Viscount and Viceroy, Monsieur and Madame, Major and –

'Welcome to Mountfathom!'

Mr Findlater, the manservant, is by the door in his best – shined shoes, maroon velvet suit, hair slicked – there to receive whichever personage with whatever present, and to make careful note of each.

One scrimshawed narwhal horn (nine feet long)

One small malachite statue in the shape of a Griffin

One pewter dish large as a cartwheel

A pair of Chinese vases, painted, telling the Tale of the Lonely Tailor

A trio of crystal vials labelled Happiness, Contentment and Knowledge

A pair of orbs (jet and jade)

A pair of sewn silver fish-scale gloves

A rattle made from bone (possibly human?) that makes no sound when shaken

A (badly water-damaged) copy of Peter Pan

A (badly fire-damaged) copy of Alice In Wonderland

A crate of mangoes

A scarlet umbrella (useless – full of holes!)

A (possibly half-eaten!) bag of boiled strawberry sherbet sweets

One rifle

One wicker basket containing a very small kitten the colour of smoke and with turquoise eyes (purring)

Clodagh: 'A very good evening! Happy to have you at Mountfathom!'

And author and auteur and artisan . . . and some with no title at all – Sullivan from the cattle farm down the Shore Road, and Billy McMaster who delivers the coal on a Monday, and Miss Bellow who runs a boy's boarding-school near Belfast –

Findlater: 'How are you? How's things? Go on ahead in! What did you say your name was? How did you spell that? Say again?'

Good thing Clodagh is there to smooth things.

'Yes, of course – I spoke to you only yesterday. No problem at all. You are on the second floor, fifth door along eastwards – your room is *Berlin*. The boys here will take your bags. And just be cautious when opening the wardrobes in your room – that's all I'll say or else I'll spoil Lord Mountfathom's surprise!'

Such excitement from the staff as they go toing-and-froing –

'Did you see the man with the gold and diamond mask?'

'See that woman with the purple parrot on her shoulder?'

'Men with needles through their noses!'

'Women leading black and white spotted cats!'

'Yes,' says Clodagh (for a change, excitable herself). 'I have seen some sights in this House, but I tell you – this is something else!'

Speech

Meanwhile: upstairs in *The Amazon* –

'*Adventure!*'

Out comes the child's first word.

'Heavens above!' This is the nanny, name of Bogram. 'Hardly six months old and listen to you – already starting with the chat!'

Child sees her reaction so cries aloud again. '*Adventure!*'

10

Not a normal first word? No normal child . . .

'Yes, I know,' says Bogram, her mood (as is usual) somewhere between amusement and dismay. 'No more talk – we need to be getting you ready for this party.'

She heaves a copper kettle from the range and fills a porcelain basin – bit of soap, bit of a stir to make a skin of suds. And she settles the child in the water. But always he wants to explore and grabble and grab – his face is a crush of concentration as his hand goes out and fingers snatch for the nearest enticing thing: a delicious and innocent-looking flicker . . .

'Not the bloody candle!' Nanny Bogram lifts the candlestick clear and scolds, 'That's burny, so it is! You do yourself an injury and I'll be in some trouble, won't I?' Would describe herself as 'no-nonsense', this woman (if she was the sort of woman to describe herself). She watches the child, and the child watches back. 'You're a strange one,' she says, not for first nor final time. The mouth of the child opens wide with excitable laughter. 'God, aye,' Mrs Bogram says, 'you're a strange enough little creature. And I tell you this: you've no idea the stranger world you've been brought into.'

Head & Heart & Haven

When the child was born six months before, the parents wept; pair of them prouder than proud! First child of Lord and Lady Mountfathom; late gift in life, longed for yet unexpected. Precious. *Treasured*.

'Has your intelligence, I'd say. Your brave heart!' said the father.

'Has your curiosity. Your level head!' said the mother.

Saw so much of themselves in the little bundle of fidgeting limb and bright looks.

'And he shall sleep in *The Amazon*!' announced Lord Mountfathom.

'Oh, indeed,' says Lady Mountfathom. 'Perfect choice!'

But some of the staff had doubt –

'Bit scary for an infant, no?'

'No end of rooms in this house so why that one?'

'Bit dark?'

'Bit odd?'

Odd indeed, yet isn't that the way of Lord and Lady Mountfathom?

The Amazon: like constant dusk despite curtains flung back, like sultry summer even with windows wide. Wallpaper a scene of lush leaf and untamed vine and keen creeper – vast rainforest, full of restless twitch and shiver.

'Now that's some crafty foreign Magic!' supplied Findlater. Stern fella, called 'Mr Sunshine' by some of the Errander boys. Swiping a hot iron across the day's papers he told all staff gathered in the cavernous kitchen, 'Oh, aye – wallpaper was a gift from a Folkmancer in Kerry. Was given to the fifth Lord of Mountfathom – he helped drive a pair of Copse Gyants out of the county and that was his reward. Must be a hundred year old or more!'

And Mrs Little the cook said, 'Ach, you're full of these fancy stories, Reginald Findlater! Always some mad idea you have!'

Well, however long it had hung for, or from wherever it hailed, the walls of *The Amazon* were more alive than they'd been for long years with the arrival of the child. And careful and watchful and looking as though they're listening in: eyes half-hidden behind branch and bough and tall grass, onyx-bright and baleful to the staff but benevolent to Mother and Father Mountfathom.

'Oh yes,' said the Lord, 'he shall have such fun in here! And know such safety.'

'Of course,' said the Lady. 'Our little boy – he will have such adventures!'

No delay; a crib was conjured quick, composed of bamboo and cord. A hood of muslin that Mrs Bogram embroidered with silver stars; blanket of cream Egyptian silk, pillow packed with goose-feather. Lord Mountfathom found two stuffed toys – capybara and tapir – to set on either side of his son. Lady Mountfathom set a Spell of Accompaniment on an old harp – the strings twitched and quivered and sent soft notes all by themselves.

And the child was settled.

Yet still the staff wondered, was a baby beyond the trusted Lord and Lady? The pair who had ventured so far, seen such extraordinary sights and crossed uncrossable countries? Courted exotic king and imperious queen? Cheered maudlin poets and manic painters? Charmed that stubborn prime minister and those inscrutable priests? Settled disputes, eased ageless grudges, brokered peace with man and beast and creature and cunning Good Folk? Was the care of a child too much?

Meanwhile, the child's mother read him *The Jungle Book*.

Meantime, the child's father read him *Curious Creatures of the Canopy*.

Midnight: the eyes of the child are wakeful, watching the walls. And the eyes of the walls watched over the child, both brimming with a mildly mutual curiosity . . .

'Such a one!'

At night The Traces come, those pale vestiges of past Lords and Ladies of Mountfathom, lingering in the dark places of the House. They curl around the crib – around cornice and ceiling-rose and whisper –

'Oh such a child! Such a wee marvel!'

'Such an oddness though! Such a one!'

'Such a good creature to carry on the name of Mountfathom!'

'He will see so much. And not all of it good.'

'It is a wonder indeed to watch him, is it not?'

'Teaches us things! Things we lost along the long way!'

'Something so easily forgotten –'

'How everything in the world was once so new.'

Who Where When?

A month before the party: head housekeeper Clodagh stood on the second floor of Mountfathom in the dark of the Gabbling Gallery. Only mirrors adorn the walls here, crowded from skirting board to ceiling. Dark mirrors. Clodagh is stationed with ledger and pencil. Good thing patience is a thing of pride for this housekeeper – needs plenty for this job.

Invitations had been out for a day, so Clodagh waited, knowing it is only a matter of short time before –

One wakes!

In the dark of the mirror are wisps of brightening white . . . eyes appear and a face too and finally a voice full of imperious enquiry. 'Major Fortflay here! Served in the Land Wars with the late Lord Mountfathom Sixth! Received the invitation – would be happy to attend!'

Now Clodagh – so pre-prepared she can't be perturbed – calmly consulted her ledger list and says simply, 'Very good, Major.'

Face of Major Fortflay dissipated.

Darkness returned, silence restored.

Clodagh made her careful notes.

Scarcely a moment though; another mirror yawned white.

'Lady Anne of Lissadell House here! How's tricks? So this shindig on Christmas Eve – what time shall I land?'

And so. And so on . . .

The arrangements were made.

Promises

'Sir, this was tucked in with the morning post.'

Two weeks before the party, Mr Findlater handed a scrap of paper to Lord Mountfathom over breakfast in the Seasonal Room. It read:

> *WE KNOW YOU HAVE A WEE*
> *CHILD NOW IN THERE.*
> *YOU THINK YOU CAN BE SAFE BEHIND*
> *ALL YOUR FANCY SPELLS*
> *AND THAT HIGH WALL?*
> *WRONG!*

WE WILL COME WHEN YOU EXPECT
IT LEAST AND FROM A PLACE YOU
WOULDN'T THINK TO LOOK!
KEEP AN EYE ON THE DARK.
KEEP AN EYE ON YOUR WEE CHILD.
THINGS ARE SHIFTING.
WE PROMISE AND SWEAR – YOU WON'T
HAVE ALL THE POWERS FOREVER.
YOU'LL REGRET IT ALL
BEFORE THE END.

'Forget we received this,' Lord Mountfathom told his manservant. He Worked his fingers in the air and Magic set the page alight – darkened and curled and disappeared. Lord Mountfathom stood from his breakfast and wandered the Seasonal Room – from Summer to Spring to Winter to Autumn. He stopped, floor around his feet littered with bronze leaves, and said, 'Keep me informed of anything you notice that is more unusual than the usual unusual of Mountfathom. These are odd and dark enough days we live in, Mr Findlater – we must be on our guard.'

Preparations . . .

Every chandelier was lowered and every shard washed! Every brass bit and bob – dish and spoon and snuffbox and doorknob – buffed and polished. Every floor swept and wetted, furniture beeswaxed and portraits touched up. Mr Hooker, the gardener, got to work pruning and keeping neat the trees in the Upstairs and Downstairs Orchards. Everywhere: elbow-grease and sweat and ache and groan as every maid and Errander boy in his livery got behind the effort of readying the place for the party. And Lady Mountfathom helped too. 'Get me a ladder and wet rag and I'll catch a few of those cobwebs!'

Lord Mountfathom does his bit: sets some Spells to surprise –

In *Berlin*, a Spell on the wardrobe that will play Bach when it is opened.

In *Atlantis*, the sounds of exploding surf when someone turns in the bed.

He wants to fill the House with sound and music and Magic! So in the hallways and passageways and galleries stone faces surmounting doorways sing an aria or recite Byron or Shelley when anyone passes by, and the patterns on the carpet of Ash-Dragons and Kelpies writhe and squirm beneath feet when anyone crosses . . .

Five Minutes to Seven

Now guests are duly gathered inside the House, but the double doors of *The World* are shut. They all ask one another waiting –

'How long till seven?'

'Is it yet?'

'Is it now?'

Agitation and clash of elbows as pocket watches are consulted. Same answer given everywhere.

'Not yet. Not just yet.'

Four Minutes to Seven

A veil of rippling smoke obscures the double doors. The guests wonder –

'What Spell? Some Weather-Working?'

'I'd say more like Smoke-Spinning.'

'Well, perhaps . . . perhaps . . .'

Three Minutes to Seven

Time for some description? Just about.

Such extravagant dress! Such articles! Which to pick out amongst the many? For a start: skirts that shimmer like wind-ruffled water; suits comprised of crimson leaves; patterned kimonos where the patterns move – carp encircling one torso and a pair of cranes picking their way across another and murmuration of starlings on one more and –

'*Two minutes!*'

Two Minutes to Seven

Everything lit with a low light.

A pair of trees on either side of the doors – candelabra, of a kind; foliage of flickering flame. Flame overhead too – chandeliers arranged with pencil-thin tapers.

Somebody cries, '*One minute!*'

One Minute More

Passes like a blink and breath and a forever. Then –
  'Welcome!'
  All attention to a face they hadn't noticed, top and centre of the doorway, carved into stone lintel. It says, 'Welcome, friends! On behalf of the esteemed Lord and Lady, welcome to the House of Mountfathom! And we welcome you most warmly to the myriad wonders of *The World!*'

Curtain Up

Smoky pall peels away; doors ease open and in they go in delighted tide . . .

The Room with The World Inside

What else but round? Above: glow of a gilt ceiling. Below: circular stone floor. And around them the wall curving smooth and begging to be touched! Lay a hand and follow and you'd find no flaw, fingers running over a frieze of green-gold-azure, a sprawling map of ocean and continent which gives way at the farthest end to glass – wall split by tall double doors that lead to . . . no, not just yet. Too much inside to see!

Every Poison

Curving table tight to curving wall, and on it are the fruits of Mrs Little's labour and all anyone's appetite could dream up –

A battalion of boars' heads with mandarins clamped between jaws; palm-sized pies stuffed with game; tarts of pear and raspberry and gooseberry with sugary crusts . . . And to wash it all down – whiskey and ice wine and port and madeira and champagne. Liveried footmen in lilac wigs go about pouring; maids in ivory caps and aprons and silver boots are busy proffering and smiling and topping-up. Mr Findlater and Clodagh keep watch, keep generous and gentle order.

And all the while overhead, some spectacular Smoke-Spinning: masses of writhing grey-white, taking shape for a second – a lion there? Sphinx? Sea snake? Certainly shoals of quick fish – darting down to skim scalps and elicit whoops and gasps. The guests remember the invitation: *Please note – you are warmly encouraged to Conduct.*

So some of the guests add their own delights – the group of ladies in kimonos raise Reeds and with a quick together-twitch they Summon soft notes, Summon an Ash-Dragon that snaps smoky jaws at the other Smoke-Spun shapes and makes them shreds. The men clothed in crimson leaves are not to be outdone – whirl Staffs with small bells that make small sounds, and sound itself brings the sight – a trio of albatross that race the dragon around and around the domed ceiling . . .

The room is soon full of tatters of smoke sifting the air like snowfall. And the eating and drinking and laughter and joy – pure *joy* – rises to such a pitch that it can only be somehow stilled by the sudden opening once again of *The World's* double doors.

The Family

Enter Lord and Lady and young Master Mountfathom. Lady Mountfathom wrapped in crushed crimson velvet, strings of cultured pearls and earrings shaped like seashells and her one simple wedding band. At her belt she wears a key clustered with crimson stones. Lord Mountfathom is more adorned – scarlet suit and tails, gold on shoe-buckle and cuff, gold thread embroidering his waistcoat in coil and curlicue and golden rings on each finger. And at his waist too a key, though his is composed of polished emeralds.

The child is in a simple blue suit. Proud mother and father each hold a hand, but truth is this child needs no leading. Only six months old, but as though he has been walking for years! Has a look on his face of such concentration: gently knitted brow and pout of mouth saying he would like to be moving faster, but is at the same time happy. Mrs Bogram walks a little behind, unnoticed by most. She sheds a single tear. Tells herself she is being a silly old thing.

And the crowd parts for the Mountfathoms –

'Aw, look at him! The big smile!'

'Such a happy child! Such a dear!'

'He'll be a force in the world and make no mistake!'

'And the eyes!'

'The eyes!'

'*The eyes!*'

What of the eyes? Colour or shape? Maybe size? Whom they take after most – greater resemblance to mother or father Mountfathom? Difficult to say. Simpler just to say this: to be looked at by those eyes is to feel investigated and examined.

The Mountfathom family reach the centre of *The World*.

And then fresh interruption –

All heads turn as the glass doors in the glass wall waft open.

Visitors

The Mountfathoms move towards the door and out into the night. Guests follow as though Enchanted.

In the garden: fullest face of moon, sky sharp with stars and the slow splash of water, fountains streaming into a pair of ponds. And soon collecting on shoulders and settling in hair and sending pleasant shivers: *snow*. But how with such a clear sky and no cloud? Surely some Spell?

The guests descend steps and land on a wide lawn and stand amongst eight towering stone pillars – eight statues of animals sit atop.

The Mountfathom family stand centre.

No one speaks.

Now some gentle movement in the dark.

One guest guesses well in a whisper: '*The Driochta.*'

First a cheetah appears – pads the length of the surrounding wall, yawns wide and then drops soundlessly onto lawn. It sits there, so shrewd of eye and sharp of claw. Sits patient beside a pillar with a cheetah poised on top.

Mere moments and then the next.

Silent swoop of a long-eared eagle owl that alights on the statue of itself. It watches the crowd, looks to the Mountfathoms.

Now something not so subdued.

Boughs groan and branches clash as some wild darkness swings fast towards the House as though promising violence and then is suddenly so present it makes some of the guests gasp and some others step back. A chimpanzee – glaring at them and rapping tough knuckles on the ground like he's enjoying the scares caused.

Now something softer.

Three forms in quiet flight – one black, one white, one resplendent. A pair of swans skims one of the ponds and slows to a stop as a peacock settles lightly on the lawn.

All assembled animals regard each other.

Eight statues, six animals: the guests look around seeking the final two, but no time to wonder more as –

'Our friends!' says Lord Mountfathom, addressing the animals. He peels away his tailcoat to show a Needle of gleaming but careworn metal bound to his belt – a thing scarcely longer than a pen, but sharp. 'Our dear friends, thank you for coming.'

'And now!' says Lady Mountfathom (notice, too, she has the same kind of short metallic rod at her waist). 'Now, we request that you show us your truest selves.'

Mogrify

Only some are watching keen or attentively enough to see. Only a few see the moment the Spell is shaken off. One of these, of course, is the child.

'Changing!' he cries.

What is reflected in the child's widening eyes: a quick shiver and wriggle as the animals become a squirm of colour, notional and undecided . . . and now suddenly become someone. Many someones.

Peacock: a tall woman with hair piled high, dressed iridescent and with opals clustered at her throat.

Pair of swans: woman dressed in black with a cascade of white hair, a man dressed in ivory with tresses of dark falling to his shoulders.

Eagle owl: small bald man with wire spectacles and an unassuming look.

Cheetah: fine man in a fine suit (first thing he does to keep himself fine is dust off his shoulders with sharp flicks of the hand).

Chimpanzee: a broad boulder of a man in his Sunday best.

One similarity in all these arrivals – same as the Mountfathoms, at their waists they have fastened short batons of a bright yet battered metal.

They step forward, footsteps a soft crunch on snow, and form a close circle.

Some gap is left, enough for two more to stand – an opening that Lord and Lady Mountfathom let their son wander through. In the centre of the circle the child stands, turning and turning so he can examine the people standing around. He smiles.

Proud parents take their place and close the circle.

All hands go to those sharp points of metal at their belts – these things the Driochta call Needles.

'And now,' says Lord Mountfathom, 'the Gifts.'

'And now,' says Lady Mountfathom, 'the Words.'

Tradition

Needles directed night-skyward – to the same point high over the child's head. And around the circle and in turn, Words are gifted –

'*Intleacht!*'

'*Paisean!*'

'*Cinneadh!*'

'*Trua!*'

'*Cairdeas!*'

'*Alainn!*'

'*Eachtra!*'

'*Gra!*'

And as one the Driochta Conduct – conjure bright trails of smoke that take the shape of the same animals that arrived moments before and that go whirling around the child, who is transfixed and adoring of this Magic. Who smiles to himself as the guests smile to themselves also – the sight of these Spells and this child sitting below feels like a glimpse of some precious peace . . .

Attack

Lord Mountfathom says, 'In sight of the Driochta, and with their blessing, we Name this child –'

Suddenly, a single gasp that multiplies into many –

Crowd parts as two figures sprint out of the dark –

Same swift shiver and distortion: in a blink two of the Driochta Mogrify and retake their animal forms, boulder of a man back to chimpanzee and fine gentleman reforming as a cheetah.

The two sprinting figures, two boys, stop. One has dark hair and the other a head of faded hair.

Mrs Bogram is in fear for the child. Wants to run forward to protect him, but the manservant Findlater holds her back.

The Driochta raise their Needles in readiness.

Lord Mountfathom tells the two boys, 'Do not ruin such a night as this – it will solve nothing.'

'Leave,' says Lady Mountfathom, her tone stronger than her husband. 'Be sensible. Depart while you still have some chance!'

The two figures say nothing.

Lady Mountfathom screams with sudden anger, 'I said go!' And she takes her animal form – a sleek panther, sharp clawed, standing guard by her son.

Lord Mountfathom says, 'I think my wife means business.' And he transforms too – into an Irish elk that towers taller than any being in the garden, regal-eyed, antlers branching broad.

Chimpanzee and cheetah inch nearer to the two boys, closing in.

The boy with faded hair takes another step and says, 'Listen to me now – none of this will last. There is no safe place, not even at Mountfathom. Remember these things!'

'Let's go,' says the boy with black hair, and he takes the other boy's hand.

Only moments more, and the two boys bolt – to the sound of more gasps, both figures run back off into the night.

Aftermath

Shock leaves them stranded. Guests recover their voices, and start to shout –

'Shouldn't someone go after them?'

'We can't let them escape, can we? They could've harmed the child!'

But one voice is loudest.

'Is the child okay? Please tell me he isn't hurt! Let me through!'

Nanny Bogram shoves and elbows everyone aside and when she reaches Lord and Lady Mountfathom and the other Driochta they have relinquished any Spells and retaken their human forms.

Child stands. Difficult to say what his expression is – worried, apprehensive? Or perhaps still curious, unsure of all this fuss? Or perhaps nothing at all – only a small child at the centre of a very strange world.

'Mrs Bogram,' says Lady Mountfathom. 'Take our son to his bedroom. I ask that you stay with him. I know you shall keep him safe.'

Mrs Bogram nods. Holds the child in her arms and turns and the crowd flows back and shifts away to allow her through. But as she goes – sound of a sniffle, small hiccup. And that rare sound, one scarcely made in any month of his life so far at Mountfathom: the child begins to cry.

PART TWO

THE BOY

First Principle of Magic –
Of Curiosity & Caution
'For a willingness to acquire more knowledge,
to better understand the world, is crucial
to any understanding of Magic.'

'Quiet! See it? Watch very carefully!'

Luke has cousins close and at his command – on their bellies in the long grass near the fern forest, sun warm on their necks and sounds of spring in their ears. Small things creep across their bare skin; limbs tickle and itch and fingers go scratch and –

'Be a bit stiller,' says Luke. 'Else we might miss it. Keep watching! It's almost time.'

Four cousins do as he bids – all eyes on a small, clinging cocoon on a single stalk. They can see something small and delicate and dark inside, and it is wanting out.

Luke holds his breath.

A cat the colour of smoke suddenly appears – threatens to leap on the stalk and ruin everything!

31

'Morrigan,' says Luke, grabbing the cat and hugging its mass to his chest. Cat squirms and complains. 'Now stay with me – be good.' Cat gives him such a look of annoyance – turquoise eyes turning sour.

Roger says, 'Can we just go inside and have breakfast now? Or do something else? I have an idea for a game.' Roger, who likes to make decisions about everything.

'Quiet,' says Ruth. 'Don't be rude.'

'What is that thing that's going to come out?' asks Rory.

'I'm scared,' says Rose.

'Don't be scared,' says Luke. He takes cousin Rose's hand. 'It won't hurt you. It will just –'

'Look!' says Ruth.

And the cocoon tears a little, like damp paper. And the thing within begins a slow inching out – small and tentative and shiveringly delicate . . . antennae unfurling, twitch of the proboscis and front legs fighting free . . .

'A ghost moth,' says Luke. 'Keep watching. Keep watching.'

But it happens too swift – one moment on the swaying stalk, taking in the world, trying to tease open its wings . . . and then away! Off into the blue air in dance and quiver and soft fall and slow rise, soon lost to Luke's sight in the shimmer of early morning sun.

Luke breathes. Morrigan yawns.

His cousin Rose squeezes his hand and hushes into his ear, 'That was amazing.'

Day before –

Luke asks his father: 'When will I start to learn Spells?'

Lord Mountfathom laughs a little. Tells his son, 'So keen! Not for a little while yet. Ten years old would be very young to start Working Magic. First you must study.'

'When will I learn to Mogrify?' he asks. 'When can I learn that?'

'To Mogrify takes time,' says his father. 'It is an odd and utterly surprising sort of Magic.'

'What does that mean?'

'It means that you shall wake one morning and very suddenly find in yourself some sense of deep and profound difference. Like a door unlocked – with utter ease and conviction, you shall be able to transform, though you may not be able to choose which animal to become.'

Luke stands by the deal-topped desk in the centre of the library. His father is off wandering; many narrow wooden paths criss-cross and bisect the floor and Lord Mountfathom looks as though he is seeking to rediscover something lost. 'Here now!' he says, and stoops and selects a fat volume from the floor – so many books in this library that they occupy not just walls but floor, so many volumes all resting with embossed and gold-printed spines upward . . . and on the ceiling too! Books packed and strapped into shelves and hoisted high.

Luke says, 'I shall be eleven years old in two months – can I not learn some simple Spells today?'

His father tells him, 'Plenty to learn and get to grips with before you start Casting.'

Luke is disappointed. And restless – wants to learn and know everything now and not tomorrow, to hurry up and be the age he needs to be! Time is too slow, he thinks. Feels as though he has been ten for a million years! And he wonders what the

33

point of these hour-long lessons each afternoon with Father or Mother are for if he isn't ready yet. (Could be playing with the cousins, he thinks. They're only here for the week of Easter. Could be having some grand adventures outside in the sun!)

Lord Mountfathom opens the books, fingers searching through pages until – 'Here now! Listen to this, son: *All Magic begins with learning. Patience can be a chore, with so much power within one's reach – but patience must be exercised nonetheless.* There now!'

Luke says nothing. Feels only impatient.

Lord Mountfathom asks, 'How many Principles of Magic are there?'

'Five,' says Luke. (Easy question.)

'Good,' says his father. 'And so you shall learn one every year.'

'One a year?' Luke repeats. 'But that'll take forever!'

'Let us not exaggerate,' says Lord Mountfathom, slotting the volume back into its place in the floor. 'It will take five years, that is all.'

Luke again says nothing – doesn't like arguments or confrontation, and certainly not with his father.

'Now, the First Principle of Magic is something a little like watching,' says Lord Mountfathom, kneeling to pluck another book from the floor – slim, sheathed in dark leather. When he speaks he speaks to ceiling or floor or walls or anything or anywhere except Luke. 'It is foremost about listening and learning! For a willingness to acquire more knowledge, to better understand the world, is crucial to any understanding of Magic. I know that this first Principle will be little or no trouble at all to you.'

'Because I watch all the time!' says Luke. 'And listen too. Mr Hooker told me listening can be like learning.'

'And Mr Hooker is quite right.'

Finally, father arrives beside son. Lord Mountfathom holds out the book he has selected – *A Photographic Account of War.*

Luke takes and opens it and lets the stiff pages flow across his fingertips – sees soldiers and landscapes scorched, sepia portraits of families with a starved look, buildings broken and heaped as rubble . . .

His father says, 'Starting tomorrow, there will be some visitors coming to Mountfathom. I want you to watch them, to learn from them. But most crucially, to attempt to understand them and their place in the world. Will you do this, Luke?'

'Yes,' he replies. 'Who are they, Father?'

Another longish pause; Lord Mountfathom smoothing his moustache, tugging his waistcoat straight and eventually saying, 'Who are they truly? Good question! That is what you must tell me, son. That is the knowledge that you must learn.'

'Who are those chaps?' asks cousin Roger.

After the emergence and escape of the ghost moth, on their way back for breakfast, the children stop. Roger likes to make a game of it: 'Quick, get down, or we shall be seen!'

They crouch by the walled garden to spy on the shingle drive: a pair of vans are parked, big brutes of things – large wheeled, bonnet and doors polished as glossy as oil, canvas-covered trailers at the rear . . .

'Cannot be certain,' says Luke, thinking of what his father told him. 'Let us watch and see a minute.'

Less than a minute: from the gloom beneath the canvas-covered trailers, boys in uniform are expelled shouldering canvas bags, eyes with an intent look and boots black that smash shingle underfoot. They have rifles held tight to their shoulders.

'They must be going to fight in the war!' says Rory. 'I want to go to war . . .'

'You're eleven,' says Ruth. 'Don't be silly.'

'I don't want you to go war anyway,' says Rose.

'Rose, stop being such a cutie-pie,' says Roger.

Rose inserts a clutch of her blonde curls into her jaws to chew. Luke has seen his Aunt Nancy tight-wrapping Rose's hair in damp rags every night, but there is no stopping it – these girlish curls are going.

Luke stays silent, watching.

Mr Findlater is stationed on the front doorstep to greet the soldiers and show them inside.

'Old Mr Sunshine looks happy to see them,' says Rory.

'How many are there, I wonder?' asks cousin Ruth.

Luke counts thirteen and whispers, 'Unlucky number.'

'Talking to yourself again, Luke?' says his cousin Roger. 'Now can we please go and get breakfast – I'm starving to death here!'

But no one moves until Luke says so.

'Yes. Let us go and see what's happening.'

'And there is talk of such unrest being planned!' says Luke's Uncle Walter. 'Such violence has been promised by these malcontents – you know the ones? Pearse and Connolly and the like. Disgraceful! A death wish is what they have, no doubt about it.'

And Lord Mountfathom says nothing and Lady Mountfathom sucks on her cigarette and Aunt Nancy sips her coffee. And Luke watches all.

'Brother dearest,' says Luke's mother, 'just eat your sausages and pipe down. Or you'll induce in yourself another heart attack.'

This is breakfast under the morning sun in the Temple of the Elements. Around a circular stone table split into the four elements and laid all over with platters of cured bacon and smoked salmon and fried sausages and potato, and neat porcelain bowls of strawberries and raspberries and gooseberries. And so hot for Easter! Though Mountfathom is always hotter than elsewhere – Luke has asked many times for the reason and many times been told the word by Mr Hooker: 'micro-climate'. He sees a dark haze of midges here and there, and fat bumblebees crawling into the daffodils, and butterflies (Cabbage Whites? thinks Luke) fawning over the flowerbeds.

'You wait and see,' says Uncle Walter. He spears a sausage on the end of his fork and removes half of it with one bite. 'Just wait and see, sister dearest. There'll be trouble or I'm a Chinaman!'

Debate starts up amongst Luke and his cousins –

Rory: 'Which game shall we play?'

Roger: 'I shall pick first!'

Ruth: 'We should all come up with a suggestion and then vote.'

Roger: 'Don't be a twit.'

Rory: 'Swimming in the lagoon?'

Ruth: 'Chase the Traces?'

But Luke is listening also to his parents and aunt and uncle; always wants to hear and understand the chat of the grown-ups.

'How long are these soldiers to be staying?' asks his Aunt Nancy. She and Uncle Walter sit in the element of Fire. To Luke, his aunt appears more strained than usual – takes her coffee from her cup in little sips. 'Not too long surely? Are they not needed right away on the Front?'

'They shall stay until they are ready,' says Lady Mountfathom. She and Luke's father occupy the element Earth. And Luke takes note of the difference between his mother and aunt: Mother's grubby cigarette, clay from her morning spent in the flowerbeds still clinging to her hair and ground into the seams of corduroy trousers and encrusted to the soles of her wellingtons. And Aunt Nancy: white dress with red tulips, red lipstick, platinum hair perfectly and immovably set (though she presses a careful palm to it every other moment as though it might fall from her head). She says, 'Well, where are these men to sleep? I have young daughters to think of.'

'In the Upstairs Orchard,' says Lord Mountfathom, from behind his copy of *The Dublin Enquirer*.

'What?' shouts Uncle Walter. 'Amongst the trees, is it? Can build themselves a lovely little tree-house!'

And the man laughs, loudly.

'Clodagh has arranged beds from Belfast,' says Luke's mother. 'So the soldiers shall be quite comfortable, don't worry.'

Some uncomfortable silence.

Uncle Walter breaks it when he prods a finger at the front page of Lord Mountfathom's newspaper and bellows, 'Could hardly get into Dublin earlier in the week! Bloody protests and so on!'

Luke reads only the bold headline of the *Enquirer*.

IRISH REBEL REVOLT SPREADS: TENSIONS RISE AS BRITISH GOVERNMENT THREATENS MARTIAL LAW

'I do agree,' says Aunt Nancy, still sip-sipping at her coffee. 'We are at war on the continent, so you would think the Irish might show a little understanding and stop this unrest.'

'Barbarians,' adds Uncle Walter. 'What do you think, William?'

Luke (and all others in the Temple) watches as Lord Mountfathom emerges, slowly, from behind the headline. Watches him fold and settle the newspaper on the stone tabletop.

'These are tough times for all,' says Luke's father. 'No doubt about it. Though I think we should extend our utmost understanding to those who feel aggrieved. It is our duty always to watch, and learn, and understand. Not to judge.'

Lord Mountfathom gives his son a wink.

And Luke watches the effect of his father's words – sees his Aunt Nancy roll her eyes, his uncle swell as though bursting with a surfeit of words but saying none. And his mother – smiling, beaming at her husband. Lady Mountfathom sees her son watching and says suddenly, 'Now, children – away and play! You don't want to be sitting here listening to such dull talk! I hope to see you all at dinner tonight and not a moment before!'

Day is golden. Day is wild and full of adventure! And Luke feels perfectly happy as he and his cousins race through the grounds. To the smokehouse where they dare each other inside, seeing who can stay the longest with the smell of fish. Or the icehouse where the Traces sometimes slumber. Or the space beneath the Rise and the Temple of Ivory where some of the Errander boys say a spiteful crone has taken up residence.

They play –

'Evade the Cailleach!'

'Secret-and-Secluded!'

'Catch!'

Roger concocts games with complex rules only he knows, but all involve saying tongue-twisters and selling their souls for tuppence and standing on their heads until they almost topple unconscious . . .

Rory: 'I know what now – let's play *War*!'

'I am the General,' says Roger. 'Luke, you can be one of the filthy Irish rebel leaders!'

Luke is dubious. But he is saved from disagreeing: sudden shadow covers them, bruised sky as though someone is Storm-Breaching, and the voice of Nanny Bogram calls to them, 'Come on in, children, or else you'll be soaked! Hurry up, now!'

And so inside. But still they find things to do.

Luke shows the cousins his newest finds in his collection of animal bones – complete skeletons of rabbit and hare and magpie and fox, the jawbone of a badger. He has all labelled with times and dates of discovery, names inked in English and Latin on small parchment slips of paper.

Ruth: 'How interesting.'

Rose: 'I don't like these skeletons. They're scary.'

Roger: 'This is rather boring. I still want to be the General . . .'

And the cousins get their game of War: Luke finds his father in the library and asks him to set the Spell on the marble staircase in the entrance hall to make it unending. So under the glass dome at the top of Mountfathom and its cerulean light, Luke and his cousins can run up and up and up and never reach the first floor – attempt to scale the staircase as though it is a mountain with Roger seated above them shouting orders, the others all battling one another and tugging at each other's shoes and tossing them down the steps with Roger telling them, 'You rebels will never conquer this mountain! Not ever be victorious so long as I have breath in my body! Never!'

And soon somehow it is six o'clock: Lord Mountfathom arrives to Dismiss the Spell and tell them it is time for dinner in *The World*.

'Tell us now, lads – looking forward to serving queen and country?' asks Uncle Walter.

The soldiers look at one another.

One says with a half-smirk, 'We're rightly looking forward to doing our bit, Mister. Oh yes. How about you?'

Uncle Walter shifts in his seat. 'I have a gammy leg,' he says, 'so no fighting for me. More's the pity!'

Luke sips his vegetable soup. Never has he sat at such a tense meal – there has always been such fun and chat and laughter in *The World*! Never a silence like this, broken only by so many sharpened words and the too-loud sound of spoons scraping bowls or being abruptly settled.

So many closed mouths around the table – not just soldiers and Lord and Lady Mountfathom and Luke and his cousins and Uncle Walter and Aunt Nancy, but also three members of the Driochta: Mr Lawrence Devine from his farm down the shore road, Lady Vane-Tempest and Mr Flann Dorrick from Dublin.

'We do greatly appreciate your efforts,' says Lord Mountfathom, and raises a goblet of claret to the soldiers.

'Hear, hear!' says Mr Dorrick.

'Quite so!' says Lady Vane-Tempest.

'A brave thing you do,' says Mr Devine.

Luke feels cousin Roger kick him under the table – painfully, on the shin. Knows well why: Rory is smirking and Rose is looking baffled and Ruth is keeping her head down and it is because the soldiers sound odd to them. They say things like, 'What's the story?' But the word 'story' comes out like 'storeee'. And when they say 'think' it sounds like 'tink'.

From Dublin, Luke decides. And he sits and whispers the words 'storeee' and 'tink' to himself, testing the sounds in his own mouth.

Roger gives him another kick.

One of the soldiers is lighting a cigarette at the table.

'I think I have had quite enough,' says Aunt Nancy, and she crumples her napkin up and drops it on the plate and stands. 'I have rather lost my appetite this evening.'

She leaves – heels sharp as pistol-shots on the floor as she moves fast towards the door, heaving it open and letting it slam shut with a sound like a cannon blast.

'I must tell you,' says Mr Dorrick, pouring himself a glass of claret, 'that you are much braver men than I. But I can assure you all that you are quite welcome at Mountfathom, and I am sure you shall have your every need catered for!'

Luke sees his father giving his mother a look.

Lady Vane-Tempest says loudly, 'Oh, you can always count on Flann here to volunteer the hospitality of another's House!'

Soldiers laugh, and Luke relaxes a little.

Main course comes – pigeon with a sticky sauce, roast potatoes, peas and carrots and green beans in tureens with plenty of butter.

The soldier who lit the cigarette during soup (now smoking another) asks Lady Vane-Tempest suddenly, 'Are you married, Missus?'

'Bit of a forward question to be asking a Lady,' says Lawrence Devine – a man that Luke's mother always describes as 'the salt of the earth'.

But Lady Vane-Tempest tells the soldier, calm as anything, 'Young man, I have no more need of a husband than a fish would have need of a bicycle.'

Laughter from everyone at the table and Luke is doing as his father told him: intensely watching and listening and examining these soldiers . . . and it happens very suddenly –

'Doesn't say much this one. Is he the son? Is he a mute or just dumb?'

Takes moments before everyone around the table realises – the person speaking is the soldier with his coffin nail of a cigarette and the person he is speaking about is Luke. No one says anything till Uncle Walter says, 'Children, I think it best you skip the sweet and go upstairs.'

But Luke and his cousins do not move – will not leave unless Lord or Lady Mountfathom asks them to.

The soldier keeps glaring at Luke.

And Luke glares back without wavering. *Know him*, he thinks. *See who he really is.*

It is Lawrence Devine who speaks. 'He is a quiet lad sometimes. But it's often better to say nothing than to talk for the sake of talking and cause ructions, don't you think?'

Takes a long time for the soldier to reply. To stab his cigarette dead into a side plate and say, 'Aye. I suppose so.'

Mr Dorrick tries to help the conversation along. 'Shall we partake in a cigar or two, lads? And afterwards perhaps the Lord and Lady Mountfathom will be kind enough to allow a spot of Conducting! My special brand of Smoke-Spinning is always very well received!'

Lady Vane-Tempest says with some enthusiasm, 'Yes, I'd say that sounds very agreeable.'

But the soldier who made such a judgment about Luke is up out of his seat and wandering *The World* – staring at the gilt ceiling, at the lacquered Chinese cabinets, arriving at the wall and with one hand exploring the vast map, walking his fingertips across the surface until he finds Ireland. He taps the tiny green island with two thick fingers.

'This place is changing,' says the soldier. 'No doubt about it – won't be the same for long.'

'Oh, I daresay some things will stay just the same!' says Dorrick, and tries to smile.

'Maybe you're right,' says the soldier, turning to face the table. 'You'll all be grand here. All sitting pretty with your money and fancy food, all hiding away from the real world in these big piles.'

Luke wishes he could leave. Has never heard anyone talk this way.

Mr Devine says, 'Sit down, son. There's no sense in being bitter.'

Soldier says, 'I'm not a bit bitter. And I'm not your son.'

And so much silence that Luke knows now must be the time for his parents to speak –

'We invited you here in order to help you,' says Lord Mountfathom. 'I made that invitation because I sympathise with your feelings – being Irish, wanting to fight, but yet not knowing which side to take.'

'The Driochta have had that experience too in the past,' says Lady Mountfathom. 'Trying to keep a balance between what we feel is right and what must be done by necessity.'

Soldier looks to his boots.

'I am sure you are trying to do your best,' says Lady Vane-Tempest, and her voice for once is soft. A softness that seems to assuage some worry in the mind of the soldier – he returns to the oval table, slowly, and sinks back into his seat.

Relief, thinks Luke. Pure relief in everyone seated!

Small amount of chatter slowly starts up.

But Luke keeps his eyes on the soldier – watches until he is seen watching, until the soldier whispers for only Luke to hear: 'I know what's for the best of this country. Just you wait and see.'

Luke is woken – a kick from his cousin Roger and a hiss of, '*Listen!*'

It is cold and not quite light; bedroom still harbours some shadow.

Luke is wondering what time it is when Roger kicks him again and says, 'Do you hear them? Those soldiers are on the march!'

Luke listens, and he hears true enough the tramp of boots going by the bedroom door. Hears some whispers –

'We can't be late.'

'Element of surprise – that's what'll get to them.'

'Get them when they tink it's all quiet – before the sun is hardly up!'

Luke sees Rose and Ruth and Rory all tangled in blanket and breathing slowly – lost in dreams. He whispers to Roger, 'I think we should go back to sleep.'

But his cousin Roger whispers back, 'Look, there is something more going on here, so I say let us make it our mission to follow these soldiers and see what they are up to. I need to practise if I am to become the very best spy!'

And Roger is out of the bed and off fast to the door.

Luke checks again his other cousins – Ruth asleep with a serious expression, Rose with the rags unfurling from her hair, Rory with his fists tight as though ready for a scrap.

'Come on!' calls Roger.

Luke goes on tiptoe to the door, eyes on the walls of *The Amazon* watching – all wide with what Luke recognises as warning.

'Can't see them,' says Roger, flat on his belly, trying to peer through the sliver of space between door and floor.

Luke presses an eye tight to the keyhole. 'Neither can I,' he says. 'Hallway is empty now.'

'Well, I'd say that means the coast is clear, dear cousin,' says Roger. 'So let us pursue with all haste!'

And opens the door and out he goes.

Luke feels the walls of *The Amazon* bristle with that same watchful warning . . . knows that if they could send out claws to hold him and keep him safe they would. But he decides: *I don't want to be kept safe always! And I don't want to just read books to learn Magic . . . I want to do something proper . . .*

He follows his cousin out into the chilly hall.

'Luke! This way here!'

Roger already far along the hall and waiting crouched at the bottom of the staircase to the second floor. Luke moves through delicate pre-dawn light but before he reaches the staircase or his cousin, Roger is away again – up the steps in a run without a bit of pause! And again Luke has no choice (he will wonder later though, *Did I? Should I have done things differently?*) – he follows.

Along the way Roger makes a great game of it all – on the second floor starts creeping, feigning, pretending someone is approaching and ducks down behind a table or statue, or slips behind a tapestry and becomes very still, like stillness means being unseen. And Luke does the same, and enjoys it.

Now the staircase that leads to the third floor and Luke knows the fun will all end now – no one but Mother and Father are allowed onto the third floor, a potent Spell of Cessation has been set and will not allow them to climb any further . . . But somehow Roger is able to scale the steps. Luke is wondering how this is happening or what might have Dismissed the Spell when he hears his father saying –

'We shall arrive exactly inside the GPO.'

Hears one of the soldiers. 'Good stuff. You still sure you lot want to come with?'

'This is the decision of the Driochta.' Lady Vane-Tempest? 'It has been discussed at length amongst us and we have made up our minds. We shall stand beside you.'

'Aye.' (*The soldier who was so restless at dinner,* thinks Luke.) 'But you'll be keeping your identities secret, eh? Unlike us.'

'Needs to be done,' says the gruff voice of Lawrence Devine.

'True, it is simply necessity,' says the unmistakable voice of Flann Dorrick. 'We need to remain –'

Lord Mountfathom interrupts. 'Needs to be now or not at all.'

Some silence.

Perhaps the soldiers answer or perhaps the Driochta discusses more, but Luke is too much caught by the panicked throw of his own heart against his ribs. Is too caught by the tone of his father – apprehensive, almost scared? A tone Luke has never heard in his father's voice before.

'Come on,' mouths Roger.

He and Luke slowly climb and at the top of the stairs stand on a dark landing with one dark corridor burrowing away to the right – flees and twists away from them into deep shadow.

No windows, Luke notices. Notices too: wall to his left painted emerald, wall to his right painted crimson.

They listen.

Sure sound of a key being put to a lock . . . more moments and a single high note like a Needle has been whirled through the air . . . now an odd silence.

Roger whispers, 'Now what the devil are those fiendish fellas up to?'

Luke feels suddenly annoyed. 'Whatever is going on isn't some game! I think we should return to *The Amazon*.'

'You are such a coward,' says Roger. 'Are you going to cry?'

Luke turns away – feels he does cry too much, but at odd things – when he sees a dead fox, or a snapped branch after a storm, or a shattered egg at the base of a tree.

Roger tells him, 'You need to grow up! Be more of a man.'

(Sounds definitely to Luke like Uncle Walter.)

But Luke isn't quick with backchat or cheek so doesn't know what to say but, 'Well, I'm not a man yet and you aren't either. I'm only ten-nearly-eleven and you're only just twelve.'

Cousin Roger rolls his eyes.

Both boys are startled at the sound of a door being slammed. Silence.

'Now let us go back,' says Luke.

But Roger only smiles – grins wide and wider as he reaches into the pocket of his pyjamas and takes out a heavy, careworn key clustered around the haft with crimson stones . . .

'When did you take that?' says Luke. 'My mother will –'

'I think we should go and investigate the greatest mystery of Mountfathom!' says Roger. He races off down the dark hallway, one hand to the crimson wall and with Luke following fast as he can, one hand to the emerald wall and wondering what storm of trouble they are stirring with this trespass.

But Luke can't help his curiosity; on the walls, group portraits with eight individuals in each. Previous generations of Driochta, seeing the Needles at their belts and all grasping wooden sculptures in the shape of their animals – hawk and warthog and lemur and emu and lion – and Luke wonders at the long history of the Order that he will one day join . . . is still wondering when he runs into Roger –

Hallway ends with a dark door. Both boys look to the only feature – a silver door handle shaped like a hand, reaching for them. Or beckoning? Silver fingers curled gently inwards.

Luke implores Roger, 'Please, Father said I was never to go through without him or Mother and the other Driochta, and even then not till I am older and have learned more.'

'Why not?' asks Roger. 'What have they got hidden behind this door?'

'Father said –' Luke starts and stops. Swallows and says, 'He told me once that there was a Monster behind there.'

'Ha!' cries Roger. 'He just told you that to keep you away! What rot!'

And again, Roger too quick. Slots the crimson key into the lock and twists it and moments later the sound of a squeal – a note like pure panic that makes Luke's heart hammer and blood hurtle . . .

The dark door springs open and within is another dark with an air of expectancy.

Neither boy moves.

Roger steps forward.

Luke grabs his cousin's arm but this is all still a game – like something Roger has contrived rules for and is in perfect control of so he announces, 'Now we two heroes set off bravely into the unknown!'

And he steps forward to be taken by the dark.

Luke waits on the threshold for an excruciating amount of time. (Thinks of going for help and doesn't. Considers calling out but stays silent. Half-turns away from the door only to face it once again.) In the end, does the only thing he can – takes the crimson key from the lock and follows his cousin Roger through the doorway and into the unknown.

A single step, the dark door slams shut behind.

Like night? Worse, more unforgiving – like the extinguishing of all light, nothing left in the wide world but Luke and the sound of his own desperate breathing. He walks the dark. And is frightened and worried, but carries also a shiver of excitement – so far he has been told nothing much of Magic or the true business of the Driochta, but now here he is . . . now he is learning. He feels so much space around him – as though he is wandering an enormous darkened room, a place teeming with possibility and adventure. And the idea comes to Luke that he can go anywhere he wants! Some enticement in the blackness seems to whisper: *I will show you what needs to be shown. I can take you anywhere. There is nowhere you cannot go! Nothing you cannot learn here!* Some presence implores him – attracts and at the same times terrifies him and Luke can think only with a shiver: *Monster*.

Now he hears something else: a whimper, a sniffle.

He calls: Roger? Where are you?

His voice sounds different – like an echo of itself, like less than a whisper.

But suddenly: crimson light rises in his hand, his mother's key glowing and laying a path on the ground that strains towards a figure standing with shoulders hunched and looking stricken. It takes many moments for Luke to recognise the figure as Roger.

Luke hurries along the crimson light, follows it like a path until he reaches his cousin and asks, You alright?

Roger nods.

Looks more scared than I feel, thinks Luke.

We are lost, says Roger, voice shivering. I don't know where to go!

Luke finds himself saying, Do not panic. We shall be fine. Most important thing now is to find our way back.

But as he turns and holds the crimson key higher, the desire comes to mind, *Wonder where those soldiers went? Wonder where Father and the other Driochta were taking them to?*

And as though in answer, the key blazes so bright both boys recoil and have to half-shield their eyes – on the blackness of the ground, a fresh red light spills from their feet and slithers off into the dark.

We follow this, says Luke.

Light meets light in the shape of a doorway only paces off – thin as a paper-cut and crimson and both boys hurry towards it and Luke notices a keyhole leaking crimson light and slips his mother's key into the lock, turns it and pushes the door.

And so much for silence – such noise! Screams and a single shout of –

'Keep firing! They'll not get the bloody better of us!'

All around stone and glass are shattering and exploding and the stench of gun smoke stings Luke's eyes and nostrils as he sees figures sprinting back and forth through toiling dust like an agitation of Traces. He thinks: *This is some place so far from home! Surely not even Ireland! And we need to get away from here . . .*

Luke takes his cousin's hand and they turn back towards the doorway.

Before they can escape they're grabbed and thrown to the floor.

A man stands over them, battered rifle in hand.

Luke recognises him – the soldier who smoked and stood and debated at the oval table in *The World*. Who whispered a promise to Luke, '*I know what's for the best of this country. Just you wait and see.*'

This soldier swears at them and demands, 'What the hell are you two doing here? Why did you follow us?'

Another door is thrown open and another man enters to swear and shout, 'What the hell is going on? Patrick, what are those bloody children doing here? And where do you think you're going?'

This last question because Roger is up and running again – dodges the man in the doorway and disappears off.

Soldiers shout, 'Stop! Wait there!'

Because Luke again has to follow.

Can hardly see – pale dust everywhere and Luke stumbles, hands out, fingertips catching on broken stone and bringing blood. Blunders on and collides with statues poised on blocks of marble – heads and arms missing, whole sections blasted away.

He has a sense of so many people moving around him.

Luke stops and leans against the wall. A sob rises to his lips as he says, 'Father – where are you? Please come and take us home.'

Crimson key once more brightens in his hand.

And as though he has Worked his first Spell and sent a Messenger to retrieve his father – Luke sees a figure approaching. A man with his father's dark hair and emerald eyes but not his face. This man stops, Works a hand in the air and this face shivers and softens and slowly deigns to become Lord Mountfathom.

'A Spell of Subterfuge,' says Luke, barely thinking.

His father nods – would perhaps be pleased at any other time that his son has been reading and learned to recognise the Spell. But the expression on the face of Lord Mountfathom is like nothing Luke has ever seen so cannot describe – perhaps frightened, perhaps worried, but so sternly powerful. Luke sees that in one hand his father holds his Needle and in the other hand he holds his emerald key.

His father speaks. 'Did you come alone?'

Luke knows his father knows the answer already but he shakes his head and says, 'No. Roger is here too somewhere.'

Lord Mountfathom says, 'Which way did he go?'

Luke says, 'I don't know, Father. I'm sorry.'

They wait moments. And the sounds in their ears Luke thinks are surely of the world coming to some sudden end – so much collapsing and crumbling and tearing down . . . And eventually Lord Mountfathom says, as though thinking aloud, 'I knew this was a dangerous stand for the Driochta to take. I knew the risk. Quickly, son – we have to find your cousin. Stay close to me.'

They move together through more smoke and explosion.

Luke catches sight of more men wielding rifles, wearing dark rags across their mouths, and soon the air around them is polluted not with pale dust but with darkness. They emerge into a wider space: a hall where the noise is loudest and close to unbearable, tables everywhere overturned and papers scattered on a cracked marble floor and pillars hewn in the shape of Ash-Dragons felled and split and so many men at a row of tall windows firing into the street beyond, feet planted on sacks packed for barricades – coal their contents, spilling free and adding darkness to the air.

One of the men at the window turns and hollers, 'What the hell is going on? Why is the boy here?'

Luke recognises something in the man's bearing – the hunch and thickset shoulders – Mr Devine? And another man nearby – tall and thin and with a gentleman's bearing, surely Mr Dorrick also under a Spell of Subterfuge to conceal his appearance – shouts, 'How did he follow us? How did he find his way through the Gloaming?'

A woman approaches them and even without the Needle in her hand Luke would still have known this as Lady Vane-Tempest as she demands, 'William, what on earth is going on?'

But there is no time for answer – Luke sees Roger and grabs his father's arm and shouts, 'There!' His cousin is huddled beside one of the fallen Ash-Dragon pillars, his face screwed tight with crying.

'Go!' says Lady Vane-Tempest. 'Take them both and go!'

But at the same time another shout from one of the men at the windows: 'Watch it! They've got Indigo Fire!'

Lord Mountfathom grabs Luke and together they run to Roger and each take an arm and wrench him to his feet –

Luke turns –

A bright blue light blossoms at one of the windows –

The sight is transfixing: almost soothing, somehow subduing the battle –

'Do not look at the Indigo Fire!' Lord Mountfathom tells his son.

But blue light becomes brighter and brighter –

Luke sees Lady Vane-Tempest and Lawrence Devine and Flann Dorrick whirl their Needles in their air but too late –

Blue fire – more like water! – explodes through glass and gushes over sills to sweep across marble floor to the sound of so much screaming from the men.

Dorrick and Devine and Vane-Tempest Mogrify – take their animal forms as cheetah and chimpanzee and peacock and leap and spring and take flight to keep themselves free of the flames –

But Luke does not move. Realises that the fire will be at his feet in the next breath –

His father flicks his Needle to sound a sharp note –

Pillar shaped like an Ash-Dragon is given life and throws itself in front of Luke and Roger and Lord Mountfathom as the Indigo Fire breaks like a wave against its stone body –

A fine spray of flame peppers Roger's clothing and he screams out as Mountfathom grabs both boys and shouts, 'This way!'

They run.

Back down the corridor, Luke feeling the Indigo Fire still in pursuit. His father is furiously Conducting, sending screaming notes into the air with twitches of his Needle, bidding the headless and limbless statues to leave their marble plinths and throw themselves in front of the flames. But they can only slow and not stop the tide.

'A door,' says Lord Mountfathom, pointing. 'The crimson key – quick!'

Luke understands and with fumbling hands works his mother's key into the lock and turns it and –

'Wait!' his father tells him, and Luke knows they are waiting for the note that signals the connection to the dark place beyond the doorway – the place of such uncertainty and possibility. But over the sounds of screaming, how they can they hope to hear?

'We can't wait,' says Luke, and turns the handle and grabs the sleeves of his cousin and his father and pulls them through and slams shut the door on blue fire and battle.

'Daddy! Mummy!'

Soon as they return to Mountfathom, Roger is away – crying for his parents. And Luke cannot pity his cousin – feels now as though he hardly knows him, or perhaps knows him better than he has done before. Luke knows this anyway: Roger will plead innocence and likely lie. Will blame and exaggerate and do anything at all to free himself of responsibility.

Luke feels a hand on his shoulder. He doesn't turn, doesn't speak – cannot look yet into the eyes of his father. He is too ashamed. He starts to sob.

He hears his father say, 'Come with me, son.'

They walk back down the dark corridor. Down the staircase with Lord Mountfathom Working his hand to reset the Spell of Cessation.

They arrive at the library. The single tall window gives a view onto the sunken garden, colours coming into their own in the light of morning. Luke is let sit in the chair behind the desk – a seat only his father usually takes. Lord Mountfathom stands, and over the sounds of the dawn chorus starts to do something like explain.

'I am sorry, son. I should have realised that curiosity would have got the better of you.'

'You told me to watch,' says Luke. Still weeping, still cannot meet his father's eye. Stares instead at his hands – bloodied and blackened, coated with pale dust and dark and still holding tight to the crimson key, its low light almost extinguished. Swallows and says, 'You told me to listen and learn.'

'I did,' says Lord Mountfathom. 'But the First Principle of Magic is not only curiosity, remember? It is also caution.'

Luke decides, 'Those soldiers were never going to the Front. They are part of the rebels, aren't they? The ones Uncle Walter was talking about. The ones who want independence for Ireland.'

'Yes,' says his father. And the tone in his voice is touched with some pride in his astute son – enough encouragement to allow Luke to face his father, to ask more questions.

'Why did you help them? Are they not fighting the Government? Is the Driochta not supposed to help the Government? I don't understand it.'

'Then you have learned an important lesson.'

Luke is surprised to see a smile rise on the face of his father.

Lord Mountfathom says, 'You have learned that things in this time we live in are not so easily understood. I expect this will be an important lesson, if I am correct in reading the signs of how things are going in this country.' A moment, then he goes on. 'For almost four hundred years, the Order of the Driochta have been loyal servants of the State. We have been mediators, negotiators – at heart, peacekeepers. Always we have used our Magic and Spell-Work for the good of this country.'

'But not now,' says Luke. He stops – worries he has misspoken. Goes on, 'This morning, in Dublin – you were fighting.'

'Yes,' says his father. 'We made a choice to side with the rebellion and fight with their cause. I do not know if this was the right thing to do. Perhaps there is no right and wrong in this? Perhaps there can be no easy answer?'

Luke knows his father and his moods – knows he likes to pose these questions as though to the air. Knows he expects no answers.

Lord Mountfathom says, 'There are many ways ahead when one steps through the dark door.' He settles his emerald key on the deal-topped desk.

And Luke settles the crimson key. 'Do the keys open that dark door to anywhere?'

'The Gloaming – which is the name given to the place beyond the dark door – contains many places, and many other things besides.'

'When I was in the Gloaming,' says Luke, 'I felt as though I might go anywhere.'

'And that is a good and proper thing,' says Lord Mountfathom. And suddenly he is impassioned. 'To feel that sense of possibility is of such importance, Luke! Not everyone would feel as you did – to be surrounded by so much dark and boundless unknown, it would likely paralyse most people.'

Luke pictures his cousin Roger: standing alone and terrified, unable to move either forward or back within the Gloaming. And as though bidden by his thoughts, a sudden cry breaks the early morning silence of Mountfathom –

'William! William, where are you? What the hell has happened to my boy Roger?'

'It seems I must go and face the music,' says Lord Mountfathom. He picks up his emerald key and pockets it. 'I am sorry you had to experience your first trip into the Gloaming in this way, son. I am sorry now that I did not prepare you.' His father leans close to say delicately, 'But remember this: no journey can be made without the risk of stepping into the dark. That has always been the way – more so now than ever, son. I believe this: for Mountfathom and all who live here, there is a long and difficult way ahead. But I am heartened by one thing – that no matter what may come to pass, I shall have my so especially curious and watchful son by my side.'

Second Principle of Magic –
Of Creativity & Consequence

*'. . . in the same way as a conductor can tease
a sound from his musicians with a twitch of a hand,
or a poet can make a sonnet appear on a blank
page with a swirl of a pen – through movement
we make what is in the mind into a reality.'*

'See the mist for what it is. Tell me.'

'It is water.'

'Come now – you can do better than that!'

'Moisture?'

'Indeed. And only moisture now – could be what else?'

Luke says nothing, for the moment, then, 'So moisture could
be rain? Could be snow or ice or lots of things.'

Says it too easily? Rhymes this off too casually.

Lady Mountfathom tells him, 'Well, then, if it so obvious,
Luke, let me see you Rework it.'

This is the early-morning sight: mother and son standing by
the lagoon beneath the golden willow. Sun already with them

61

but shrouded – the mists that settle and collect in the bowl where Mountfathom sits have not yet been burned away. So everything has a vagueness to it – things glimpsed as though through the thinnest leaf of paper.

Luke shivers.

It is summer, a year since the events of the GPO and the Rising in Dublin; mere seasons since the kind of dark headlines Luke couldn't stop himself reading and rereading.

LEADERS OF EASTER REBELLION EXECUTED
MAJOR FORTFLAY VOWS:
"NO MERCY TO BE EXTENDED TO THOSE
DISRUPTING THE PEACE OF THIS ISLAND!"

'Concentrate!' his mother tells him.

Luke allows his eyes to shut. Tries for stillness – feels the tickle of damp on his cheeks and brow. And slowly, allows his arms to drift upwards and fingers to peel free from palms. He mutters the Spell, and straightaway feels some obliging and obeying tell-tale shift – some strangeness in the atmosphere . . .

He hears his mother say, 'Good. Not bad at all.'

Luke opens his eyes to see his Spell Worked.

Mist that lay soft as down over the surface of the lagoon has taken a shape. A flock of herons now picks its way silently across the grey water.

Luke smiles to himself – the detail is sharp, he thinks. Bodies and legs in proportion, behaviour utterly characteristic . . .

'Very pretty,' says his mother. 'Indeed that is how I would describe it: *pretty*. Though you should now be pushing yourself to Work more than pleasing sights, son. Even without use of a Needle, you should be attempting to Work the elements into more substantial shapes – this will be essential for Summoning Messengers, for example.'

This is a gentle admonishment though; the sight is altogether too convincing, much too intoxicating. And so mother and son stand together and watch these birds composed only of mist and Magic as they walk the lagoon. Watch with pleasure until sunlight spills into the grounds of Mountfathom and Luke lifts his arms as though in farewell. He bids the flock of herons fly, sends them off into clean, unclouded morning . . . watches them until they are no more than pale shapes against blue, shedding their Spell to drift and part, nothing more than memory against the sky.

And what else next? Inevitably this –

'When can I begin to use a Needle?'

Spells Worked through the weaving of a hand? Powerful and potent enough, if performed right. They have kept him engrossed for twelve months – such Spells of Enclosing and Cessation, of Fleeing and Seclusion. He has advanced quickly (his parents privately wonder, *Too quickly?*). But he has been dedicated and patient and attentive. And curious.

'Would I not be better to start practising with a Needle as soon as is possible?'

'Such nonsense!' says his mother. In the Downstairs Orchard, she is busy pruning an apple tree.

Mr Hooker, holding her ladder tight, says, 'Are you sure now you wouldn't like me to do that, Lady Mountfathom?'

'Do not patronise me,' she tells the gardener. 'You were the one who fell off the ladder last month, not I.'

'True enough,' says Mr Hooker, one finger touching the tender bruise on his brow.

Lady Mountfathom points her secateurs at Luke as she says, 'You are a knowledgeable and very dear and special child, but you have not yet lived nor learned nor seen enough to handle a Needle. No member of the Driochta has ever been given such a thing at the age of twelve! All Magic is in the mind, and you must first learn to Cast without one. The Magic you can tease from your mind with a Needle has yet a greater weight to it; you will not be ready for that for some time, Luke.'

Luke doesn't doubt his mother's wisdom. But even so . . .

'Well, can you please teach me more about the elements?' he asks her. 'And so when I do get a Needle I'll be able better to use it.'

'Is this because your cousins are arriving tomorrow?' Lady Mountfathom asks him.

Luke is always amazed – and a little vexed – at how well his mother can read him.

'Now did you ever hear such demands, Bartemius?' his mother asks the gardener, all mock scandal and shock.

'I never did, my Lady,' says Mr Hooker, and he gives Luke a wink. 'But the boy is keen to grow up and prove himself, and nothing wrong with that.'

'Except that a child growing up too quick is the heartbreak of every mother in the land,' says Lady Mountfathom.

'As you said this morning by the lagoon,' says Luke, 'I need to Work more substantial Spells. I want to learn something a little more . . . *dramatic*!'

Mr Hooker chuckles.

'You boys,' says Lady Mountfathom, 'always craving drama. Well, how about this: when your cousins arrive tomorrow, we shall go to Loughreagh for a spot of boat racing, see how well you can Work the water there. Agreed?'

Luke knows this is the best he shall get.

So when his mother spits in her hand and extends it, Luke strains on tiptoe for the handshake so as to seal their deal.

Since the previous spring, Luke has had his wish for more learning – soon as his cousins departed Mountfathom (his uncle somewhat placated after much discussion with Lord and Lady Mountfathom, his Aunt Nancy nothing but silent and furious) a lesson plan was agreed. Daily classes from members of the Driochta, a timetable crammed tight.

Mondays: Mr Flann Dorrick lectures on history and politics – his government work at the Castle in Dublin giving him plenty of insight and information into both, though he doesn't always convey it as clearly as Luke would like. On his first day, Dorrick describes history as, 'Akin to a series of dominos toppling, one never falling in isolation without striking the next . . . and so on and so forth.' To illustrate, he says, 'The cries of the Banshees were so constant during the Great Hunger that the Gards were given permission by Westminster to hunt the creatures down and exterminate them, which led to the Extraordinary Breeds Bill of 1897 – masterminded by Major Fortflay and in conjunction with the church, it sanctioned the destruction of the Faerie Raths and the purging of the Gyants. The Driochta opposed this Breeds Bill, and so consequently the first Cooperation Bill of 1729 was rescinded, marking the end of civil dealings between the Driochta and the church.'

'Consequences,' continues Mr Dorrick. 'Nothing in isolation – no single thread tugged without another coming with it. Yes – I rather like that analogy . . . you know, I surprise myself sometimes with my fine grasp of words!'

Tuesdays: The Halters, husband and wife. Mr Halter is a botanist and Mrs Halter an anthropologist. They take lessons together and are prone to swapping from subject to subject. Luke keeps two leather notebooks – one blue and one green – and swaps fast between, making notes . . . Mr Halter teaches how to recognise Irish Moss in a bogland, and then warns always to avoid it; Mrs Halter lectures at length and with great gusto about the tribe mentality of the old Irish Gyants (how they defined themselves not only by race but by their own notions of county and border and townland); Mr Halter then on the healing qualities of many native Irish plants – Vandal Root and Faerie's Thumbs; Mrs Halter on the word "Faerie" and its origins, and some sage advice for Luke – 'It is said you should never enter a Faerie Rath without at least three clean shillings in your pocket to barter with. And I believe that is a good general rule for life!'

Wednesdays: Favourite day! Luke leaves Mountfathom and walks the three and a half miles to the farm of Lawrence Devine and is put to work. 'Good honest labour,' Mr Devine calls it. And Luke learns things without knowing he is learning – how to milk a cow and muck out a pigsty, sharpen a knife and shoe a horse. He helps deliver a litter of terrier pups (begs to take one back to Mountfathom but Mr Devine rightly says that

Morrigan wouldn't tolerate another animal in the House). And he reaches home at nightfall mucky and exhausted and unfailingly happy.

Thursdays: Lady Vane-Tempest lands, always late but bursting with information about people. 'Word is that General Pakenham and his wife are planning to leave Limerick for London! Afraid of their tenants, I do believe. Did you ever hear such a thing? Cowards!' 'Did you hear about the estate at Lissadell? They have point-blank refused to rehire anyone who went to fight in the war! Such short-sighted madness!'

And so on – a litany of these types of tales!

Luke tries not to think to himself, *Is this not just gossip?*

Yet after a number of lessons, some minor revelation – Luke realises he is hearing about people and their ways and to the (sometimes distinctly Irish) habits for snobbery and idle prejudice, for struggle and blood-grudge. He is learning about people of importance beyond Mountfathom, and is suddenly attentive as anything . . .

Fridays: Mr Gorebooth, who refuses a label for his lessons.

'Yes, some poetry,' he tells Luke. 'Yes, plenty of mythology. But more generally, we shall learn of the world and the world of words within it!'

Luke feels some impatience with this vagueness – he is eleven, and so is craving things definite and decided; needs to know what can be learned and used and repeated. Sonnets give no certainty, plays neither. But he applies himself, because it is his nature. Though he is a little relieved one long afternoon (after so much reciting and philosophising on the tales of the warrior Cuchulain) when Mr Gorebooth sinks into a leather chair and tells Luke in an exhausted whisper, 'Do not worry too much – you will see in time that these words I speak are merely a passing whisper! Sometimes it is enough simply to let words wash over you, and perhaps later you shall remember them, and feel enriched by the memory. Often times it is preferable simply to be peaceful – to listen, and to dream . . .'

And suddenly, Mr Gorebooth is asleep and snoring in his chair.

But this is the weekend now, and his cousins have returned to Mountfathom. Over a year and not a single visit, not till today . . . but as though no time has passed between –

'What game shall we play?'

'Catch!'

'Chase the Traces!'

'Luke, can you stay with me if we play Secret-and-Secluded?'

'Let me decide – I have a game I have been thinking of!'

But Roger has no say, not on this afternoon.

Luke: 'We are going to Loughreagh to boat race!'

They set off: beyond both walled and kitchen gardens, beneath eucalyptus and bypassing the kiwi bushes, they come to the stone staircase. The Winding Stair, Luke's mother calls it. Contrary and oddball thing – won't descend straight, juts one way and then the other, angles like sharp elbows and bent knees . . . and when you think it's about ready to drop you at the bottom it twists in another direction! Eventually it leaves you at the limestone wall that surrounds the sprawling demesne of Mountfathom. And here an archway: a tunnel thick with webs of spun Spell-Work, invisible and only able to be unpicked on this Saturday afternoon of summer by Lord or

Lady Mountfathom, taking Luke and his parents and cousins and Uncle Walter and Aunt Nancy through to arrive on a shore of shattered stone.

All eyes on Loughreagh – surface untroubled, water the colour of cool slate and cut by a causeway of dark stone that stretches from the shore to a small crannog and stone tor. And beyond, surrounding all – the collar of the blackberry-coloured Mountains of Mourne.

The cousins whoop and cry out and cheer – breathless with excitement.

And Luke adds this place – perhaps this very moment – to the list of times and places he has been happiest.

'Last one to the isle is a very rotten egg!' calls Uncle Walter ('Biggest child of them all!' says Aunt Nancy often), and things begin: Luke and his mother and father and the four cousins and their father race across shattered shore to commandeer three rowing boats lying with their bright undersides to the sky – yellow and red and green. Luke and his mother and cousin Rose take the red boat, cousins Rory and Ruth and Uncle Walter hop into the yellow. Lord Mountfathom and Roger take the green. (No one can entice Aunt Nancy to join – she pleads a migraine, wants to simply sit in the shade and relax.)

Uncle Walter bellows another threat: 'Last one to touch the tor on the Isle of Solitude is a filthy woodkerne!'

Into the water and only moments before Luke overhears his father say to Roger, 'Perhaps a little extra help?' And Lord Mountfathom takes his Needle from his belt and flicks it and a single loud note makes the surface of Loughreagh swell at the stern of their boat and push them on faster!

Rose (whose curls are long gone) says very calmly to Luke, 'They're cheating, aren't they?'

But Luke is watching his mother – they share a long look, wordless. And finally Lady Mountfathom tells her son, 'Oh, go on then! Show your cousin and I what you have learned.'

So Luke kneels in the stern of their red rowing boat, holds his hands above his head, a foot apart, and starts to weave and Work the air . . . and at the same time feels the water beneath begin to respond; in prod and poke it begins to nudge the underside of their boat.

And he wills it to will and coax them on –

'No! Too much too soon!' his mother calls to him, but too late –

Sudden rush of water leaps from the lough and soaks Luke and his mother and cousin through. Rose laughs about it and says, impressed, 'Did you do that, Luke? That was amazing!'

'Wasn't meant to work like that,' says Luke, and raises his hands once more.

'Enough for now,' says Lady Mountfathom. 'Let me try!'

A whirl of her Needle, a long, shivering note, and a responding swell sends their boat speeding forward –

Luke settles in the stern, feeling sullen.

Far behind – Uncle Walter and Ruth and Rory shrink from sight, scarcely further than the shore and too far behind to be in the race any longer without the benefit of a Spell.

'Faster!' shouts Rose. 'Faster!'

And another twitch of the Needle and Lady Mountfathom sends their boat hurtling on –

Luke and Rose lower themselves and hold tight –

They draw level with Lord Mountfathom and Roger, and Luke's mother and father are crying at one another, 'Cheat! Foul play here! Not fair at all!'

And suddenly both boats run aground on the Isle of Solitude, and Luke and Roger leap forward and sprint fast towards the tor. But Luke knows he has lost before he has lost: Roger is older, taller, bit faster and fierce as hell –

Luke falls. Face meets damp earth and he thinks, *Was I tripped?*

And Roger is the first to reach the tor and plant a palm on its grey stone.

Luke has a distressing realisation: *Roger tripped me.*

'Bad luck there, cousin!' says Roger, and he takes Luke's hand and heaves him to his feet. 'Bit of a novice mistake not to keep an eye on the ground and see where you're going, is it not?'

And Luke thinks of lots of things he could say. And decides it best to say nothing at all.

'I say we shoot the lot of them!'

'*Walter!*'

'Do not try to tell me you disagree, Nancy! Not if you were completely honest. Our tenants have us run ragged at Goreland Hall now – want to see me every other bloody day to discuss lowering rents and whatnot. Think they have rights to just come up and knock on the door and make demands!'

Lunch is on the shore of the lake, courtesy of Mrs Little and Lady Mountfathom – a small fire conjured by Luke's mother, fried sausages and fresh bread and pitchers of iced tea with slices of peach and fat raspberries floating on the surface brought to them by the cook. The waves of Loughreagh venture close, now retreat; rise and fall.

Luke thinks, *It is true – it does breathe.*

'Well,' says Lady Mountfathom, waving a cigarette, smoke making an elegant tangle, 'you are their landlord, brother dearest. And as it happens, they do very much have rights.'

'And does that mean I wish to discuss the weather or pass the time of day with them?' says Uncle Walter. 'Is that a so-called right? Isn't something I voted for! You agree with me, William? Tell me you do and restore some sanity to the general conversation!'

Luke's father takes his time to say, 'I have personally collected the rents from each and every one of my tenants for the past ten years. They come on the first Tuesday of every month and if they wish to discuss any arrears or personal worries, I listen to them. I think it the very least we can do.'

Uncle Walter spears another sausage from the pan.

Luke thinks, *So much like last year. So little changes!*

Uncle Walter tells them all loudly, 'Well, I shall say one thing: that woman of yours in the kitchens is a miracle-worker! Not at all like our dozy old cook at Goreland Hall! Are you sure you haven't delegated some Spell-Work to her, Edith? Must be something uncanny about this servant to conjure such a magnificent feast with such speed!'

And Lady Mountfathom breathes smoke as she says, 'Firstly, she is not called a "servant". We see all who work at Mountfathom as family. And the fact is that our dear Mrs Little is simply well accustomed to hard work. Being a banker, Walter, that concept is likely something you are not familiar with.'

Aunt Nancy's mouth slips open.

Uncle Walter laughs loud, once – a bark that bounces across the lake.

Luke watches: Aunt Nancy shifts herself a little away from Luke's mother, tucks her skirt beneath her legs; Roger sighs and manages the feat of looking more bored than he did a moment before, and Ruth and Rory and Rose say nothing and keep their eyes on their food.

And Luke watches all, trying to learn to see.

'Who is that?' asks cousin Rose.

She and Luke are on the causeway together – they race along dark rock, forward and back and feeling a little self-conscious in their game of Catch. (Roger spares a moment to shout at them, 'Grow up, you two! Catch is for children!' Roger who has decided this year to follow his father into the world of banking.)

But they stop only at this sudden sight – a man standing alone on the Isle of Solitude. From their distance, halfway along the causeway, Luke can take note of only three things: the dark eyes of the man, the palest face, and a head of faded hair.

Luke tells his cousin, 'I do not know who that is.'

'I thought the isle was deserted,' says Rose.

'Used to be used by monks,' says Luke. 'And the Driochta too, for studying.'

They wait as though the man might greet them – trusting children; they expect no threat and certainly none here, not so close to Mountfathom.

And the man on the isle raises something in the air – *a Needle?*

Something stirs in Luke – a sense of some gathering Magic – and he has only a moment to tell Rose, *'Run!'*

But too late and not quick enough –

From either side of the causeway waves leap high –

Shadow cast – water obscures the sun . . . and then the waves falling, crashing so hard on both Luke and Rose that they are pinned to the rock –

Luke hears his cousin plead, 'Help! Help!'

But Luke cannot respond as more and more waves break upon the causeway, and Luke knows some powerful Spell is commanding Loughreagh. His mind strains towards some Spell as his hands and fingers strain to weave it in the air. He manages a Spell of Enclosing and for some short time it holds, keeping them free of the rush and clamour of the waves. Enough time for Luke to hear the thin scream that escapes Rose –

'Help! Help us!'

Enough time for him to look towards shore and try to see what help might come for them, but he can make out nothing –

A squeal from the Needle on the Isle of Solitude –

Luke's Spell is shattered.

Once more the lough is hurling itself on them and his cousin Rose has stopped screaming, ceased protest. He sees: she is no longer moving.

And Luke does the only thing he can – holds tight to her hand.

Now newer sounds – the squeal of more Needles, and are the waves being battled back? Luke sees enough now to see two figures approaching from the shore: his mother and father side-by-side on the causeway, both with Needles held high and twitching and jabbing and Conducting with such speed and precision.

Luke turns towards the isle – the man there is battling just as furiously.

And the scream of Needles is a torment to Luke's hearing.

Hands and fingers of water grab at Luke and Rose, try to drag them from the causeway as Lord and Lady Mountfathom conjure from the waters of the lough an Irish elk and panther that leap over Luke and Rose and charge at the man on the isle.

And in all the tumult and battle, Luke loses his grip on waking – slips and falls, and is suddenly lost.

'Rose! My Rosie!'

Luke wakes to this screaming: to the dazzle of sun and the sight of Aunt Nancy running barefoot down the causeway, Uncle Walter trying to keep pace. And she is shrieking, 'My Rosie! My Rosie!'

Luke sees his father kneeling beside Rose. Sees that she isn't moving.

He tries to sit up more and speak but his mother is beside him to settle a hand on his shoulder and say, 'Do not move. Say nothing.'

'Get away from her!' shouts Aunt Nancy, arriving at her daughter and pushing Lord Mountfathom aside. Luke can see Rose's face now – the cheeks pale blue, the lips slightly parted and dark. Watches as his aunt gives her daughter the kiss of life.

Luke's father says, 'Please let me help, Nancy.'

And he holds his Needle up but Aunt Nancy shouts, 'No! There's been enough trouble because of your silly Magic already!' And keeps pressing her lips to her daughter's lips.

Uncle Walter arrives, so out of breath he can't say a thing.

In the distance, on the shore, Luke can see his cousins – waiting where they've been told to wait.

Rose does not move, does not stir, will not wake.

It is too much: Luke closes his eyes, is held tighter by his mother.

Sound of sudden coughing and gasping!

Luke opens his eyes –

Aunt Nancy turns her daughter on her side as Rose retches and a throatful of grey water leaves her mouth. Aunt Nancy starts only now to weep, sobbing more softly, 'My Rosie. My dear Rosie.'

Lady Mountfathom breathes, 'Thank goodness.'

'Who did this?' says Uncle Walter, relief now giving him speech – making him want to incriminate and blame. 'Who is responsible for this?'

And Luke turns his gaze towards the Isle of Solitude – but there is no man there with dark eyes and pale face and faded hair. There is, for now, no one to blame.

The lack of a clear culprit is no obstacle to Uncle Walter.

'This is your fault! This is what you get for being so lenient with your servants and tenants! They think they can get the better of you!'

'Try not to overreact, brother dear – you shall give yourself another heart attack.'

'Do not patronise me, Edith! My daughter almost died because some lunatic thought he'd have a go at the people in the Big House!'

Sun is sinking and Luke sits on his windowsill, Morrigan coiled on his lap – the cat so unconcerned, bored by it all. Luke listens to his mother and uncle flinging words back and forth one floor below in *Valhalla*.

'You should have better defences around the place! To go boating on that lake was the worst idea, the very worst!'

'Walter, no one could have predicted what was going to happen today.'

'I thought you had ways of predicting things!'

Some silence from Lady Mountfathom.

Luke thinks, *Uncle Walter has a point*. Maybe his mother or father should have done some Mirror-Predicting – consulted the patterns in the ink and seen what was to transpire. Sensed this impending trouble?

And Uncle Walter starts up again like an airplane engine. 'With what happened to Roger last year and Rose today, I can tell you we will be thinking long and hard about coming back to Mountfathom!'

And Luke's mother says, 'You think you shall be safe if you lock yourself away in Goreland Hall? You think danger will only reach you here in this House? You are mistaken, Walter.'

A slam of a door. Some final silence.

Some minutes and the door of *The Amazon* opens.

'Best stay away from your mother when she is at war.' It is Luke's father. He slinks in and quietly closes the door behind him. 'How are you, son?'

Luke does not wait – starts straight into his questioning.

'That man I saw on the isle. He wanted to kill us.'

Lord Mountfathom stops halfway across the room. Nods.

'Why would people want to kill us?' asks Luke. 'Who was he?'

'These are the very questions you should be asking,' says his father. Folds his hands behind his back and half-lowers his head – stands like an Errander boy summoned for discussion. 'And if only I knew how to answer them for you.'

Luke opens his mouth to mention the Needle, then decides not to, wonders whether he imagined it.

'I want to know what is going on outside Mountfathom.' Luke stands, lifting Morrigan aside; she complains, gives a groan and tries to snag small claws on his trousers. 'Uncle Walter keeps talking about things being dangerous and changing – he is right, isn't he?'

Lord Mountfathom nods once more. His gaze wanders to the small crib still kept in the corner of the room – muslin hood scattered with sewn stars.

'I knew this day would come,' he says. 'Yet, in my foolishness and naivety, I thought it would come much later – the moment when Mountfathom would no longer be enough for you.'

'It is not that,' says Luke. 'It is just living by the First Principle – to have curiosity, to want to learn.'

His father smiles, says, 'I believe you are picking up the Principles very well. Today, I think you saw a rather dramatic show of the Second.'

'The man had a Needle,' says Luke. 'I am certain I saw that.'

'And with such anger and bitterness in his mind he was able to use the Needle to Summon such power. You witnessed that too – you saw how thought becomes act, and the havoc it can wreak.'

Luke turns back to the window, burnished with the slow sunset, sees his own reflection on the bright surface. Pauses, then says, 'Will you let me go with the Driochta on a mission? Can I go back into the Gloaming?'

A long of time of waiting, and finally father concedes to son.

'Yes,' says Lord Mountfathom. 'We shall show you, Luke, how to move between Mountfathom and the rest of the wide world. We shall teach you how to leave the safety of home behind, and show you how to return – how to explore the Gloaming. And, when time tells us it is right, you shall embark on your first mission of Magic.'

Third Principle of Magic –
Of Action & Inaction
'No, we must not act! We must force
ourselves to do nothing!'

Lady Mountfathom asks her son, Are you getting a sense of the dark now?

Yes, he says. I believe I am.

(Luke thinks: After a year – at long last!)

He holds not so much of fear – same queasiness, little less worry. With each excursion over the last twelve months, Luke has become better and better able to negotiate the Gloaming. But today is different. He is not just wandering with his mother or father, but has a purpose – is beginning his inaugural mission for the Driochta.

Good, says his mother. Though do stay close. We are almost there.

Crimson light from Lady Mountfathom's key stretches towards a sudden doorway in the Gloaming, its outline rising like an opening wound.

Be ready, she tells her son. Major Fortflay and his Gards may not be receptive to our sudden appearance.

So Luke holds in his mind (and in readied hands) a host of Spells, should he need to Work them.

Key into lock.

Door opens and mother and son step out onto a blustery hillside.

After the Gloaming – so much of a nowhere and no place, silent and containing nothing like weather – Luke feels the shock and attack of the elements: their fur-lined capes lift and snap, eyes stream with cold. Luke wants to prove himself: quickly Works a Spell of Enclosing to shield them both and instantly they are let be, capes settling like leaves after a gust.

'Well Worked,' says Lady Mountfathom. 'Though I think things may have escalated since Mr Dorrick sent his Messenger.'

The passage they have used belongs to a half-collapsed cottage – the door they have stepped through slowly parting company with its hinges. A famine cottage, thinks Luke, balanced on a bald rise from which they can survey things.

Below: fields blue with dawn frost, drystone walls interrupting the ripple of hills, blue roads looping and meandering the cold countryside. And in the field below them, Luke sees so many Gards from Dublin Castle – guesses at a hundred or more, all clustered tight together. All in formation, they face a stark forest – watching it as though the bare trees themselves might rally themselves to battle.

'They have driven the Boreen Men all the way into the forest?' asks Luke.

'I would say so,' says his mother. 'Fortflay used some Magic from the Politomancer in Whitehall to lock these workers out of Dublin, then pursued them across the counties and now the Gards have them here. Have them surrounded.'

Lady Mountfathom sighs.

'All the Boreen Men wanted was to work?' says Luke.

'Not enough money to pay them,' says his mother. 'All are not as fortunate as us, my son.'

Luke wants to say: *I know this. I know more than I did a year ago when some stranger stood on the Isle of Solitude and tried to kill cousin Rose and me. I know there are others in the world not so well off.*

His mother continues. 'It was – and still is – a great struggle for many in Dublin. The Boreen Men are fathers, sons, husbands simply wishing to provide for their families. They have no interest in Magic or the machinations of the Government. The Driochta tried to help, we tried to negotiate – but the Castle decided on its own methods, as they are wont to do.'

Luke says, 'What does Major Fortflay plan for them?'

His mother says, 'He will wait. And when the Boreen Men are forced – either by hunger or thirst or pure desperation – to leave the cover of the trees, they will have to surrender.'

'And if they do not?'

'They will be slaughtered.' Lady Mountfathom looks at her son. 'May sound a touch harsh, but Fortflay and the Castle in Dublin, and Whitehall too, are desperate to put an end to these rebellions.'

'And the Driochta must try to play peacekeeper in all this,' says Luke. Says it with a sigh.

'So it has always been,' says his mother. 'Better get used to it, son – this is our role and we must play as best as –'

Stopped by the sound of a voice hollering;

'Hold your ground, lads! No daydreaming or slacking. We shall not move one inch unless we see surrender!'

'Major Fortflay?' asks Luke.

Lady Mountfathom nods. 'Fool,' she says. 'Well-educated, I believe. But still, in so many subtle ways, a fool.'

'Mother, I thought we had to be impartial?'

'Let that not stand in the way of the truth! Just don't tell your father I said so. Now: let us go. Let us see what we can do.'

So Luke and his mother find a frozen and well-worn farmer's path to follow down the slope and into the field – tramping brittle grass, earth hard as marble. As they descend, Luke sees to the west a glimpse of some different blue: the languorous shrug of grey waves. A sudden thrill of excitement.

'We are near the Dragon Coast!'

'Do not be getting any ideas about going to look for Ash-Dragons,' his mother tells him. 'Poor creatures, they want nothing more than to stay asleep under the ground, and we should leave them that way.'

But it is not long before –

'Stop where you stand or I shall have you shot!'

'Calm yourself, Major Fortflay!' Lady Mountfathom shouts. Tries to sound a touch jocular as they walk into the midst of the Castle Gards. 'I would venture that your bullets would have little chance against my infamously swift brand of Magic!'

Luke and his mother move amongst the battalion – some scowl, some stagger-recoil. But most shiver, despite the benefit of greatcoats. And most, Luke thinks, look pleased and relieved. He even catches one young Gard whispering to his mate, 'It'll be sorted now they're here. This needs Spells and not shooting.'

Major Fortflay greets Lady Mountfathom with salute and a handshake. He is a tall man, wiry – big moustache growing grey at the tips as though touched with the same frost that clings to the ground. He tells them with a bite in his voice, 'Doubt there is much you can do now.'

'I would hate to think that was true,' says Luke's mother.

'Two of your number have already attempted mediation,' says Fortflay. 'And failed.'

'*Edith!*'

Someone is pushing through the crowd and a voice shouts again, '*Edith!* Out of my way, if you please! Go on – move it! Stood on your foot? So sorry – though I daresay you'll live!'

And Luke sees Lady Vane-Tempest. Always so well dressed – long cloak of turquoise with silver trim, black boots with a sharp heel. She has her Needle in hand and tells them without wait, 'The Boreen Men have taken Flann.'

'What?' asks Luke.

'Yes,' says Lady Vane-Tempest, with a sour curl of the lips. 'His own fault though, I say. Told the Major he knew how to speak the "lingo of the common man". And then went marching off to negotiate with the Boreen Men! Usual story with Flann Dorrick: determined to make a hero of himself, ends up making a show of himself!'

'So,' says Fortflay, mouth making a grim smile, 'one of the Driochta already taken hostage – hardly a promising beginning to negotiations.'

'I think "hostage" is a little melodramatic,' says Lady Mountfathom.

'I quite agree,' says Lady Vane-Tempest. 'I can assure you – no being in their right mind would choose to have Flann Dorrick as a hostage!'

'We need to speak with these Boreen Men, Major,' says Lady Mountfathom.

'They are beyond discussion or reasoning. My intelligence tells me that they have moved deep into the forest and are hiding in an abandoned Faerie Rath. They have barricaded themselves inside and no amount of pleasant chat is going to bring them out.' And Major Fortflay turns away, shouts to his men, 'Be ready! Stay alert! We can take no chances!'

But Luke's mother will not be ignored.

'Major Fortflay, need I remind you of the second Cooperation Bill?'

Fortflay stops.

'I do not need a history lesson,' he says, half-turning back to face Lady Mountfathom. 'And I do not need laws quoted at me either. What I need is –'

'Let me refresh your memory for the sake of clarity,' says Luke's mother, in that tone that her son so marvels at: somehow both soft and stern. 'The bill states that the Driochta are to be allowed, in potentially violent or aggravated political circumstances, to serve as mediator between the present Government and any other party. I believe, therefore, that we have a duty and a right to attempt talks with the Boreen Men.'

Luke watches the Major for reaction – hands tight at his side twitch towards fists, knuckles pale purple. His breath makes swift scraps of white in the air and he says with such coldness, 'As you wish, my Lady. Go and speak with the troublemakers and malcontents. I shall give you one hour, and then my men shall storm the forest.'

Luke asks, 'Mother, should I Work any Spells to Seclude or Enclose us?'

'So keen!' says Lady Vane-Tempest.

'I know,' says Lady Mountfathom. 'Does it not take you back, Helena, to being thirteen years old and the heady empowering days when we first learned Magic? So ready to Work or weave Spells!'

'I just want to help,' says Luke.

'Now don't sulk,' says his mother, and rubs a hand over his hair.

'Just teasing,' says Lady Vane-Tempest. 'It is a very sensible thing to be so prepared.'

Luke feels as though he has been somehow snubbed; promises himself that if the need arises, he will prove himself.

Three of them move on through the trees: silver birch, branches snapped and some scorched, grim signs of the battle that forced the Boreen Men to retreat into the forest. All seems so simple to Luke, so clear: the behaviour of the Major and the Castle is wrong, the decision to hunt the Boreen Men down so abhorrent that he suggests, 'Can we not simply Work some Spell to send the Gards away? Leave the Boreen Men alone?'

'Surely,' says Lady Mountfathom. 'And also start all-out war in the process.'

'Would put a stop to things,' says Luke.

'For now,' says Lady Vane-Tempest. 'But do not forget, as our fool of a friend Flann Dorrick would say: *consequences*.'

'One thing you should remember,' says Luke's mother, 'is that violence and Magic cannot coexist. The Driochta may fight, but only when it is unavoidable. We fight only with a greater goal in mind. Remember the Third Principle, Luke – the value of knowing when to act, and when to restrain oneself.'

Lady Vane-Tempest adds, 'The day this land chooses battle and blood over discussion will be a sorry day for Magic, and a sorrier day for all in Ireland.'

Luke recites his mother's words to himself, attempts, as he does with so much, to learn and commit them to memory.

'Not far now,' says Lady Vane-Tempest.

Luke sees no sign of the Rath yet. Wonders aloud, 'How will we get into the Rath if they have it so well protected?'

'Well now,' says Lady Vane-Tempest, 'I have an answer to that!'

She says nothing more.

They walk for another minute or more till suddenly Luke sees an ancient rowan standing tall at the centre of a small clearing. *A Quicken Tree*, thinks Luke. A species favoured by the extinct Faerie Folk.

'Here now,' says Vane-Tempest, and lays her hand on the trunk. Luke and his mother move close and, only just, discern a carving: two figures, both with human heads but the torsos and lower parts of foxes.

'An entrance,' says Luke. He recalls a woodcut illustration in a book he finished only two or three weeks before.

'Continue,' his mother tells him.

'I read in *The Lost Ways of Faerie* that some colonies of the Folk could Mogrify, and so they used to create these small entrances that led into the Raths – they would transform into foxes or badgers or sometimes birds and get inside. Is that correct?'

'Such a smart boy,' says Lady Vane-Tempest.

'No grown man could gain entry,' says Lady Mountfathom, 'but only an animal or one of the Folk who had Mogrified. Or, sometimes, a stray child.'

And Luke knows what he must do, has no hesitation in saying, 'I'll go in. I'll speak to the Boreen Men and do my best to get them to agree to some kind of discussion with Major Fortflay and the Castle.'

'Such a brave boy too!' says Lady Vane-Tempest.

'Do you know how to bid the tree to open?' asks Luke's mother, as though this is all a test – something organised, contrived.

And once more, no hesitation in Luke's answer: 'By whispering a wicked wish.'

'Go right ahead,' Lady Vane-Tempest tells him. 'We shan't listen!'

So: Luke lays both hands on the trunk of the Quicken Tree, leans in close and in an intimate whisper offers, 'If I could, I would Work a Spell to shrink Major Fortflay to the size of one of the Faerie Folk he destroyed and see how he likes it.'

And the Faerie tree favours this confession – trunk instantly splits open as though on a sprung hinge! Opens onto nothing – cool cavity choked with a dripping darkness. Luke hesitates, wonders – realises he is slowly developing a sense for the presence of Spells, for the vestiges of Magic – and he senses something ahead, something perhaps already in the process of being Worked . . .

'We do not have much time,' says his mother urgently.

'Good luck,' says Lady Vane-Tempest.

And Luke stoops and steps into the tree, and discovers a muddy slope to start down. Soon on hands and knees he goes, and has less than a minute of light before the trunks shuts and he is lost to the dark.

Luke could conjure a little light, but Spells of Illumination are temperamental. Any attempt Luke has made hasn't done as bid: flared too bright, taken on a displeasing colour, fizzled and died. And so difficult to judge – he could mean to conjure only a tiny flicker and instead Work a forest fire! So best not to, not yet.

Now suddenly the slope levels out and leaves him in a tunnel – Luke stands taller, scalp touching a damp ceiling sprouting whirls of feeble grey-white roots. He looks both ways. A stinging coldness rushes down the tunnel and makes him draw his cloak closer. And he walks in the direction the cold is coming from; is only minutes along when he hears shouts from somewhere ahead –

'We're only asking for our rights! Some basic rights for workers, that's all we want!'

'Not to be treated like animals!'

'We need food to keep our families!'

'Fourteen of us in my house in the tenements! Fourteen in a place with three rooms!'

His tunnel takes a sudden turn, and now Luke is exposed to a chamber carved out of the earth, so throws himself to the wall and keeps still and thinks of Working some Seclusion but thinks again – any weaving of a hand might get him noticed. He watches.

At the centre of the chamber: the rambling and heavy-knuckled roots of a tree, its furthermost tips hung with lanterns. One broad man stands nearest the roots and in the low light it is he who gees up two dozen (perhaps more? Hard to tell in the dimness) other men. 'Are we gonna let them silence us now? Gonna let them lock us out of the city and force us to live rough like a pack of barbarians or Woodkernes?'

Such roars! They bring the stutter of soil from the ceiling –

'Not a bit of it!'

'No way!'

'Not so long as I've got breath in me!'

Luke sees men mucky in the face, clothes faded and boots split. But their spirits blazing. They shake hands and smack one another on the back and open dark mouths to roar as their leader shouts to them, 'We are gonna go out there and show them we won't be silenced! Show them what the Boreen Men are made of!'

But Luke sees one not joining in: a figure folded on the ground with his knees dragged tight to his chest, and appearing appalled not just at the rabble around him but the state of his clothes.

'Mr Dorrick,' Luke whispers to himself.

And as though he has been greeted aloud, Flann Dorrick looks up and sees Luke and says (too loud), 'Oh, thank goodness.'

Fool, thinks Luke, shrinking back into the shadows, but too late –

The leader of the Boreen Men stops – his sight wanders and he sees Luke in the tunnel and straightaway shouts, 'A bloody spy! Grab that boy there!'

Luke lets himself be taken – thinks that any Spell now would only enrage the men further – so allows himself to be half-lifted and dragged towards the roots of the tree and the man in charge. Luke is dropped, stays there on his knees in the wet.

'My name is Malone,' says the leader, and waits. Has such blue and assessing eyes. Now shouts, 'I've shown you some decency by introducing myself, so you should do the bloody same!'

'Luke Mountfathom.'

And of course, some shiver of recognition passes through the cavern.

'One of the Driochta, is it?' asks Malone.

'Yes,' says Luke. 'I have come here to help start discussions between yourselves and the –'

But barely gets beyond starting when the tumult rises once more –

'The nerve of that bastard Fortflay!'

'Who does he think he is sending this boy down here!'

'Coward that he can't face us himself!'

'Quiet,' says Malone, quietly. And the Boreen Men settle themselves. He turns to Luke. 'Your father tried to help during the Lock Out – tried to get us back into the factories and back to work and earning even a measly crust. He tried to start discussions between us and the Castle and none of it did a button of good. We shall fight, and not give in!'

'What is the alternative?' says Flann Dorrick now. He stands, straightens his tie and tugs at his cuffs. 'I mean really – it simply cannot go on like this. What you need to do is –'

'We don't *need* to do anything!' shouts Malone.

'No,' says Luke, speaking before Dorrick can say another word. 'You don't need to, but would it not be better for all if you tried?'

'We shall fight,' says Malone. 'Fight and not give in!'

'You cannot keep fighting – Major Fortflay has a hundred Gards on the borders of the forest and if you do not enter into talks he will storm into this Rath and destroy all of you.'

'Even he wouldn't dare do that!' says the leader of the Boreen Men, though some doubt sounds in his words.

Luke tells him, 'He will. He did it with the Gyants and the Good Folk and plenty of other creatures, and he will do it to you without thinking twice.'

Luke stops. Wishes his words had more weight – that he could speak like his mother or father and have in him their special brand of authority. Yet as he watches he sees his words take some unexpected effect – as though he has uttered a Spell, the attitude of the men is shifting. Does he discern some softening in their looks?

But Luke knows that all depends on the feelings of their leader.

Malone rests a hand on Luke's shoulder and says: 'For the sake of my friends here and to stop their blood being shed, I shall go and do my best to reason with that gobshite of a Major.'

'Oh, thank goodness,' says Dorrick.

'Not that it was anything that you did,' says Malone, sharp once more. 'It was this boy who spoke some sensible words, not you! I still don't have trust in all this Magic, specially seeing as Fortflay has been organising for some extra power to be brought from across the water.'

'What?' asks Luke.

'You know well he has favours he can call in from that Politomancer in Whitehall,' says Malone.

'That was simply a one-off,' says Dorrick, stepping forward. 'Mr Malone, when Magic was used to close the boundaries of Dublin and keep you out – that was merely a one-time request.'

'Is that right?' says Malone. 'And how can you be so sure?'

'We were promised,' says Flann Dorrick, straightening his spine as much as it can be straightened in such a small space. 'The word of Whitehall was given to the Order of the Driochta that no more Magic would be used without consultation with the Driochta! This is an absolute –'

'Quiet,' says Luke suddenly. He feels some change, some sure instinct that Magic is being Worked: same feeling as when he stood on the threshold of the Quicken Tree. Malone, though, pays no heed – is keen to go on, perhaps to further goad Dorrick on his ignorance.

'Well, you were lied to, weren't you? Did Fortflay not bother to say? Shame. He wrote to Whitehall two days ago and asked for some extra help; that Politomancer fella who helped during the war and used Spells to keep us out of the city would be very happy to send some more wickedness to try to finish us off!'

The voice of another Boreen Man resounds in the gloom. 'Malone! What the hell is that?'

And before Luke can turn to see, his sense of impending Spell-Work tells him: *It is here. Whatever dark Magic the Politomancer has Worked, it has arrived.*

'Stay back! Don't touch it whatever you do!' says Malone.

Luke sees: from a second tunnel some dark mass is edging into the chamber – dark earth moving like a dark river, creeping with the languor of serpent, its surface full of a gentle writhing and twitching.

'Don't go near it, I said!' cries Malone.

But his comrades won't listen: will not back away or be intimidated and they lift whatever instrument they can find – spade or shovel or blade – and face the darkness like it is something that can be beaten back.

'We must leave,' says Flann Dorrick, retreating towards the same tunnel Luke entered by. 'We must get out of here now!'

'No,' says Luke. 'We need to help them!'

He sees: the dark tide touches one of the Boreen Men.

A scream of such agony from the man as though he has been touched by fire!

Slow tide that suddenly snatches at the man's legs.

And the Boreen Man is stopped, stilled as though petrified, as though stone, the darkness climbing his legs like a canker and spreading across his abdomen and chest as others try to free him and are infected too.

Luke can think of no Spell to help and the space is too small to contain all the screaming as Flann Dorrick Mogrifies into a cheetah and takes Luke's wrist in his jaws and drags him from the chamber –

Luke turns to take a last look: sees Malone trying to supress his own screams as he attempts to wrestle free of the darkness, but in vain. Malone falls to his knees as his whole body is seized, transformed, skin darkened and enclosed and encrusted with earth. The leader of the Boreen Men starts to cave under the weight of the dark, to shrink – limbs being cracked and crammed close and closer to his body . . .

Tunnel turns –

Luke sees no more – only hears the final screams of the Boreen Men as the ceiling caves and the chamber collapses.

Cry of Lady Vane-Tempest: 'What happened? We heard such screams!'

The trunk of the Quicken Tree is quick to release them. Luke falls to the ground, the cheetah of Flann Dorrick alongside him.

'What happened?' asks Lady Mountfathom, rushing to Luke, running her hands over his face. 'I sensed some Magic being Worked – such a darkness of a Spell.'

Luke chooses his words carefully, decides on the most important thing he must say to his mother. 'Major Fortflay lied to us. He was never going to give us time to talk to the Boreen Men. He's asked the Politomancer in Whitehall to help him – some Spell invaded the Rath and when it touched the Boreen Men it transformed them.'

'Into what?' asks his mother.

'I do not know,' says Luke. 'I didn't see it all – just that they were all being shrunk. Their bodies looked to be transforming, growing dark – turning to earth.'

Lady Mountfathom looks to Lady Vane-Tempest.

'It is true,' says Flann Dorrick, returning, with a shiver, to human form. 'I saw it also. It looked to me like a Spell of Humiliation – though I confess I have never seen anything so merciless.'

Lady Vane-Tempest grabs Dorrick by the lapels and shouts at him, 'Did you know about this pact between Fortflay and the Politomancer? You work in the Castle – it cannot have escaped your attention!'

'I didn't know of this!' says Dorrick.

'Well, you should have done!' shouts Lady Vane-Tempest. 'You should have kept your ears open!'

But Luke feels some sympathy for Dorrick (would feel sympathy for anybody being confronted by Helena Vane-Tempest), though feels a cold disappointment as Flann Dorrick says, 'There were rumours – but there are always rumours of deals for more powers with Whitehall. I did not think it true! I did not think it would come to this.'

'None of us would have,' says Lady Mountfathom calmly. Her words loosen some of the anger of Lady Vane-Tempest – she releases Dorrick. 'It is not your fault, Flann. We did not know how far the Major would go to retain control of matters in Ireland.'

'But now you are enlightened.'

All turn – Major Fortflay, a dozen Gards with rifles grouped around him.

He says, 'Magic can solve some problems, I will own to that.'

'Not Magic of this kind,' says Lady-Vane-Tempest, and Luke notices that her hand is hovering close to her Needle. Notices the same action elsewhere – his mother and Flann Dorrick also ready to act if they need to. 'It is a clear violation of the second

Bill of Cooperation! You cannot allow such Magic into Ireland without consulting with the Driochta. I shall see to it that –'

'Listen,' says Luke. Beneath his feet a tremor, some small shiver.

'What on this good earth – ?' starts Dorrick.

Lady Mountfathom shouts, 'Run!'

And the ground around the Quicken Tree drops: earth falling-folding into earth as Luke and his mother and Lady Vane-Tempest and Flann Dorrick flee.

'*Fire!*'

Rifles raised as the Gards start to shoot into the ground.

Luke is forced down by his mother but turns and sees now the results of the Politomancer's Magic.

Boreen Men fighting their way free from the ground like rabbits flushed from a warren, but scarcely distinguishable from the surrounding ground: their bodies small and enclosed in earth, eyes the only slips of humanity left and mouths wide and pink and screaming with anger and agony as they are gunned down by the Gards.

'We have to do something,' says Luke, and fights to his feet and lifts a hand, preparing to Work whatever Spell to stop the Fortflay and his Gards but –

'No,' says his mother. She grabs his wrist and holds it tight. 'No, we must not act! We must force ourselves to do nothing!'

Luke faces his mother. Sees tears in her eyes as she tells him, 'We cannot interfere with this.'

He turns to Lady Vane-Tempest – surely she will do something? Or even Flann Dorrick? But both remain, hands loose at their sides, faces almost impassive.

'These men are fighting for their rights,' says Luke. 'We should help them. Is that not the job of the Driochta?'

No one answers. No one acts.

Luke turns last of all to Major Fortflay – sees in his face no compassion, only a sense of cold duty. And Luke understands. *We cannot act. If we do, then Fortflay and the Castle will see us as enemies.*

'Back into the Rath! Back below, lads!'

Luke is sure this is the voice of Malone commanding his men into retreat – sees some of the surviving Boreen Men making an escape back into the shattered ground. Is certain he recognises one set of blue eyes; meets them and feels their hurt and horror before Malone vanishes back underground. Humiliated, broken – Luke understands this now.

Fourth Principle of Magic –
Of Utterance & The Potent Word
'Listen, and let me tell you a story . . .'

In the nights following, Luke sees the Boreen Men – dreams them. Relives in vivid nightmares the moments below ground, wakes in *The Amazon* drenched in sweat. He leaves his four-poster and crosses the floor and slips behind the curtains to sit on the deep sill and look out over the silent grounds of Mountfathom.

He is sleepless much of the time now – cannot stop his brain whirring with worry. So much shifting in the country, and Luke feels unable to understand it.

Morrigan leaps onto the windowsill. The cat gives him a (rare) consoling look.

And then the headlines.

FURTHER MAGIC NEEDED
TO QUELL REBELLION:
BOREEN MEN KILL THIRTY GARDS IN
BLOODY BATTLE NEAR DRAGON COAST!

99

'Liars,' says Luke. Disappointed more than angered: saddened more than riled by what he reads in the papers. 'Not a single Gard was killed – that is patently untrue.'

It is a Thursday, and Mr Gorebooth is happy to let the lesson digress into other territories.

'The *Enquirer* needs to toe the line, as they say. Needs to print what the Castle and Major Fortflay needs it to print.'

'How can the people at that newspaper live with themselves?' asks Luke.

'I do not know,' says Mr Gorebooth. 'Though this is one of the many reasons why poetry is preferable to the writings of the press.'

Fire of rebellion in the following year – each day the newspapers reporting on gun battles in bogland, skirmishes between Gards and rebels that destroy homes and leave bodies drifting in dark waters. And the Castle in Dublin struggles to contain what refuses to be contained – may as well try to capture shadows.

The Driochta have scarcely been more active.

Luke joins his mother and father on missions of a more ambassadorial nature: to the Aran Islands to meet with the Faithful, an attempt to forge some new civil agreement with the monks there; then on to the monks of Skellig, the so-called First Believers, in the hope of kindling some new cooperation. Both sects on both islands are disquieted by the business with the Boreen Men, and express their wish to be kept informed of any further Magical interference by the Politomancer at Whitehall. They make a sombre vow to let the Driochta know if they hear of any troubling plans by the Castle.

Will they tell us? asks Luke, as he moves through the Gloaming with his mother and father. Are they on our side?

It is not helpful to try to split matters in that way, says Lady Mountfathom.

True, says Lord Mountfathom. There are no such things as *sides* any longer.

And as though to mark the arrival of his fourteenth birthday, a realisation arrives too with Luke: *We are not simply working with the Government in Dublin Castle any more – the Driochta needs to work to look after itself.*

And it is now, so suddenly, that Luke becomes ill.

Happens too quick.

First day – Everyone knows there is something wrong with Luke before he knows himself; he sleeps late. This is the first odd thing, so unlike him. When Nanny Bogram finds him still in bed at eight o'clock and asks him why he isn't up and about, he tells her he is tired and needs more sleep. When she brings him his breakfast tray an hour later he cannot eat it – again pleads for sleep, some quiet and more rest. Morrigan lies across his chest and purrs deeply.

Second day – Sudden rise of fever, a continual cough, wild sweats . . .

Third day – Will hardly wake; is gabbling about Spells he needs to learn and how the walls of *The Amazon* are withering and the Boreen Men need to be rescued and returned to their families and he needs to be the one to do it or Mountfathom itself will crumble to dust . . .

'Can we do nothing?' Nanny Bogram asks Lord Mountfathom. She will not leave Luke's bedside. 'No Magic to help him?'

Lord Mountfathom says, 'There are Spells, of a sort, that can ease pain. Of Inertia and Dreamless Slumber, of Soothing and Consolation.'

Lady Mountfathom says, 'But they will only ease things, not cure. They are Spells for the mind, and this illness is a matter of the body.'

'We have to do something!' cries the nanny. And she holds the child's hand tight and vows not to let him go.

Fourth day – The Traces arrive in *The Amazon*. Nanny Bogram would ordinarily be keen to shoo them but she lets them be. Is comforted to some degree by the sight of them – faintest figures, like pale fingerprints on a dark pane. And their mutterings too somehow soothe her –

'Such a thing to happen – let him defy this illness!'

'He has such things ahead of him . . .'

'Such a special child . . .'

'Such a one . . .'

'Let him find his way back from the dark.'

And all the while, the House of Mountfathom itself is grieving – any lantern that is lit keeps a low light; candles stutter and weep; any fire begun in a grate soon shrinks and dies; Errander boys and maids cannot speak their prayers; any small Spell Worked by Lord and Lady Mountfathom will not take; food is spoiled and milk curdles in the can and cold creeps into every room, windows shivering in their frames and doors trembling when shut and boards groaning underfoot. As though the entire House is in such agony.

And now at night, Luke begins to scream.

Fifth day – The Driochta assemble in *The World*.

Sombre gathering. Mr Jack Gorebooth describes it, 'As though some precious light is leaving the place. As though some key and enduring Spell is beginning to fade!'

Flann Dorrick agrees. 'Yes – so true.'

Lady Vane-Tempest tells him, 'Let us not aggrandise this illness with such poetry, fancy words.'

Mr Halter: 'Perhaps words are what we need?'

Mrs Halter: 'Perhaps such words can be put to use?'

Lawrence Devine: 'He is fond of the words, the boy – fond of stories. Maybe too much! I remember when he used to be out getting mucky all day – collecting bones and dead animals.'

There is a stretch of silence.

There is much time without speech before Lord Mountfathom says, 'What makes any illness thrive is silence – we must find a way to fight back.'

Lady Mountfathom says, 'Our son loves his stories. So perhaps there is some answer there. Perhaps with words we can lead him back into the light?'

Later, a Spell seeps beneath the door of *The Amazon* – a mere thread that snakes its way across the floor, arriving with Mrs Bogram. She is snoring in a rocking chair, a small Bible in her hands. The Traces arranged by the bedside see the Spell, and respectfully withdraw to the shadows.

The thread of Spell slowly encircles and eases the Nanny from her chair, lifting her to rise towards the ceiling, to enclose Bogram in a complete, dreamless, undisturbed sleep. And when this Spell of Inertia has done its silent work, the door of *The Amazon* opens.

'Well cast, my love,' Lord Mountfathom tells his wife. 'As always.'

'Thank you, my dear,' says Lady Mountfathom.

'Jack?' says Lord Mountfathom. 'Are you ready?'

Jack Gorebooth says, with a slight shake in his words, 'Yes, I am ready.'

He steps into *The Amazon* and the door eases shut behind him. The room is almost dark, a lantern by the bed holding a humble flame. And such dampness in the air, such a heady sourness – an atmosphere that can only be attributed to sickness.

Morrigan stands on the bed: bristles with back arched, tail straight.

'Who's there?' cries Luke. 'Malone? Is that you?'

'Do not fret,' says Gorebooth, crossing the floor in small, near-silent steps. Morrigan settles – lies down and curls herself tight on the counterpane. 'It is only myself – Mr Gorebooth. The poet, you remember?'

'Owl,' says Luke. Sighs and says once more, 'An owl.'

'That is quite correct,' says Gorebooth. 'My animal form when I choose to Mogrify is an eagle owl.' He lowers himself into the rocking chair where Nanny Bogram had been keeping her vigil – glances up to see her drifting so serene, just below the chandelier.

And when all things feel right, Mr Gorebooth begins to talk to Luke.

'Do you know what the next Principle of Magic is? The Fourth?'

'Utterance,' says Luke. A struggle to swallow – coughs and winces, one limp hand crawling to his chest and throat and settling there. 'And the Potent Word.'

'That is quite correct. And in my humble opinion, there is no more important a Principle than this Fourth.'

Luke coughs and coughs, for such an extended time Mr Gorebooth feels as though it may never stop. Or perhaps stop suddenly, horribly. He takes Luke's hand and holds it between his own and says low, 'Listen to me now: let words weave their own Spell. Listen, and let me tell you a story . . .

'In the county of Fermanagh – which, being such a learned boy, I am sure you know is the most Magical of all counties in Ireland – there once lived a Magician of great intelligence and power. He lived alone in the shadow of the Forlorn Mountain, in a cottage of stacked limestone. And, as I say, he was a most intelligent man – wrote long and erudite pieces that were published in many a Magical journal.'

Luke groans – struggles to half-turn away and Mr Gorebooth knows he needs to shift his story, to find some detail to hold the boy's attention.

'He was a most creative man – invented many things, but his most infamous invention was a Skeleton Key that he fashioned from the bone of a Lough Gyant, and which allowed him to open any door and to step into the Gloaming.'

105

Luke settles. His eyelids part a little – he is watching now, he is listening. He is waiting. And so Jack Gorebooth goes on.

'These journeys into the Gloaming allowed the Magician of Fermanagh not only to travel anywhere he wished in the material world, but also to more numinous places: he was able to visit or revisit any part of his own life. So, he could choose to return to his boyhood to set eyes on his long-dead parents. Or to see his future wife, long deceased – to witness once more their very first meeting. But yet more of a wonder, the Magician had taught himself to travel so far from his own present self that he could travel into the future years of his life, meet himself as an old man . . . It allowed him to feel as though, perhaps, nothing in this world could truly be said to die. For if he could return to it – could see again his wife or parents – did that not mean that they lived still somewhere? Somehow endured?

'But for all these wonders and achievements, the Magician of Fermanagh was a solitary and isolated man. The locals in the surrounding countryside had little care for him. They thought him unsociable and rude. Though the reality (as is often the case) was very different – in fact, this Magician spent a great deal of time interacting with the people of Fermanagh, though not directly. For example, he had a rod of ivory and gold he had been gifted on his travels in the East, which acted something like a Needle. Being able to exert some command over the elements, he used this Needle of ivory to Conduct the weather – to Summon showers when the crops were crying out for rain, or to part the clouds and allow warm sun when that was what the people of the county desired. Or to drive

106

back dark waters when rivers burst their banks. Any number of acts small and large he undertook to benefit the lives of these strangers who so derided him.'

Jack Gorebooth pauses, plotting his next move. Luke squeezes his hand and whispers, 'Go on, Mr Gorebooth. Please.'

'Well,' says Gorebooth, 'the years passed in such a way – the Magician Working his thankless Spells and fashioning more and more intricate inventions from Faerie branches and lough water and fallen stars. And making his frequent excursions into the Gloaming, which was where he felt most contented – amongst the past, amongst those he had loved so dearly and lost. But this was not to continue. One cold morning, very suddenly, something changed. The solitary Magician of Fermanagh realised that he was not only alone, but unbearably lonely. He asked himself, "What is the point of a life if so much of it is lived in the past? What is the point of Spells Worked without care or appreciation?" For ten years, since the passing of his wife, he had been bereft on the mountainside beneath his stack of limestone. But no more, he vowed. The Magician decided that it was time for things to change.

'So, on this fateful morning, he stepped out onto the slope of the Forlorn Mountain and from the ground conjured a group of thirty-two Messengers.'

'What form did they take?' asked Luke.

'Why, they took the form of Peak Gyants. All thirty-two of them were thirty-two feet tall! Now, the Magician thought long about what words he wished to impart to the Messengers – this would be the message they would carry across Ireland, and he was a man who prided himself on the precision of his words

107

and so wanted it to be worded perfectly. And after much thought and deliberation, this is what he simply told his Gyant Messengers: "If there is any on this island who through words can help an old man mend his broken heart, then send them here and I shall hear what they have to say." And so the Magician of Fermanagh sent forth his group of thirty-two thirty-two-foot tall Messengers to each of the counties of Ireland, in search of someone who might cure him of his isolation and grief.

'Now, you shall not be surprised to hear that such phenomena does not go unnoticed. Messengers as tall as Peak Gyants moving across Ireland? People were both frightened and deeply fascinated. The matter was discussed in all counties – in pubs and fields, bogland and townland – and, eventually, in the Castle itself in Dublin. And I am rather ashamed to say (human nature being as it is), many people began to wonder at how the plight of the lonely Magician of Fermanagh might profit them.'

'Did anyone go to see him?' asked Luke. 'What did they say?'

'Nothing less than hundreds upon hundreds descended on Fermanagh! The roads of the county were packed with people coming from all over, and the locals of Fermanagh were not best pleased. They cursed the Magician for bringing such disruption to their lives when all they wished for was a bit of peace and quiet. So many came, and the Magician resolved that he would see each and every one of them. A long, long queue formed on the mountainside – snaking all the way through Florencecourt and the island town of Enniskillen and ending at the small doorway beneath the stack of limestone that was the Magician's home. And he invited each person in and gave each person precisely one minute to tell him of how to cure his loneliness and heartache. And the stories they came out with! Some told him he needed to invest in their farms and he would surely feel the benefit of having helped someone less well off than himself. Some said he needed to Work Magic on them to make them finer of voice and more pleasing to the eye, and surely the joy that would bring would make his heart lighter. Or (said a man from the Castle in Dublin who had attempted disguise) he should concentrate on offering his services to the country at large and Work widespread Spells of Reclamation to bind the land more firmly to the Big Houses!

'Thankfully, none of these entreaties were listened to. Each person was dismissed, and each night the Magician went to bed more firmly convinced that there were simply no words in all of Ireland powerful enough to lift him from his grief.'

Jack Gorebooth pauses. Notices that Morrigan appears as attentive as Luke in wanting to know what happened next.

'It is very fortunate indeed that one of the Magician's Gyant Messengers arrived here at Mountfathom. A whole season later, in spring, your great-grandfather Francis Mountfathom was out seeing to his vegetables in the kitchen garden when suddenly he was cast into shadow. He looked up and saw the thirty-two-foot tall Messenger standing over him. And he listened as the Messenger whispered the message he had been charged with. Your great-grandfather Francis was a tenacious and bold man – prone to all kinds of sudden passions and obsessions. And so he decided instantly that he must heed the message given him, and so threw down his trowel and readied his horse and made haste that very day for the Forlorn Mountain of Fermanagh!

'When he arrived, the crowds of people awaiting an audience with the Magician were much depleted, though still your great-grandfather Mountfathom had to take his place at the rear of the line and wait for a full week and a half for his turn to see the man in his limestone cottage. Whilst waiting in line, he listened to the chat of the others around him. Much he discarded as nastiness and hearsay and gossip, but one thing he did find of interest: talk of a Skeleton Key the Magician had invented, its ability to take a person into the Gloaming, and how it could lead them anywhere in the world and anywhere within a person's own life.

'And when his moment came to enter he was full of nervousness and concern, which was not at all like him. But within moments, he felt he had the measure of this man. The Magician was seated deep in shadow, appeared sunken and so very weary. He was surrounded by so many towers of books that they appeared as pillars holding up the ceiling! And the room was packed with so many ingenious inventions, stacks of paper marked by intricate Spells and mirrors stained with ink from so much Predicting that your great-grandfather thought the whole place a very sorry sight – no life, he believed, should be so devoted to Magic. For there is so much more to the world than time spent alone and imagining. And so, your great-grandfather Francis felt only great pity for the Magician of Fermanagh.

'"You have already expended half of your allotted time gawking around!" the Magician shouted at your great-grandfather. "So speak up for yourself now, or you may as well get out and give another their turn!"

110

'And your great-grandfather thought long about his words. He checked his pocket watch – watched the small hand tick away the seconds until he had only ten remaining to him. And only then did he speak. "Sir, there is so little that can truly cure a broken heart. No amount of time – or moving forward or backward through it as someone would swim through a treacherous sea – will help you. Though if you so wish it, here is my offer: I would be your good friend so that you should not have to live so alone in this life."'

Jack Gorebooth stops.

Luke has fought his way upright; is no longer coughing, his breath leaving his body more cleanly. And the eyes! His eyes have reclaimed some of the remarkable curiosity that burned in them since birth. The child sounds more like himself too as he asks, 'And what did the Magician of Fermanagh do?'

Mr Gorebooth smiles. Laughs a little and finds that a single tear has left his left eye. He wipes it away gently as he says, 'The Magician of Fermanagh made a decision – that he would leave his limestone mound on the slope of the Forlorn Mountain and go with your great-grandfather. Decided that he would abandon his many instruments and inventions of Magic, and that he would in fact and from that day on give up Magic entirely!'

'What?' asks Luke. Morrigan once more rises with back arched and tail poker-straight – the epitome of outrage at the words of Mr Gorebooth. 'How can that be true?'

'It simply is,' says Mr Gorebooth. He stands – Works his hand in the air, Dismissing the Spell of Inertia holding Nanny Bogram and steers her back into the rocking chair where she resumes her snoring. 'And as to the answer why . . .

Why leave behind Magic? Why would the Magician leave behind his journeys into the Gloaming? Why abandon the chance to see again those long lost? Well, I shall leave that with you to wonder about, my boy. I shall allow you the very simple yet essential joy of finishing this story as you so wish.'

Fifth and Final Principle of Magic –
Of The Necessity of the Unknown
'No matter what awaits you in the great
unknown of the world, there is nothing worse
than being afraid of stepping into the dark.'

At the end of the hallway on the third floor, between one emerald wall and one crimson, hoards of portraits holding generations and generations of previous Orders of the Driochta, Luke and Lord and Lady Mountfathom stand before the dark door.

'But how shall I know where to go?' asks Luke. It has arrived. Five years – sounded such an interminable time when he was younger, and now he marvels at how suddenly it has come. He is fifteen, and to become a member of the Driochta, he must now do this last thing.

'You cannot know for certain,' says Lord Mountfathom. 'When you step into the Gloaming on your own, there are a great many distractions and potential wrong turnings.'

'What kind of distractions?'

'I always try to think of it in this way,' says Lady Mountfathom. 'Imagine yourself a pioneer landing in a strange, uncharted country! No map, no compass, just a dim sense of landscape and shape. You do not know the correct way to go – perhaps there is no correct way. But still you must move on – navigate obscure roads and pathways, passing through light and dark. And in the end and when you are ready, you must find your way home.'

'You must trust,' his father tells him.

'You must be brave,' says his mother.

And Luke has no certainty, and doesn't like it. But has learned well how to transform his fear into something else.

'Alright,' he says. 'I am ready. Let us begin.'

And his mother takes from her pocket the crimson key and inserts it into the lock and turns it with a snap. A moment, now a long, echoing note: the silver handle shaped like an outstretched hand is turned and the dark door opens onto deeper dark.

'Take my key,' says Lady Mountfathom. 'Use it well. Respect it, and it will lead you true.'

Lord Mountfathom says, 'We shall see you very soon, son.'

In Luke's hand, the crimson light of the key is inconstant – imparts only a little, though when he holds it tighter and thinks *I must do this*, it burns that bit brighter. And he feels braver.

'Now or not at all,' he whispers.

And so steps through the doorway and into the Gloaming.

Nothing now –
No one nowhere –
Luke's breathing has a shallow sombre pitch –
sounds unnecessary.

114

And he waits, tries not to hold his breath –
Realises: *I cannot wait.*
Realises: *No Spell will help me here – this is instead
something else, something different. This is the point
of the Fifth and Final Principle – this is something
that cannot be learned.*

Luke walks.

As he walks through the unknown of the Gloaming, he thinks
on the words of his mother as they climbed the stairs together
to the third floor, unpicking the Spell of Cessation that was once
set with the purpose of protecting him. She said, 'Knowledge
is not moving towards a place of smug satisfaction – not at
all! That is not true learning. If anything, the opposite is true.'

'Then why have I been learning for the past five years?' he
had asked. 'What was the purpose of it all?'

His father told him, 'That is for you to decide – it is merely
a beginning. Though I would say this: if you are very fortunate,
you will live long enough in this life to achieve a complete
and blissful ignorance.'

What do you see?

Luke stops now. He hears a voice deep and cold and full
of echoes –

What do you wish to see?

Luke holds the crimson key higher, but the light will not lay
a path as he has seen it do for his mother. He has been told not
to wish for a destination – not to desire certainty and things
familiar, but to crave this unknown. To stand and be and only
endure in this undecided dark.

The voice of the Gloaming tells him –

You are frightened. And I have so many secrets to show you.
Will you follow me? Will you learn the last and final thing?

Luke walks on – wanders, not knowing what is ahead but
knowing that to stay in safety is no longer possible. The world
has changed – he has grown and must take his place in the
Driochta. No more games in the grounds of Mountfathom,
no more time for such play.

And all the while he hears a voice telling –

You come from such a familiar place – somewhere you have
hardly ventured from all your life. You have been happy there,
content and safe. And this is nothing to bemoan – it is a great
thing to feel so safe. But it cannot last. It will not last!

These final words shouted in a growl that shakes Luke's
spine and he fumbles the crimson key and is almost parted
from it. He shouts back –

I am not afraid of the unknown! I am not afraid of leaving
Mountfathom! I can leave if I wish and return if I wish and I –

And what, says the voice, *if it is not there to greet you when*
you return?

Luke stops; his breathing has become a frantic thing, like
the worrying of so many wings, a flock of dark birds panicked
into flight and –

If the place you call home is not there, then where do you go?

The voice grows quiet. But Luke senses some close presence –
feels on the back of his neck the breath of something wild and
gloatingly full of knowledge and threat, and bloated with the
wish to disabuse him of his threadbare ideas and petty learning.

Voice whispers –

I shall show you.

Something blooms in the darkness – a scene pale and washed of all colour. Luke moves towards it, recognises the Temple of Ivory that stands on a rise overlooking the grounds of Mountfathom. It is where his ancestors rest, where their bones are buried beneath ivory slabs and ivory casts of the Veiled Ladies. Closer and closer he moves and then stops – sees that the Temple itself is made not of cool ivory but human bone.

This is what you will one day know. This is what will one day undo you and all your wondrous learning – this is the end of all things.

The Veiled Ladies turn to face him.

And Luke can only cry out and scream for home.

Flees from the sight as the crimson key lays a livid path in the dark for him to follow, feeling all the while as though he is being pursued by this creature, this thing, this voice –

Run, Luke Mountfathom – but you will someday return to face me.

Now a doorway outlined in crimson light; Luke unlocks it and escapes to that place so familiar – to home, and the awaiting arms of his mother and father.

'What is the creature in the Gloaming?' asks Luke.

So much later, he is sitting in *Valhalla* with his parents – they play cards together, his mother almost always winning.

Lord Mountfathom says, 'My own father called it only "The Monster". I do think he was being a little melodramatic –'

'So unlike his son,' says Lady Mountfathom, and smiles.

'Or perhaps,' Luke's father goes on, 'he simply wanted to put me on my guard, which was no bad thing I suppose.'

'Has anyone in the Driochta ever found out what it is?' asks Luke.

'What makes you so certain we can ever know what it is?' asks his mother, glancing at her cards. 'Have you learned nothing today, Luke?'

A pause.

'I am sorry, Mother,' says Luke.

'This Monster,' says Lord Mountfathom, 'if we are going to call it that, is a something every member of the Driochta has had to face. From when the Order first began, each person selected from whatever field – medicine or science, agriculture or politics – has learned all Principles and then stepped into the Gloaming.'

'The aim of it is not to work it out and so settle the matter in your mind,' says Lady Mountfathom, sipping some claret. 'It should unnerve you, Luke. There are many things in the world that should make you question yourself.'

She lays down her cards – wins once again. Full house!

Luke's father leans back in his chair with a yawn. 'The creature is akin to the Gloaming itself and also not unlike your mother's extraordinary skill at poker,' says Lord Mountfathom. 'Both are a great and fascinating mystery.'

They sit quietly for a moment, contented. Though one question still turns and turns in fretful circles in Luke's mind. He must ask it.

'I shall have to face it again someday. It said it had some truth to tell me – something it wanted to show that I needed to see.'

'Do not worry yourself,' says Lord Mountfathom.

But Lady Mountfathom takes a different view.

'You may worry, Luke, but do not let it stop you from being adventurous in life. No matter what awaits you in the great unknown of the world, there is nothing worse than being afraid of stepping into the dark.'

A Saturday in early summer and cousin Rose has come to visit. Chaperoned by a sour-looking maid from Goreland Hall, Rose is thirteen and tall for her age. Curls have softened into a sheet of sheer auburn. She is dressed in red with yellow socks and gloves and (it seems) likes to speaks her mind.

'You never invited me back!' she tells Luke by way of greeting. Then she smiles, embraces him on the doorstep. Some awkwardness – caused mostly by Mr Findlater hovering nearby, holding Rose's bag and not the three years since they've last seen one another.

But suddenly, as though they are children again –

'Want to play Secret-and-Secluded?' she asks, and sprints off across the wide shingle drive. And Luke – fifteen years old and telling himself he is too old for such things – follows fast.

Past the labyrinth, around Mr Hooker with his head in a flowerbed and the Errander boys and maids playing tennis on the lawn and by the blank gaze of statues – previous Lords and Ladies of Mountfathom – and towards the lagoon and the unruly patch of rhubarb spreading wild by the waterside.

Suddenly Luke loses sight of Rose, as though she has Worked a Spell of Seclusion.

He stands beneath the golden willow and watches bright dragonflies swerve and dart over the blue-green surface of the water.

'*Here!*' A whisper harsh as a summons. '*Under here!*'

Luke stoops to see beneath the rhubarb – his cousin Rose crouched. She smiles and crawls off, moving deeper into shadows pink and green. He follows, and feels no shame in it – no care for how childish this is, how much an indulgence. He thinks of the last message received from Flann Dorrick in Dublin – seventeen Big Houses burned by the Land Grabbers in Mayo and Galway, more being destroyed each night. Thinks of the Driochta journeying to the remaining Big Houses to draw Spells of Reclamation – Magic that binds the property to its owners, repels any invader or attempt to destroy it. Thinks too of the uproar in Dublin and Major Fortflay's threats of retribution for what he called in that morning's issue of *The Dublin Enquirer*, 'The law-breaking miscreants who would see this country burn!' Luke leaves all this behind – sheds responsibility and worry like an unwanted skin as he joins his cousin in cool shadows.

Some more of that awkward silence. Luke breaks it by saying, 'Here is an interesting fact, cousin – did you know that if you listen terribly hard you can actually hear rhubarb growing?'

And they sit together cross-legged and chat about any topic that arrives. Sit for how long? For some amount of time Luke would not be able to decide, but he feels each second as precious.

'What Magic have you learned?' Rose asks. 'Can you change into an animal yet?'

'No,' says Luke. And then finds himself saying, 'But I will soon.'

'How do you know?'

He smiles.

'I just do.'

And because Rose pleads with him, he shows her only some of what he has learned: Conjures shapes from the air – pale forms of starlings and stoats, fox and hare; Works a Spell of Subterfuge to change the length of his hair and nose; makes it rain, makes it snow; makes the leaves of rhubarb wither and then ripen once more . . . all trifles, nothing too serious. But Rose is mightily impressed.

'You've changed so much,' she says. 'Learned so much.'

And they talk on.

Conversation stumbles to a stop only when Rose says, 'Father wants us to leave Ireland, to go and live in London. Says he is going to give Goreland Hall one more year and then to hell with it – is going to get on a boat and get away from here.'

'I could never leave Mountfathom,' says Luke. And means it: cannot conceive of walking away from this world, from the house where his parents and grandparents lived, from Nanny Bogram and –

'Is that your father?' whispers Rose, pointing to a place beneath the leaves. 'And your mother too? Those are her wellies!'

Luke watches through the smallest sliver of space – sees indeed his mother and father's feet passing by. They are moving slowly. And he moves just as slowly on hands and knees back towards the lagoon.

'Stay here a minute,' he tells Rose.

'No, stay with me!' she says, and snatches up his hand. 'Let's stay here a bit longer, pretend it is still like it used to be.'

Luke says very calmly, 'I just need to know where my parents are going. I'll not be long. Please now?'

Slowly, she lets him go. Says as though it still a game, 'Good luck! Come back safe!'

Luke sets off.

When he returns to the bank of the lagoon, the air around him is darker – swollen grey clouds move slowly across the sky, stealing sight of the sun. And he sees standing on the other side of the lagoon – a man with dark eyes and a pale face and faded hair. It looks to Luke like the same man who three years before stood on the Isle of Solitude and tried to kill him and Rose. And Luke's first instinct would be fear – to raise the alarm and cry for help – if he did not also see his mother and father standing beside the man with faded hair. They are talking to him.

Luke watches.

They stand near the statue of King Glotsickel, the last King of the Faeries.

And Luke still watches and waits and wishes he could hear what was being said. He wonders, has the man with faded hair broken into Mountfathom? Fought through their Spells of Seclusion and Security? Is he to be reasoned with? Are Lady and Lord Mountfathom trying, as always, to be diplomatic and peacemaking – perhaps helping their home to escape the fate of the other Big Houses?

One thing Luke notices about the man though: he looks almost defeated. Is smaller perhaps, or does he imagine that from such a distance? Older? Sadder. Has all the melancholy aspect of one of the Traces. Or worse – of a ghost. And suddenly

Luke wonders, *Is it in fact the same man from that afternoon on Loughreagh?* Decides in an instant: *No. He looks more like a boy.*

And the dragonflies continue to dance, robbed of bright colour by dark sky.

A breeze rattles the boughs of the golden willow and suddenly –

A rustle of thunder –

A scream –

Rose runs from the rhubarb shouting, 'You said you wouldn't be long!'

The scream makes Lord and Lady Mountfathom and the boy with faded hair look across the lagoon. Luke feels a shiver in his bones, as deep and uncanny as when the voice of the Monster spoke to him in the Gloaming.

And it begins to rain.

'Is the game over now?' asks Rose.

Luke turns to her. Says, 'No, the game is not over.'

And turns back – his mother and father and the boy have gone.

'No, Rose – I think the game is just about to begin.'

PART THREE

THE WITHERING

Disputed Land: undoubtedly the most
disagreeable when responding to Spells.
On a whim will take whatever
damnable allegiance it likes!
Or stubbornly decide to take
no allegiance at all . . .

Guide to Agrarian Spells
(Lesson XVII: When Spells Refuse to Take)
Lawrence Devine

LUKE

Watch closely now.

A single starling settles on a windowsill. Restless thing, hops along and along, looking anxious and peering through the smudged pane. But the inside of Goreland Hall is the same as out – only dark. Starling's head is a twitch of curiosity, a ceaseless left-right-left-right-left . . . sudden stop.

A clock somewhere inside groans twelve.

And the starling becomes a boy.

All happened so suddenly one morning at Mountfathom. Luke awoke before dawn and felt instant excitement, leapt from bed and ran to the window and this time did not bundle himself onto the sill to sit, but instead twisted the latch. Waited some moments, Morrigan regarding him from the bed – sceptical cat, eyes half-shut, head barely raised. And then Luke was gone – off through the window and away . . .

In the weeks since, he has taken well to Mogrifying – each time easier, taking pleasure in becoming something other than what he is.

Now: window is luckily off the latch, so out on the windowsill Luke elbows it open and stretches one leg through. His foot finds the floor firm enough so he brings the second long leg alongside. He stands and listens; some sound from downstairs? From the front drawing room – sound of laughter and scuffing of boot against bare boards?

He thinks, *Now, quick! Need to get to work . . .*

His coat starts to squirm and he fumbles open two brass buttons and out pours a cat the colour of smoke. It lands soundlessly as he puts a finger to his lips for *Shh!* The cat gives him a bland look, starts to wash herself.

'You do lookout,' says Luke. 'Give me a signal if you spy anything, Morrigan. That agreed?'

The cat gives only a lazy wave of the tail. But eventually consents; ups and pads off to stand sentry by the door.

Goreland Hall is not like Luke remembers it – his trips here to visit his cousins and aunt and uncle are part of a drifting, fading and almost obsolete past. But this is his mission: he must tether it, try to save and restore it. And with the other Driochta working in the grounds, busy in the dark, he knows what is expected of him.

So from his coat Luke takes a leather notebook and sharp charcoal pencil. Inside the notebook: pages already torn loose in preparation. He kneels and lays the sheets out like cards – one, two, three, four, five . . . five chances for the Reclamation to take, five chances to save Goreland Hall from the Land Grabbers. To save Uncle Walter, Aunt Nancy, Rose.

'Now,' he says to himself. 'Let's keep everything crossed that this works. Right, Morrigan?'

The cat gives him no kind of look.

'There's the spirit,' he says. 'Stay alert. Let us hope we don't get discovered too soon.'

Luke settles the dark point of the pencil on the first sheet of paper and slowly starts to draw his Spell.

KILLIAN

Something desperate in somewhere dark; a handful of damp newspaper smashes a window, and in snakes a hand to flick the latch free.

Has to be done, he thinks. *Needs must!*

The boy is inside and across the shop floor in a couple of seconds. Silent on bare feet, he goes straight for the rack of cigarettes. He knows the old man owner lives above with the wife and two plain, polite daughters – knows that if he's caught this time he'll be for the children's home.

A voice outside says, 'Stop hanging about, son! Hurry up!'

His father (poor fella) has a gammy leg so is waiting outside. Will soon have to retire from the business of thieving altogether, so he's trying to get his son trained up well. 'I don't intend to spend my last days on some street begging for smokes,' the father said to the son before they set out. 'You're the one who's gonna have to look after me!'

The boy in the dark shop also takes a copy of a *Dodgy Dom* comic and two big bars of Bryce's chocolate and –

Father says, 'Would you come on?'

The boy stops – sees a shadow on the staircase. Surely the shadow of the old man owner and shadow of a shivering rifle in his hands and the owner shouts, 'I've had enough of this! Fifth time this year and I've had enough. Do you hear me, lad? I'm going to put an end to it and I don't care what happens!'

The boy says plainly, 'Look, times are hard in Belfast. And sure I'm only ten years old!' (A lie: he is fifteen.) 'And I'm only stealing these bits for me mam because she's fierce unwell, Mister!' (Another lie: his mother has been in Heaven since he was two and three-quarters.)

'I don't care a damn! You've no bloody right!'

And the shadow of the owner steps towards the boy called Killian, rifle raised and sure as anything ready to fire and put a stop to it all once and forever!

LUKE

A pistol pressed tight to his temple and a voice tells him, 'Don't you move a feckin muscle!' Luke is still crouched with his charcoal pencil and one sheet of paper remaining. 'Gimme that!' Pencil snatched and snapped, paper taken and torn and Luke feels the Reclamation Spell slowly dissipate – an hour of work wasted! And thanks to Morrigan for no warning! He thinks, *Where is that lazy cat, anyway?*

Pistol presses again at his skull and the same voice asks, 'What the hell are you doing here? Get up!'

No choice but to rise.

'Look me in the eye!' shouts the voice.

Luke turns; too dark to see the fullness of a face, he sees only eyes wide above an open mouth and bared teeth. Pistol is prodded into Luke's belly and the eyes look him up and down and the mouth says, 'You're very well turned out here, aren't you now? Big warm coat and heavy boots and all. Look to me like another Lord of the bloody Manor!'

A shout from downstairs. 'What's going on up there? Who is it?'

Man with the pistol shouts, 'It's a lad! Dunno how the hell he got in!'

'Well, is he for the Free State or against?'

Another, calmer, voice from below. 'Just bring him down.'

Jab of the pistol to Luke's stomach. 'You heard the man – let's go!'

KILLIAN

Simple as this: the boy is quicker than the old man owner.

He drops the chocolate and cigarettes and comic and grabs the barrel of the rifle but it goes off and blows a hole somewhere behind his shoulder. There is screaming from upstairs – owner's wife and two lovely daughters in a terror. Screaming too from Killian's father who is screaming nothing helpful. 'For Godsake get the better of him, son! Come on or the Peelers'll be here!'

Killian thinks, *Thanks for the advice, Da!*

He wrestle-wrenches the rifle from the owner and at the same time sends the old man sprawling onto the shop floor, and as he falls, there's a sound of a *thwack-crack* – skull against stone floor. And the owner goes still, doesn't move. Killian watches him.

'What the hell are you doing gawping!' shouts the boy's father. 'Come on! The Peelers are busy elsewhere but with our luck they'll probably turn up especially to collar us! And don't forget them fags.'

But Killian crouches and puts his hand on the shop owner's chest, same way he did when he found his mother cold on that cold morning. But this time is different – he feels the jerk of a stubborn enough old heart and breathes a bagful of relief.

A sudden blast right by his ear just misses him!

A new shadow on the staircase – the wife with another shotgun and she's shouting, 'You bloody murdered my husband! You thieving little –'

All else lost in rifle shots as Killian snatches up the cigarettes and runs for the window and feels broken glass graze palm and sole and thigh as he squirms out into the air, his father grabbing him by the arms and dragging him free saying, 'You're a halfwit if ever there was one, lad!' Father takes the fags and jams them into his pocket. Killian hears the sound of a whistle. Alarm raised for the police? Or just the continuing sing from the gunshot that almost took his ear off?

'See now?' says his father. 'The Peelers! Come on, quick! Run for it!'

LUKE

So many voices shouting –

'That joke for a Government in Dublin think they can outsmart us?'

134

'This is our land and we're taking it back fair and bloody square!'

'Who sent you, anyway?'

'Who are you here with?'

'I said WHO bloody sent you?'

Luke surrounded. Moonlight shows Luke how many? Maybe twenty, maybe more . . .

'What are we gonna do with you then?' says the man with the pistol.

Luke says nothing. He stands now in the old drawing room – remembers it well enough from his few visits to Goreland Hall when he was young. Familiar faces in photographs. He sees signs that this Land Grabber occupation has been days long at least: blankets for bedding across sofas and chairs, family portrait over the fireplace used for a dartboard, stack of empty bottles, furniture broken for use as a barricade against the tall windows.

Someone suggests, 'Tie him up with the family?'

Luke feels he should speak so he says, 'I came here to help.'

The men swear-heckle-mock –

'Help!'

'*Help?*'

'Bloody help yourself!'

Luke starts, 'I only wish to –'

But gets a boot in the small of his back and falls on his face on the marble fireplace. A pair of placid-looking caryatids propping up the mantelpiece peers down at him.

Man with the pistol says, 'Bit rough for you? Well, how 'bout let's reunite you with some of your own kind? The endangered species!'

Sound of scuffling and more men arrive from the hall – at gunpoint they have Uncle Walter and Aunt Nancy and cousin Rose. Their faces are darkened by bruise and blood. Luke's instinct is to call out to Rose, but he keeps silent. Only watches as Uncle Walter gets the same blow to the back of the legs as Luke and he topples. Aunt Nancy and Rose crouch down beside but don't cower.

'Now look!' says the man with the pistol. 'You're all together!'

And only now does Aunt Nancy notice her fifteen-year-old nephew – boy she hasn't seen in three years. Recognises, but is shrewd enough not to say. Instead she gets some sudden steel and shouts, 'This is our House! And even if it wasn't, you could have the decency to let us go and not keep us here for your amusement! What good is it doing?'

Some sniggering amongst the men and the one with the pistol says, 'We're going to keep you here in order to send a message, your Ladyship!'

The other men all about agree with –

'Lady Muck and her thief of a husband!'

'Too right! Bloody thieves!'

'You've had it too long your own way! Setting whatever rent you like!'

'Living here in the lap of luxury and us all going without!'

Man circling with his pistol says, 'It'll show the others in their Big Houses that we won't be beat! We're not going to let this matter go, you see. We're not going to just roll over like obedient dogs and –'

'Oh, give over!' shouts cousin Rose. She looks as fierce as her mother. 'The other Houses are all being burned out! Why

136

not just get on with it? You're only hiding here so you don't have to be out fighting! Cowards!'

Aunt Nancy says, 'Rose!'

Luke notices Uncle Walter hasn't moved.

And no laughter now.

The man with the pistol makes way for another – larger, with the build of a double bass, dressed in a neat suit and tie and clean shirt. All business, he kneels by Rose and Aunt Nancy and says, very clearly and as mild as May, 'It is simple as this – we are the ones in charge of this House now. We shall stay as long as we like because it is our House by right and always has been – it belongs to a fully independent Ireland. And when we've finished, when we've done with these rooms, we shall leave it to stand or we shall burn it to the ground. And I promise you this – if I feel like it, I shall leave you inside to burn with it.'

KILLIAN

'Hurry up, in the name of God, or you'll be caught!'

'I am hurrying!'

'Bloody fool of a boy.'

'You try running with a foot and leg cut to bits!'

'Not my fault, is it?'

Two shadows: son trying to keep pace beside father.

And behind, some other shadow in determined pursuit with a shrill whistle going off and a voice between times calling, 'Stop! Stop where you stand! Thieves!'

Father: 'Bloody Peelers. Have they not better things to be doing with all the fighting tonight? This way, son!'

Sharp turn by St George's Market, Killian lagging with a stitch in his side and bleeding free from too many places. He spies smoke and climbing fire only a few streets away and wonders what more trouble they're running towards.

Shriek of a whistle still and, 'Thieves! Stop, thieves!'

'He's not for giving up, Da!'

Father calls back, 'In here, quick!'

Gap in the locked gate of the market takes the skinny shape of Killian's father but the boy himself is too far behind and the Peeler too close – if he stops to slip inside he'll be caught and is no fit state for fighting.

'Wait!' the son shouts to his father. 'Wait on me!'

No use – he knows his father will have mingled with the shadows so expertly . . . always can when the need is there.

And that Peeler behind – 'Stop! Don't move! *Thief!*'

'*Thieves*' now '*thief*' and Killian thinks, *On me bloody own now, like always!*

'Come here, you Lagan Rat!'

A hand lands on the scruff of his shirt but the boy twists away – is injured but still willing to spit-thump-kick-bite if he has to. But he sees this Peeler up close and sees how fat he is around the middle and Killian only has to smack him once on the face and is released – easy escape and he's off!

'Stop! Stop, thief!'

Ah, give over, you fat fool, thinks Killian.

He abandons one street for another, down an alleyway and turns a corner –

Into such heat and noise!

Onto a packed street with so many Peelers on one side and on the other side so many men hollering and smashing shop windows and flinging fire inside, finding stones and mortar and shattered bricks to hurl at the police.

And Killian stands between – stranded in the middle of the riot not knowing which way now to run.

LUKE

'See anything?'

'Nah – nothing more. No movement.'

'Good. Keep your eyes sharp though.'

'Yes, sir.'

Land Grabbers at the windows with rifles are watchful and wary of the dark.

Luke watches all with a mind clogged with questions. Where are his parents and the other Driochta? Have they had enough time to lay their own Spells? Will the Reclamation even take without him working to secure it?

Some shiver underground? Some tremble in the walls?

Luke watches the Land Grabbers – they haven't noticed. Watches Aunt Nancy and Uncle Walter (now with his eyes open but unmoving) – they don't seem to have noticed either. Only Rose shows some sign, small wrinkle on her brow to signal some small wondering. She watches Luke. He nods as they both feel again a small rumble beneath them.

'You think I don't know what's going on.' Broad man in

the neat suit kneels close to Luke and says so neatly, 'I'm not stupid – I know a Spell when I feel it. I know the Driochta are out there on Government orders. They're trying to Reclaim this House, trying to secure the boundaries. And what'll happen then, do they think? The floorboards will open and the earth will just swallow me and my men up? The House will spit us out? This place is too conflicted – like the rest of the country, doesn't know what it is any more. You were upstairs scribbling away, trying to establish the Spell from the inside, but I'm telling you now – those Spells will not take.'

Luke can only ask, 'How do you know about Spells?'

Man only smiles.

One of the men by the window shouts suddenly, 'I see lights down about the gates! Should we go and – ?'

Undeniable to any this time – deep shiver of the ground and the men stagger, windows vibrating in their frames and ornaments falling to shatter. The man in the suit stands, eyes still on Luke. 'They will destroy the House if they keep this up,' he says. 'They'll bring it down with us all inside. How will that look for the Driochta?'

The Land Grabbers hear and shout –

'We should've just been burning the place to the ground!'

'Let's shoot them and be done with it!'

'Calm down, fellas,' says the man in the suit. 'We'll do no shooting of anyone. We don't need to. That's not our way. Our claim on this House is sound. This building won't turn on us no matter how hard they try to Reclaim it. We've nothing to fear. And sure anyway, we've our own Magic, remember?'

KILLIAN

Someone shouts to him, 'Don't just stand there, lad! Make yourself useful!'

Killian joins the crowd of men facing the Peelers and reaches down and lifts the first thing he finds, enjoys the heft of the stone in his hand and takes careful aim and hurls it hard . . . watches it fly far far into the crowd of oncoming police . . . and hears it hit home. Score! Just like in the films!

And as though his was a signal – more stones and bits of brick and broken bottles follow his effort but they fly wide. (No one has aim as true as his.) A young protestor comes close and slaps him on the shoulders and says, 'By God, you're a good shot! We need more like you!'

Around them the bellow of the protestors, words barely distinguishable –

'– no longer divided!'

'– be giving us back our country!'

'– and we won't bow to the Crown!'

On one side – more armed police than would be needed if they could organise themselves right. And on Killian's side – hardly a hundred but plenty of anger and grit. *These Peelers are unprepared*, thinks Killian. *And you can do a lot when you catch someone with their kecks down.*

So he says to his new mate, 'Tell everyone to get their hands on something sharp or heavy and get ready to charge!'

The man looks a bit taken aback, bit impressed. He nods once and says, 'Right you are, lad. Good idea! I'll pass the word around!'

And the mounting shouts from the crowd go –

'– bullied any longer!'

'– second-class bloody citizens!'

'– any orders from over the water!'

But a sudden roar that covers all else; Peelers charge with firelight gleaming on badge and boot and belt-buckle and baton –

Sudden blood –

Sound of baton on skull and limb: breaking bone and more and more blood.

It is all too much for Killian, who didn't plan on getting involved in any riot tonight, so says to himself, 'To hell with this!'

He turns and runs and hears the man that was his best friend for two minutes shouting to him, 'Where you going, lad? Come back! Coward! *Coward!*'

LUKE

Whole House shakes like it's being tugged in two and into the room waddles a creature the size of a child, but bald and well wrinkled in the face. Dressed all in dark that drags across the floor, a pair of eyes iridescent. Luke knows: a Cailleach. In one hand the crone holds a jar containing a slosh of bright blue: Indigo Fire.

The leader of the Land Grabbers tugs his lapels straight and says, 'We'll use the same stuff that they used on our comrades during the Rising – see how they like that!'

'Oh, indeed, indeed!' croaks the child-woman. Her gaze settles on Luke. The Cailleach's fingers go twitch and squirm and Luke knows she is skimming the topmost thoughts from his head. 'This boy has not come here by chance or happy happenstance. Oh, there is more to this! Indeed!' Luke tries to keep his thoughts close or think other things that will not incriminate but he can't keep himself hidden, has no talent for dishonesty so – 'I see now!' says the Cailleach. She smiles and shows small brown teeth. 'This little one has come to save his relatives.'

Land Grabber in the suit says, 'Is that so?'

Land Grabber with the pistol kicks Uncle Walter and says, 'You know this one, do you?'

Uncle Walter finally speaks, spits out, 'He is no family of mine!'

Luke doesn't know how to feel – not hurt, not betrayed. In the end feels more sorry for Uncle Walter than anything else.

Goreland Hall shakes again as though in the hands of a Copse Gyant, and the Land Grabber says calmly, 'I believe it is time we departed. Let us leave the old place to the flames.'

'Wait!' cries the Cailleach. She shuffles towards Luke, peers into his eyes and his past and his whole self and says, 'This is the son of Lord and Lady Mountfathom!'

The Grabber in his neat suit smiles. 'Well, now,' he says, 'that changes things a bit. Mountfathom – the seat of all privilege and Magic! So perhaps we shall be taking one hostage with us? Someone tie him up.'

'My pleasure,' says the man with the pistol.

Then so much at once –

'*No!*' Rose cries out and launches herself at the Land Grabber –

A sudden storm of gunfire at the windows –

Rose thrown aside –

And Morrigan chooses this moment to reappear;: leaps on the Cailleach to attack with a flurry of claws –

Luke takes his moment too –

Mutters the first Spell of Fleeing he can recall and presses his fingers to one of the caryatids. Marble statue springs free of the fireplace and swings a marble fist at the Grabber holding the pistol and knocks him cold. Luke adds the same Spell to the second statue and –

'Gimme that, you old crone!' cries the man in the suit and he snatches the jar of Indigo Fire from the Cailleach and hurls it across the room to shatter against the opposite wall –

Silence: all air sucked from the room to one spot –

'Fool!' cries the Cailleach and slaps the Land Grabber in the suit.

Explosion! A wave of Indigo flame rushes across floor and walls –

Quick Working of the hands and Luke bids one caryatid to lift Uncle Walter from the ground and the second to hoist Aunt Nancy and Rose into its arms –

Cailleach: 'Stop the Lord of Mountfathom! Don't let him escape!'

Luke scoops up Morrigan and climbs onto the back of the statue carrying Aunt Nancy and Rose –

Man in his suit pulls a pistol from a pocket and aims –

Now a shower of smashed glass –

From the window arrives something sharp-toothed and sharp-clawed; sleek blue-black body and gleam of green eyes, it swipes the gun from the Land Grabber's hand and sends the Cailleach shuffling off squealing.

The panther turns eyes on Luke. He says, 'Sorry, Mother. I didn't have time to complete the Spell from the inside. I tried my best.'

Flame sweeps and submerges the floor and the panther has to turn and leap back through the same window it entered as the ground beneath gives a groan and starts to sag –

Rose smacks Luke on the arm and shouts, 'Get us the hell out of here!'

Luke whips his hand through the air and bids both statues sprint across falling floor to leap high – to crash through the wall of the drawing room and out into the night.

KILLIAN

'There he is! Stop him!'

Killian thinks: *Whole city wants me! By God, I'm in big demand!*

'Come back here you, Lagan Rat!'

Still that same fat Peeler in pursuit!

Killian finds an alleyway, bare feet splashing through muck and whatever else you wouldn't like to look at in daylight – trip-stumbles over something and someone unseen grumbles, 'Watch where you're running there!'

Hears a Peeler shout, 'Go around – cut him off at the far end!'

He thinks, *Maybe a bit sharper than usual, this lot. But not sharp enough!*

Killian sees a stack of empty crates and climbs high and pulls himself higher – up onto a low rooftop and he stands and tries to see. A layer of soot makes it near impossible for sight – the riots are raging, violence spreading wild and insatiable and he has never seen Belfast City like this before.

'Up there he is! Get him!'

On tiptoe Killian walks the spine of the roof, teetering but still scampering fast. He reaches a gap and a leap to another roof that sheds tiles under his feet but is up and hurrying on . . . but he is running out of things to run on and encounters too wide a gap to leap. And still below those Peelers are not for giving in.

'You two – stay with me! And you other three – keep watch at the far end of the alley! Has to come down sometime!'

Heart and head hammering, Killian swallows and slaps his hands together and tells himself, 'Right! You can do this without a doubt! Here you go!'

Backs up . . . runs and leaps . . . falls through the air with hands and feet scrabbling but he lands well enough on only a tin roof with a tin chimney sending up a fish-smelling stench. He scrambles up and crosses the roof in three strides and is down once more to re-join the ground and a more solemn street. No protesters here, but plenty of shadows slumped in doorways. He feels for a moment more at home.

But the same cry Killian is getting sick of. 'Stop that child!'

Runs on and down High Street – avoids a cart of grey vegetables and skips around a woman with an armful of limp stalks and swerves an old fella with a sandwich board shouting about some film showing at the Ulster Hall. But as though they've been spawned – more Peelers!

He thinks, *So what now for our brave hero Killian? Is this the end? Surely this cannot be his final hour?*

LUKE

Loses his grip on the statue and tumbles onto scorched lawn and Morrigan lands lightly beside, managing to look heroically bored. As Luke abandons the statue so does the Spell – the caryatids topple and Uncle Walter and Aunt Nancy and Rose tumble likewise to the ground.

'What do we do now, Luke?' asks Rose.

Luke tells her, 'I think we best get out of here.'

Blue-white firelight is throwing itself wild across the open grounds of Goreland Hall. Land Grabbers are climbing from the windows with fire on them but some who've got free without harm are gunfiring, desperate, into the darkness.

Beside Luke again is the panther – a shiver and in less than a second the animal Mogrifies and becomes his mother, Needle tight in her hand.

'The Reclamation?' she asks. 'Are you sure it wasn't completed?'

Luke shakes his head.

'No matter,' says his mother. 'I told your father this wouldn't work.' She looks to Aunt Nancy and Rose standing together, then turns to her brother Walter still sprawled on the ground and tells him, 'You either get up and walk or I leave you – your choice, brother dearest!'

'Edith,' says Aunt Nancy. 'I think my husband needs –'

'I know what he needs,' says Lady Mountfathom. 'But that can keep for later, don't you think?'

Nancy nods.

'Can you walk, Uncle Walter?' asks Luke.

'He'll walk,' says Rose, and she gives her father a dig with her toe.

'Rose,' says Luke's mother, 'I believe I rather approve of the young woman you've grown into.'

'There they are!' Cry of the Cailleach directing the Land Grabbers. 'Mother and son Mountfathom! Get them!'

Gunfire that Luke protects them from with a swift Spell of Dismissal.

'Hurry now,' says Lady Mountfathom. 'We don't have much time.'

KILLIAN

Now he likes to think Lady Fortune tips him a wink – sickly yellow light sweeps through soot and smoke, accompanied by a squeal of wheels . . . Killian sees a tram take the corner onto High Street, so many bodies packed onto its open upper deck it looks like it's under siege.

'It's all in the timing,' Killian tells himself.

He waits for just the exact right moment – an instinct he prides himself on – and when the conductor turns away he leaps and is on, slipping in amongst passengers as easy and snug as a card back into its pack.

He likes the confusion he hears from far behind.

'Have you seen a boy pass through here? Have you seen a child? A Lagan Rat running around – he's wanted for thieving!'

He thinks, *Fools! Can't catch Killian so easy!*

Only off-putting thing in the tram is the smell. Something like sweat-grease-smoke all mixed up and stewed, and maybe something else too. He has time to wonder where his father is – maybe made it free and is sitting smoking his way through his cigarettes? *Better save me some. Better keep me a pack after all that hassle!*

Tram approaches the pale face of the Albert Clock.

'Hold it there!'

Tram slows and stops and all inside lurch.

Shout from outside. 'All off! Now!'

Those bloody Peelers!

Killian half-ducks down; officers are scanning the contents of the tram and shouting, 'Off! All disembark now!'

But there's plenty of complaint back from passengers –

'Give it rest, would you?'

'I'd think you've better things to be doing!'

'Some of us have homes to get back to!'

'Aye! And some of us have done a decent day's work too!'

But in all the shove and squirm and shout Killian shrinks – makes himself smaller and smaller with eyes only for the exit . . .

'We have reason to believe that some of those involved in the trouble tonight are aboard this tram! I ask that they surrender themselves now without fuss! If they do not, then we will bring upon their heads the very sternest of Her Majesty's Justice!'

This brings such outrage from the men on board! And in the fresh racket Killian forces himself free and jumps out . . . and into the arms of an awaiting Peeler who lifts him clear off the ground and announces, 'I've got him! I've got the Rat here, captured!'

LUKE

They run.

He and his mother and aunt and uncle and cousin.

And more members of the Driochta join them – cheetah sprinting beside transforms into the dapper Flann Dorrick; chimpanzee drops from the boughs of a towering oak and assumes the stout shape of Lawrence Devine; owl alights and Mogrifies into a small and bespectacled (and breathless) Jack Gorebooth; bright swoop of blue-green that in mid-air becomes Lady Vane-Tempest who lands light and elegant. All have their Needles in hand and with their other hand are Dismissing bullets as though they're newspaper pellets.

Flann Dorrick says, 'I thought we could reason with the Grabbers! They have a code of conduct!'

'They also have a Cailleach,' says Lady Mountfathom.

'She commanding them?' shouts Lawrence Devine.

'Please tell us the answer is no!' says Jack Gorebooth.

'Has at least added her poison to their thoughts,' says Luke's mother. 'I think I see my husband – almost there now!'

Luke is more concerned with below than what is ahead – earth softening underfoot, ready to swallow, not far off becoming a swamp. He knows the land is resisting the Reclamation Spell, is too conflicted to know what it is any more and is sinking under the pressure of Magic.

'Don't slow or stop!' Lady Mountfathom shouts. 'Keep going!'

Lord Mountfathom is in sight – kneeling with his Needle planted in sodden ground and hands submerged to the wrist in damp earth.

All stop. And none of the Driochta wants to speak the question.

Luke's mother allows some moments and then says, 'How much longer, my dear?'

'Not long enough,' says Luke's father. 'I sense the Spell inside was not completed?'

'No,' says Luke. 'I'm sorry, Father.'

A sigh from Lord Mountfathom.

And everyone knows it now: Goreland Hall cannot be Reclaimed, nor rescued nor saved. The Driochta turn to watch blue-white flame encase it.

'What next?' asks Luke.

'We leave,' says his father. 'Quick – to the river.'

KILLIAN

But the boy has spirit and fight. And fast fists – he punches the Peeler in the eye and kicks him in the privates and is dropped.

'Don't let him go!'

Killian thinks, *I'm away again, lads!*

No shadows to dive into though – the river Lagan is hogged by barges, gantries overhead throwing pitiless light on so many bodies busy loading-unloading and opening-stowing. Killian races across gangplank and gangway, shoving workers aside as he springs between one barge and the next. Bad idea; now he has more men who want him. And he reaches a dead-end and has to double-back so –

Faces the very same fat Peeler from the beginning of all this who tells him, 'You've nowhere to be running to now.'

He's not wrong.

'Be sensible now, lad,' says another Peeler behind, closing in.

Sensible my feckin eye! thinks Killian.

And he decides there's only one way out – takes a big breath, hopes for some of that good luck he always manages to find, and throws himself into the river.

LUKE

Distant cry from the Cailleach: 'Cut them off! Don't let them escape!'

'I see at least one Spell has decided to be compliant!' says Lady Mountfathom.

Luke sees too: Smoke-Spun bridge not far ahead, still spanning the river that runs through the grounds of Goreland Hall. But it is faltering too – unravelling in pale and paler wisps to rise moonward. He leads cousin Rose and Aunt Nancy and his huffing and puffing Uncle Walter over, the smoke of the bridge hardly retaining their footprints but holding strong enough for the Driochta to cross. When all are on the other side, Lord Mountfathom whips the bridge out of existence with a casual hand.

'Quickly now,' says Luke's father. 'Make for that groundskeeper's cottage near the gates.'

Luke takes the chance to tell his father again: 'I'm sorry. I –'

'We shall talk of it later,' says Lord Mountfathom.

In the dark they discover the stone cottage and its small door with a rust-eaten lock. Luke's mother slots her crimson key in and waits for the tell-tale sound –

'You're not getting away that easy!'

The shout makes Luke turn first – Land Grabber in his no-longer neat suit raises his pistol and fires and it is Luke who is quickest to wave a hand to try to Dismiss the bullet but instead sends it astray –

Uncle Walter shouts out and crumples.

Aunt Nancy and Rose each take an arm to haul him up and Luke wonders how badly is he hurt? Will he be – ?

More gunfire from more of the remaining Grabbers.

Lord Mountfathom whips his Needle into the air and the river rises like a ribbon . . . he lets it remain and the eyes of the Land Grabbers widen to watch it . . . and then lets it fall – graceful and devastating, a smash of silver that snatches most of the men away like matchsticks.

Now the longed-for sound – the high, singing note as the crimson key finds home.

'Quickly!' cries Lady Mountfathom, opening the door.

More gunfire as Luke takes Rose's hand and drags her through the dark doorway as she asks him, 'Where are we going? What is this place?'

And Luke answers –
It is the Gloaming: the great unknown.
And we are going home.

Pen poised so elegantly above;
only a single dark drop needed.
You see, so much wisdom springs from so little.
Like words riotous across a page – read quickly!
And (whether it be great or grievous)
watch some future unfold . . .

Reflections on the Art of Mirror-Predicting
Lady Helena Vane-Tempest

LUKE

'I do not care what your wonderful plan was, Mountfathom – you failed! And failure is failure no matter how you try to dress it up! You should be ashamed!'

The reply of Lord Mountfathom is slow, and so delicate. 'Major Fortflay, these things cannot be Worked quickly. Spells are complicated, and my colleagues and I did our utmost to save Goreland Hall. In the end, there were elements simply beyond our control.'

But the Major bellows, 'I thought you had ways of seeing the future!'

'Only the immediate future,' replies Luke's father. 'And it is not a precise art – these things would not have been interpretable on any mirror.'

Fortflay gives a snort.

Uneasy silence in *The World*; sighs and a restless shifting of limbs, a long night still not ended. Around an oval table, the Driochta face a tall mirror holding the face of Major Fortflay. He tells them, 'I am running out of options of how best to deal with these rebels and Land Grabbers. I confess I simply do not know how to deal with you people!'

Luke hears Lady Vane-Tempest whisper, 'No change there.'

Hears Flann Dorrick say, 'Will he be finished soon? I'm exhausted . . .'

But Luke isn't a bit tired. Instead feels each moment as a passing opportunity; that he should speak up, explain the circumstances – the surprise of the Cailleach and the Indigo Fire, the determination of the Land Grabbers. He doesn't want the Major to pass this casual blame. And Luke marvels at his father's patience.

'The point is this,' says Lord Mountfathom, leaning forward, palms together, 'the Reclamation Spells are not taking. The land of this island is now too much contested – the wish for independence in this country is too strong. With the political situation so much in turmoil we have to consider –'

'No!' says the Major. 'The point is this: because of your ineptitude we've lost yet another House!'

Luke chooses now to speak. 'Might I add that what was lost was a much-loved family home. Goreland Hall belonged to my cousins and aunt and uncle.'

'I do not see how that is of any particular importance,' says Fortflay.

'A Big House is a home as well anything else,' says Luke. 'All the Big Houses are linked, whether they know it or not. If they continue to be burned then the Driochta will continue to be concerned.'

'Why?' The Major pauses, almost scoffs. 'Worried it might happen to yourselves?'

Luke opens his mouth to speak but his father says, 'Enough now, Luke.'

Father and son share a glance. Luke sinks back in his chair, into reluctant silence.

'Listen,' says the Major. 'There are tempers flaring up everywhere across this island – Belfast wasn't far off a warzone last night. So while you sit comfy in your cosy House reading your books and getting cream teas brought to you, I am in the thick of it here. I need to know I can rely on people! I need my soldiers not mild-mannered but merciless if needs be.'

'Two of our number are keeping watch on the Dragon Coast,' says Lord Mountfathom, and in his father's tone Luke hears a slight quiver of exhaustion. 'The Halters are endeavouring to ensure that the Ash-Dragons are not woken and recruited by the Land Grabbers. Our numbers, therefore, are somewhat reduced.'

'Yet another excuse!' says Fortflay.

Lord Mountfathom opens his mouth for more words, but it is Luke's mother who says, 'Major Fortflay, the Order of the Driochta have endeavoured always to keep the peace. We were there to offer help during the Great Hunger; we acted as ambassadors and brokers to establish the Land Bill; we attempted to heal the deep scars caused when your soldiers destroyed the Faerie Raths and purged this island of the Gyants. We offered our services during the aftermath of the Lock Out as we tried to negotiate with Boreen Men – we were ignored in favour of some wicked Magic from across the water. Always we have mediated and discussed and advised and resolved. And – if we deem it necessary and utterly unavoidable – we will fight. But what we will not do is thoughtlessly slaughter. To put it in simple terms, good sir: we are not soldiers.'

Pale face of Major Fortflay goes tight.

Luke feels the satisfaction of the Driochta, their pride in Lady Mountfathom!

And for some moments – silence.

Fortflay's mouth finds some slack and he spits, 'I don't need a history lesson.'

'It was not a lesson,' says Lady Mountfathom, staying so calm, so sympathetic. 'I was merely seeking to make our position clear. And, on these clear terms, I hope we can continue to work together in the best interests of the people of this country?'

'Look now,' says the Major once more, face already beginning to fade from the mirror, 'my concern is keeping the peace and defending the honour of our monarch. And it is your job to use your hocus-pocus to help. There is little enough Magic left in this island and, as far as I can tell, most of it is in your hands to use. But if you can't fulfil that duty, then I may need to look elsewhere.'

Luke leans forward to ask, 'Meaning what, Major?' Yet knows already: the dark Magic Fortflay has been employing from across the water. Thinks: what more of this will there be?

'Meaning this, lad: there are more persuasive types of Magic we may have to consider employing.' Fortflay allows some moments of silence, of a slow sinking-in. And as dawn at last seeps into Mountfathom, the Major departs with these words: 'I must do what is necessary to stamp out these rebellions, whatever the cost and by whatever means. I shall not stand by and see this island overrun. And I would be wary, if I were you – nowhere is safe from these Land Grabbers. No one can sit on the fence in this war. Soon you'll have to decide where you stand.'

KILLIAN

'Waken up now.'

A slosh of frigid water in the face and a tap-slap on each cheek and he opens his eyes. And without thought or wondering, only on innate instinct – Killian starts fighting. From sitting to standing in seconds with fists flying, ready to take on all comers! But too quick off the mark, it turns out – a bubble of nausea swells in his skull and makes him blunder into a wall and bang his forehead on something low-hanging. He feels the floor tip beneath him but before he topples is caught, and strong arms steer Killian back to a low stool.

The same voice as earlier tells him, 'Calm down a bit, lad. You came very close to death last night, so I'd take it easier if I were you.'

Killian closes his eyes: shivers, hears his own frantic heartbeat like private thunder. He wets his lips and asks, 'Where am I?'

'Safe,' says a voice. 'That's all you need to know for now.'

'I've got rights,' says Killian (knows all the lines, been well rehearsed by his father). 'You can't just lock me up without evidence! I'm only a child so you can't just –'

'Save it,' says the man. 'I'm no Peeler. Far from it.'

Killian senses this someone standing close. He smells tobacco smoke and something else – can't place it, reminds him of the fireside at home when it was lit in winter. So he asks again, 'Where are we?'

'Dogged little thing,' says the voice, sounding amused. 'You're on a turf-barge heading inland.'

'Why did you – ?'

All Killian manages – again the floor shifts and his hands snap out to hold tight to the stool. He decides, *I need to see*. So he half-opens his eyes and sees some of the cramped space he sits in. Everything has a grey-blue tinge, and he guesses it's only early morning. Killian strains his senses further: hears water breaking against the barge and then hush-rushing away, a sluggish progress but still enough to make his stomach sick. Some trace of blessed breeze though – a window has been drawn back to let in fresh cold.

'Where you taking me?' asks Killian.

'On a little trip,' says the man. 'To a rather fine old residence. Going to pay a visit to an old friend. To some people who think they are our superiors.' It sounds again to Killian like the man is smiling to himself.

'Why did you bring me?' asks Killian.

'We plucked you out of the Lagan,' says the man. 'And I took a guess you wouldn't want to be facing those Peelers that were after you.'

Killian knows his next line. 'Them Peelers got the wrong man. They thought I was thieving but I –'

'No lies,' snaps the man. 'That's the first and only rule I'm going to make. Otherwise you make fools of both of us. I know your da. I know that you and him have a habit for thieving, so no use trying to tell me any untruths.'

Fine, thinks Killian. *Fine and well; if you want to play like that –*

'I don't take orders from nobody. And my da is gonna be looking for me so you better –'

'Your da won't be looking for a single soul,' says the man. 'My guess is he's currently sitting pretty in a cell somewhere. I was told very reliably that he was picked up by the Peelers, full drunk.'

Killian sees a bit clearer now – the man sits across from him on another low stool, a crooked smoke smouldering between his lips. 'You know an awful lot for some turf-cutter,' says Killian.

'Something told me you were sharper than all this,' says the man. His words make the cigarette wag in his mouth. 'I said we were on a turf-barge, but that don't mean I spend my time cutting the stuff, does it?'

And the next thing that happens is a thing that Killian is sure he must be imagining – the man weaves a hand in the air and the blue-grey smoke unfurling from his cigarette twists and shapes itself into a set of jaws and a snout and long ribbon of a body. It does a quick whirl around the man's head, and then dissipates.

Christ, thinks Killian, *must've hit my head some knock when I fell in the Lagan!*

The man laughs a little, and his smile is wide as he says, 'I think we're going to get along well. You know why? For some reason you remind me of my son.'

And Killian sees more clearly now: the man across from him has dark eyes deep in a white face, and a head of faded hair.

LUKE

'Why can I not come along?'

'You would do well to rest now, Luke. You are tired, I am sure – you have not slept. And we need someone at Mountfathom to keep watch on things.'

'I want to come – I wish to help.'

'And you will be helping greatly by remaining here, son.'

Luke has come to the Seasonal Room to confront his father – Lord Mountfathom stands with his back to his son, filling a leather satchel with books and materials for Spell-Work. Morning sunlight is given a different quality at the four Spell-Worked windows of the room: cold, golden, bright, breezy. And father and son stand in separate and adjoining seasons – Luke choosing winter, Lord Mountfathom busy in autumn.

Luke says with his head down, 'I know it is because I failed at the Reclamation Spell.'

His father sighs.

'Should I escort the young master to his room?' asks Mr Findlater. The manservant is hovering between spring and summer.

'I can escort myself,' says Luke. 'I know where my own bedroom is, sir.'

'Findlater,' says Lord Mountfathom, before anyone else can speak. 'Could you please be so kind as to go to the library and fetch my copy of *The Worship Ways of Spell-Work*?'

Findlater remains for a moment. Bob-bows a little, and leaves the room (thinks Luke) with such slow reluctance. Soon as the door of the Seasonal Room has shut –

'Always wants to know what is going on,' says Luke. 'Always hanging around and listening.'

'It does us no good to start complaining of the habits of the staff,' says Lord Mountfathom. 'I know you are keen to play your part,' says his father, turning back to his books, his packing. 'And you are an invaluable help on our errands, but now things are becoming more complicated – you know this.'

'Is Mother going?'

'Your mother has already departed into the Gloaming – she and Lady Vane-Tempest are going to meet with the families of the five largest Big Houses in the South. They are going to help strengthen their Spells of Seclusion and Security.'

'And where are you going to?' asks Luke.

'I will travel to the monks.' Lord Mountfathom faces his son, and for a moment Luke feels sorry for his mood – he sees on his father's face such fatigue. 'I shall speak to them and try to convince them that we need their help now.'

Father and son come together.

'Luke, this is not the end of anything,' says Lord Mountfathom. 'I know it can seem that way – I remember that feeling well from my own boyhood. But it is only a time. All things change, and we must do our best to decide how we can adapt to that change.'

'What should I do in the meantime?' asks Luke.

'Take some time to think and to learn a little more. And to appreciate Mountfathom. Remember: whilst your mother and I are absent, you are the Lord here.'

A knock on the door as Mr Findlater returns with the requested volume.

Lord Mountfathom says, 'This House is in your care, and all within it. There are things we cannot know, shadows we must keep careful watch on. Understand?'

'Yes,' says Luke.

'Here is the book you asked for,' says Mr Findlater, and the manservant steps between father and son.

And Luke thinks to himself, *Yes – I understand very well indeed.*

KILLIAN

In the afternoon, they idle by a waterside pub. He is allowed fried whiting and stout and knows he is being buttered up like a burned crumpet, but doesn't care. Only knows that he needs to keep himself sharp. The man from the barge has introduced himself only as a 'Mr Gassin' (some fake name, Killian knows. Wouldn't expect anything else). And they sit together outside the pub, on two barrels, watching other barges shunt by. And Killian asks his questions.

'What's this place called we're going to?'

'No names are needed,' says Mr Gassin.

'Then tell me why we're going.'

'To teach some people a lesson; you don't need to know any more.'

Killian doesn't like not knowing but stays silent.

There are two other lads nearby who Mr Gassin is calling 'the muscle'. Not much muscle on them, Killian reckons – red haired, pair of them only a little older than himself – but they know how to work a barge and have been seeing to the business of getting them to wherever they're going.

Killian makes a guess. 'You have a score you want to settle?'

Mr Gassin takes a sup of his stout. Says, 'Aye, but not just for me – for a whole lot of people.'

'You can do Magic,' says Killian. 'What you did earlier with the smoke from that fag – that a Spell or what?'

Mr Gassin lets out a big sigh and says, 'Have you ever felt you should be better off, boy? I'm sure you have. You're a smart lad. I'm sure that if you were given the chance, you could do better by yourself. Talent should never go to waste. We should all have a chance to maybe make a better way in the world, don't you think?'

Killian nods. Thinks of his father and his constant scheme for betterment. 'Aye,' he says. 'I know that feeling.'

'Well, let me tell you,' says Mr Gassin, 'there used to be a time not that long ago when Magic wasn't just for the posh sorts of this island but for everybody. Anybody at all could learn a Spell! Fishwife or farmer, no odds what you were! Anyone at all! Including myself.'

'What happened?' asks Killian.

'Was taken away from me,' says Gassin, and for the first time sounds a touch agitated. 'And now where's all that knowledge? I'll tell you where – all stolen. Hoarded and stuffed into places where no one except the well-off can get to it.'

'Places like where we're heading?' asks Killian.

'Exactly right.' He downs the last dregs of his pint and stands. 'And pretty soon, they won't know what hit them.'

LUKE

He hasn't slept at all. Instead he stands by the lagoon in the blue hour before dawn. A delicate web of mist has laid itself over the water, the surface beneath crowded with fallen leaves. Boughs around him naked and grey. Autumn has arrived too early; so many things already fading, failing. Luke could weave a Spell of Restoration – it is not so difficult to return a leaf to a tree, to reattach and restore its green. But what is the use? Things could be Restored, but only to lose their colour and detach and once more fall. All Magic is temporary, thinks Luke. All Spells can be undone. The failing of Goreland Hall proves that; even if he had managed the Reclamation it wouldn't have lasted. And it this lack of permanency that is vexing him – why bother with anything, if all of it ends up ending?

Suddenly, a summons –

'Here! I'm under here!'

A whisper from where? Luke turns to the patch of wild and wilting rhubarb.

Whisper tells him, 'Underneath!'

He crouches and beneath spies his cousin Rose. She is smiling. 'Want to play Secret-and-Secluded?' she asks, and creeps off further into shadow. On all fours Luke follows – crawls and crawls until he rediscovers both his cousin and the same space where they hid at the beginning of the summer. Rose has a face of such excitement. As though she's uncovered buried treasure – the pleasure of returning to a certain place, to a certain memory.

She asks Luke, 'Did you know that if you listen terribly hard you can actually hear rhubarb growing?'

'Is that right?' says Luke, sharing her smile.

'Oh yes,' says Rose. 'That's what they say.'

They sit close beside one another and pull their legs to their chests.

'Aunt Edith and Uncle William have left?' asks Rose.

Luke nods. 'Yes,' he says. 'Gone with the Driochta on some mission.'

'Busy time for you here,' says Rose.

Luke says nothing. Knows his father has entrusted the care of the house to him, in the meantime; but thinks only how he wishes he could be with them. Closes his eyes and decides he better ask, 'How is Uncle Walter?'

'He'll live,' snaps Rose. Seems to become aware of her tone so adds, 'Sorry, but he's always complaining. Says he can't wait to leave here. We're going this afternoon. Doesn't realise that he's likely to be better off at Mountfathom than anywhere else.'

Luke has an urge to say, *I am not so certain about that.*

'We're going to England,' says Rose. 'Probably to London. Ruth and Rory went to stay with our Aunt Dolores there a few months ago. And Roger is at Cambridge so we'll be closer to him too.'

A moment, and Luke lies: 'I'm happy for you. You'll all be together.'

Rose makes a sound like a scoff.

Luke opens his eyes.

She says, 'Roger always told me you were too nice for your own good. He said you'd rather be nice than say the truth sometimes.'

169

Luke can find no reply.

'But Roger was always a prat,' says Rose. 'I think you always just said the thing people needed to hear.'

And rain starts.

'Just like before,' says Rose. 'Same as it used to be, me and you playing a game. Remember?'

'Yes,' Luke says. He closes his eyes once more. 'Yes – just like before.'

KILLIAN

By now the sun is skulking behind purple hills, and the barge slips out into open water – a wide grey lough with an ornamental island in its middle.

'Not far now,' the man with faded hair says. Shouts to the two lads, 'Turn a bit more south.'

The barge begins to lean towards a broken, stony shore.

Killian fills time with as many more questions as he can.

'But why bother bringing me? I know nothing about Magic or Spells.'

'Because you have certain other talents,' says Mr Gassin. 'And as I said, if there is one thing I cannot abide, it is seeing good talent go to waste.'

Killian knows enough about himself not to feel flattered – knows he can slip silent into many a place and steal and escape and not be seen, so doesn't need some fella to tell him so. He starts to wonder now, *What can I get out of this?*

'How much of a cut for me?' he asks.

'A boy who knows what he wants!' says Mr Gassin. 'I like that.'

'No stalling – how much?' asks Killian.

'Half,' says the man.

Instinct makes Killian say, 'Not enough. I want three-quarters of whatever you make from selling the stuff we steal.'

'Look now,' says the man, trying to sound mild. 'I have two other lads here hardly older than you and they'll need paying.'

'From what you've said,' Killian tells him, 'they aren't going to be the ones climbing through windows and unlocking doors and all. That'll be me. That means danger and that means more money. So – three-quarters.'

He sticks out his hand.

Mr Gassin rubs a hand over his face.

'You drive a hard enough bargain,' he says.

'I do indeed,' says Killian. 'Hard but fair.'

They shake on it.

'I've not much interest in money anyway,' says Mr Gassin. And he is smiling to himself once more. 'There's more precious things to be had in this place than gold and silver. There's things in there that could unlock a whole new future for you and me, just you wait and see.'

LUKE

'Now,' he says, 'let us see.'

Near midnight but still Luke is sleepless – sits at the desk with Morrigan on his lap as the pair of them peer into a circle of spotted mirror, a lantern with a pick of flame beside.

He thinks to himself, *If I'm not allowed to go along with the Driochta, then maybe I can be some good here; perhaps I can prepare myself for what might be coming.*

Now Luke holds a pen high, its nib loaded with ink. Now shakes it a little and lets one solitary drop fall and as soon as it meets the mirror it plays – goes coil and split and shiver, like a child racing around a garden it makes nonsensical and gleeful shapes. Luke weaves a slow and intricate hand and slowly the ink settles, stills, makes for him a bold Impression in the form of a tall figure.

Luke thinks, *Is it Father? Mr Dorrick? Or some unknown other? Looks a little like Mr Findlater.*

'Trouble always is,' he says to Morrigan, 'it could be illustrative and not literal – merely indicative? What do you think, lazy cat?'

Morrigan offers nothing but a slow blink of the eyes.

Such an imprecise branch of Magic – doesn't rely so much on learning or knowing of facts, so Luke doesn't like it or trust it.

Morrigan offers a small mewl of consolation or concern or (more likely) impatience. She sits up straight and stretches and Luke scratches her behind the ear and at the same time his fingers flick through *Reflections on Mirror-Predicting*. He is no further than *Chapter Two: The Poetry of Patterns*: the page is populated by lines of print so minute Luke brings the lantern closer and as he does so the word *Dismissal* leaps out at him again and again. So he sweeps a decisive hand over the mirror and starts again – ink flees to the fringes of the mirror where it trembles in fat globs. Morrigan extends an exploratory paw to the ink, tries to leap onto the desk and Luke has to drag her back.

'One more time,' says Luke, 'then sleep.'

Now the word *Recall*, and a helpful diagram of the needed gesture – another slow sweep of the hand brings ink racing back into the centre of the mirror.

'And now what can we see?'

Only this same tall figure, though now joined by someone smaller – a boy? Must be. The ink settles, relaxes, losing its slight shiver as if to tell Luke, *Yes. Very good. And what else . . . ?*

A mumble-whisper comes from one of the Traces.

'Magic cannot cure all ills – makes one infinitely short sighted. Should always be on the sharp lookout for low-flying Ash-Dragons and the terminal risk of dry-rot!'

Must be a dozen or more Traces tucked tight under Luke's desk. They've taken lately to following him – spending increasing time under his bed or in his wardrobe or beneath the firedogs. More and more they dislike any light – sun or lantern or tallow – and more and more gabble with such little sense. The same Trace says, '*Careful! Spend so much time looking one way and from the other comes the threat! From the other comes the blade or the bludgeon or the stray bullet or –*'

'I hear,' says Luke. 'I'm listening to you. Don't worry yourselves.'

Like anxious children – more accurately, worrisome old men – the Traces are soothed into silence.

But when Luke turns attention again to the mirror, the ink has left him a new Impression – the tall figure has shrunk and now there are two small forms. Two boys? Luke lets his fingers twitch, gently, over the mirror. He tries to tease out some more meaning. And a small slither of ink joins the two figures – like a pair of children holding hands.

Morrigan lets out a small, mournful meow.

Luke frames a question in his mind, and asks of the mirror, 'Where will the threat come from? What will become of Mountfathom?'

The ink does not answer, will not change its shape. And Luke can interpret nothing more from the Impression. Yet something about it makes him shiver.

One of the Traces whispers, *'You would do well to heed me: it is when we, the past keepers and custodians of this ancient House, decide to leave it that you will begin to worry. When the past has no place in the world, that is when things begin to burn.'*

KILLIAN

On the shore, Mr Gassin gives Killian some stern advice.

'Listen now, lad, you can't just walk into this place like you would walk into anywhere else.'

'I don't need telling,' says Killian. 'I'm an expert at this, you said it yourself!'

'You've never broken into somewhere like this. It has some rightly vicious Spells on it. Believe me – I know what goes on here. They're secretive, these people. They keep themselves to themselves because they don't want anyone coming in and sharing any of their treasures.'

They are standing on the shore of small stones, in shadow beside a wall of sheer limestone. Killian sees no way ahead. 'So how're we gonna get in?' he asks. 'How do we get past all this Magic and these dangerous Spells?'

The man with faded hair tells him, 'We'll get in because we've been invited.'

From his jacket pocket he produces a folded sheet of paper and shakes it out. Killian cannot see what is written there but watches closely for what comes next. Mr Gassin lays a palm on the limestone, muttering to himself whatever words are on the page, and pushes . . . and slowly shadows mass and swarm around his hand, darkening and delving till they form a narrow opening. A sudden rush of cold lifts Killian's hair.

'Easy if you have the knowledge,' says Mr Gassin. He weaves a hand in the air, startles Killian and the other two lads as the sheet of paper suddenly catches fire. Gassin holds it between fingertips until the page is almost consumed, and then casts it aside and steps into the tunnel.

Killian looks at his red-headed comrades – no weapons, not even a bit of wood to defend themselves with. Older than him, but they look as though they've not seen much of the world, no wiles about them. Their eyes keep flicking back to the barge so Killian decides to tell them, 'If anything goes skew-whiff, just run back here and head on. I know how to handle meself.'

'We haven't all night!' Mr Gassin calls back to them. 'Our invitation won't last forever and this tunnel won't stay open forever either!'

'And I've a feeling,' Killian tells the other two, 'that this fella with his faded hair knows how to handle himself too.'

All three step into the dark, and soon as they are over the threshold the limestone wall seals up behind their backs.

LUKE

He steps into the cool, stone passageway – sees no one, realises that anyone sensible is surely asleep. But he calls for her anyway. 'Nanny Bogram?'

A creak of bedsprings, quick footsteps across stone floor and a door halfway along the corridor opens and her face appears.

'What you doing down here?' Bogram asks. She's in her nightdress and cap and is dragging on a dressing gown. She has a small Bible in her hand. 'You should be asleep! What's worrying you now?' She is padding towards him, arms folded tight. 'Not still fretting about the business at your uncle's house?'

Luke says nothing – can't lie and can't admit.

Nanny Bogram settles one hand on his shoulder. 'I know you don't agree but your mother and father have put too much on you, and too soon. That's what I think and I don't mind saying it.'

Luke doesn't want to disagree. Instead asks, 'Can I have a drink?'

'Let me guess – some of my special hot chocolate?' says Bogram. She sounds stern but Luke can see her starting to smile. He nods. 'Alright!' she says. 'I'll go find some. You stay here though! You shouldn't be down here at all – catch your death!'

She tucks her Bible into the pocket of her dressing gown and heads off down the passageway.

He does as he's told. Stands and inspects the row of brass bells with their enamel plaques – *Berlin, The Amazon, Valhalla, The World*, the Seasonal Room . . .

'Young sir, what are you doing down here?'

Mr Findlater now, appearing from another doorway and not dressed for sleep but still in his starched shirt and tails.

'Getting a drink,' says Luke. 'Mrs Bogram is fetching it for me.'

Does Findlater look a bit flustered? Does Mr Sunshine appear a bit strained at the sight of the young master and future Lord of Mountfathom below and not safe above in bed? He has such a strong notion of etiquette and decorum, Findlater, that Luke even admires the manservant sometimes; cannot imagine Mountfathom ever fading with someone like this so keen to keep things in order. And yet . . .

Luke asks, 'Are you not going to bed, Mr Findlater?'

'No,' replies the manservant. He sighs. 'No, I was trying to prepare some things for your father, for his return. He wants brought out of the attics the oldest maps we have of Ireland – wants to see where the old Faerie Raths and Gyant Towers were situated.'

'Did he say why?' asks Luke.

'No,' says Findlater. 'At least, not to me. Though I have no doubt he knows what he is doing.'

'Yes,' is all Luke says.

'Well, I shall let you get your special drink and then I would advise bed,' says Findlater, very quickly, and then returns to his room and shuts and locks the door.

There is a minute more of waiting, and then, suddenly, the shatter of glass.

'Nanny Bogram?' calls Luke.

No reply.

He starts down the corridor – starts to run.

KILLIAN

Favourite old trick: fistful of something to smash with (shirttail this time), but he worries he might've made too much noise. He is remembering last time too clearly, in the shop – owner and owner's wife and the gunshots. But he slips in anyway and lands on a cold, stone floor. Sees a large table and dark range and empty fireplace and an array of copper hanging from hooks on the ceiling.

'Don't stand about!' Mr Gassin tells him.

'Where now?' asks Killian.

They speak in fierce whispers through the broken window.

'Go out and then left,' says Gassin. 'Along the passage then up the stone spiral stairs and they'll bring you out in a hallway with loads of maps and oddball drawings on the walls. Go to the end of that, then down another hall with loads of stuffed animals, strange-looking things, and then across the entrance hall and open the front doors – the lads and me will meet you there. Then we head to the library.'

Man with the faded hair nods to his two other boys and they hurry off.

'Go on,' says Mr Gassin. 'I've got your back, don't worry about that.'

Killian takes some steps across the kitchen, not stirring a sound. But he hears something: sound of someone approaching, someone shouting. He sees a knife in chopping block and snatches it up –

LUKE

'Mrs Bogram! Nanny Bogram, are you alright?'

He stops – peers into the scullery and moonlight shows shattered glass on stone floor. Luke doesn't think, just steps inside . . . and gets perhaps two steps before someone grabs him from behind –

LUKE & KILLIAN

'Don't shout out. If you do I'll cut your bloody throat!'

A calm enough voice, and truthful – Luke feels the blade tucked tight against his Adam's apple. He doesn't dare swallow, let alone shout out. And even trying to throw some Spell at the person behind him might mean a risk . . . might not be quick enough, or not as quick as the blade.

But Killian doesn't move much either. He's never cut someone's throat, though he has witnessed it done umpteen times. He makes the only decision he can. 'Stay quiet and you'll not get hurt. We're here for the valuables and that's all. Understand?'

Luke manages a mumble. 'Yes.'

'You're gonna guide me upstairs,' says Killian, though he needs no guide; still sees clear in his mind all the directions Mr Gassin gave him. The boy he has by the throat doesn't budge so he says more forcefully, 'I'm not messing! Now move!'

Together they shuffle slowly towards the door. Killian stays sharp for any sound and Luke waits, waits – is awaiting the right moment . . .

A shout of, 'Luke, where are you?'

Whoever holds him from behind stalls.

'I've got this hot chocolate here! I said not to be wandering off!'

And Mrs Bogram's shout is enough of a distraction – Luke whips his hand through the air and mutters a Spell of Release and the boy cries out and is hurled backwards as Luke races down the passageway and through his panic and with hammering heart he shouts, 'Intruders! Intruders in Mountfathom! Raise the alarm!'

KILLIAN

A hand takes him by the collar and hoists him up, spits: 'Stupid little shit! Was it really that bloody difficult to just go upstairs and open a door!'

Killian can't think or move – whole body fizzing not just with pain but with confusion. Senses feel scattered! (If he'd ever experienced the effects of a Spell before, he would recognise these symptoms.) But he has enough sense in his head to say, 'We have to leave. Now. Have to go or else they'll catch us.'

'Like hell,' says the voice of Mr Gassin. Drops Killian to the floor. 'I didn't come this far to leave without doing some damage.'

Killian hears the crunch of glass as the man with faded hair leaves the kitchen. Watches as Mr Gassin reaches into his coat and draws out a short pistol.

LUKE

'Wake up! Wake up!' He is hammering on the door of Mr Findlater but there's no answer. He feels though the whole House has been paralysed with a Spell of Inertia. Races to the spiral stairs that lead up into the House and settles one foot on the bottom step as –

'Luke, what's going on?'

Turns back to see –

Mrs Bogram emerges from a passage on the right. In her hand she has a mug, faint tendrils of steam rising. And from beyond, another figure. Stepping clear of the dark is a man so tall Luke almost takes him for Mr Findlater. But not. And it is as though his heart is failing, as though memory has been rendered real – seasons and years nothing and he feels as though he is back on the causeway as he watches the man with dark eyes and white face and faded hair approach. Sees the man, now, raise a pistol.

181

Mrs Bogram registers Luke's fear so turns; sees the man and the pistol and with no hesitation throws the mug at him and rushes forwards shouting, 'No! Stop! Get out of it!'

A single gunshot, too loud in the narrowness of the stone corridor.

It makes something in Luke unlatch – he falls against the wall and sinks to the ground. And he sees Nanny Bogram fall too. The echo of the gunshot takes a long time to die as Luke locks eyes with the man for a long moment – he sees no pity there, only anger and cold spite and bitter resolve.

Any Spell Luke might use to stop the man has deserted him – he cannot think, can scarcely breathe.

Now footsteps from above? Surely some help descending the stone steps? But arriving too late – Luke watches as the man with faded hair turns and vanishes back into the dark.

Now friendship founders on such rocks –
Lone footsoles find stone and sand.
Now light sends solace across the stars –
Now a word, now an outstretched hand.

'On the Shore of Loughreagh'
Returning to Mountfathom & Other Poems
Jack Gorebooth

KILLIAN

'I didn't know what I was getting into! Was bloody tricked into it! Some fellas snatched me by the docks in Belfast and brought me here on a turf-barge. I was running away from all the rioting in the city, did you hear about that? Yeah, well . . . got lost and couldn't find my da. So I got caught. Got knocked cold. And when I wake up I'm on this barge and the fella in charge says to me that he's taking me somewhere safe. But when we arrived here he pulls out a shooter and starts telling me I have to break into this House!' He allows a pause. Wonders, can he muster some tears? 'He sticks the gun to my head and I have to do what he says or else. I didn't know anyone was gonna get killed! I've never seen anyone shot before.' And he trails off and lowers his head and presses the heel of his hand to his face and wipes his eyes. Because sure enough – here come the tears and the sniffles. He thinks: *You are too good! You should be on the stage, boy! Or better – on the silver screen!*

He hears the man with the moustache telling someone, 'Go and check Loughreagh for this turf-barge. Perhaps they are still on the water. If they are, do not approach them – come back and inform me.'

Killian hears another voice say, 'Can we not send a Spell of Finding after them? Track them down that way?'

'Luke,' says the man with the moustache, 'I shall do all I can to apprehend these men. But now is not the time – we must secure Mountfathom. When I am finished here I will require your help in setting fresh Spells around the borders of the demesne.'

'But how did they even get in?' the boy asks.

Killian peers out between fingers – sees the man with the moustache and the boy (this father and son) sharing a look. The boy is holding himself, is shivering. His face is red and he looks as though he would be happy to fold up like a newspaper and fall *smack* to the ground. The father tells his son, 'We shall discuss those matters later. I would be only too happy to hear your theories. For now, I want you to join your mother in the Gabbling Gallery and send messages to the other members of the Driochta. Tell them what you experienced. Let them know what has happened, that Mountfathom has been compromised. I shall meet you by the walled garden in half an hour.'

'Gabbling Gallery' and 'Driochta' and 'Mountfathom' aren't familiar things to Killian, but he tucks them into his memory; in situations like this, as he well knows, he has to keep himself sharp for any knowledge he can pick up. Looking and listening – these are the best tools he has. Killian sees the boy called Luke watching him, so shuts his eyes and sniffs a bit more.

'Yes, Father,' says the boy, and he leaves the room. As obedient as anything! *Must remember that*, thinks Killian. *Could be useful later on.*

186

'Now then,' says the man with the moustache. Killian opens his eyes. He makes a brave attempt at a brave face and sees that he and the man are alone. He takes some quick looks around. They are in a library. Huge place, whole room teeming with books! Even more than in the Linen Hall! Killian has been sat down at a desk with slips of paper and a fancy pen and small towers of books with titles such as *Seeking to Storm-Breach* and *The Rise of the Politomancer* and *Shillingham's Guide to Protective Spells*.

The man takes a step towards him and says, 'Now that we are alone, I was wondering if you could find it in yourself to tell me the truth of what transpired here tonight.'

Killian holds the man's gaze. Decides on playing a bit dumb. 'Sorry, Mister – I don't know what you mean. What was that word you said? "*Transpired*"? I dunno what you –'

'I am the Lord of Mountfathom,' says the man. 'And tonight, in my absence and under my roof, a long-serving member of my staff has been murdered. I do not wish to contact the police. I daresay they have enough to be dealing with, and given the current climate I feel the murder of a member of staff at a Big House will arouse alarm with which we do not wish to contend. So I shall deal with this in my own way – you are an intruder in this House, you have proven yourself a practised but deeply flawed liar, and you are a fool if you think I shall believe such lies.' Killian sits up straighter. 'Now ponder this: if you are confident that you can break through the various layers of Spell-Work surrounding this House and not tell me how, then that confidence is misplaced. If you think you can sit there and implausibly fabricate for the benefit of your own

187

pride and amusement, you are very much mistaken. You will tell me the truth, or I shall Work a Spell to make you spill all your secrets. Do we understand each other?'

Well, I'll be damned, thinks Killian. He almost has some respect for this Lord of Mountfathom for seeing through him so easily! He knows when he is beat. He knows – if only for now – that he best be dutiful and say, 'Oh yes, Mister. Of course I shall tell you all the truth I can.'

LUKE

Luke stops at the top of the stairs and listens to the faces of the Driochta in the Gabbling Gallery –

'If Mountfathom has seen violation, then I don't know what will be next!'

'Don't be so melodramatic! This is not one of your plays, Jack!'

'No need for such personal insult, Lady Vane-Tempest!'

'The Spells were so well set, I believed.'

'There's no telling what way land will go, Spells or no Spells.'

'Too true, Lawrence.'

'But Mountfathom! Surely the land knows to whom it belongs?'

'Do I hear some doubting there, Flann?'

'Not at all, Helena! I am simply concerned . . .'

'Aren't we all! So, what is the plan, Edith?'

A moment before Luke hears his mother say, 'Firstly, Dublin must not hear of this. Major Fortflay must not be told – that is the priority. Word that the Spells of Mountfathom have been breached must not travel. Agreed?'

Only firm agreement –

Face of Jack Gorebooth: 'Of course!'

Face of Helena Vane-Tempest: 'Absolutely.'

Of Flann Dorrick: 'Won't say a word to anyone! Though you should know – eleven more Houses have been lost to the Land Grabbers this night.'

Face of Lawrence Devine: 'I heard that too, on the wireless – five in Mayo and six in Clare.'

'Also by Indigo Fire?' asks Luke's mother.

Dorrick: 'From what witnesses are saying, yes indeed.'

'Then that Cailleach is still helping them,' says Luke. He can't stay silent – walks into the Gallery and stands beside his mother, swiftly returned that night, along with Lord Mountfathom. Sees the four pale faces of the Driochta swimming in their dark mirrors. All eyes turn to watch him. He goes on. 'They've clearly made a decision to use Magic. The Land Grabbers don't care that it's something they swore they'd never use.'

'Indeed,' says Lady Vane-Tempest, 'attitudes are changing. If they can find a way to empower themselves, they will take it.'

'How are you, lad?' asks the Lawrence Devine. Luke wants to say he is fine, or that he will be – that he will cope. But he says nothing. His mother places a hand on his shoulder and Lawrence Devine says, 'I knew Mrs Bogram for forty years and she was some woman.'

'Oh yes!' says Vane-Tempest. 'Very formidable!'

'So very kind and attentive too,' says Jack Gorebooth. 'Always at your side, Luke. Always there to –'

'What is the plan?' asks Luke. Has heard enough talk – needs some sense of action.

'We must do nothing to arouse suspicion from the Castle in Dublin,' says Lady Mountfathom, addressing the Driochta. 'I hope you will agree that we cannot place our entire trust in Fortflay any longer – he has lost his belief in us, and so we must be cautious.'

All faces agree.

'And my requests to each of you are as follows,' says Luke's mother. 'Helena – I wish you to track down this Cailleach. We need to know what her next move will be.'

'I accept your request and will begin at once,' says Vane-Tempest, and instantly she departs her mirror.

'Flann,' says Lady Mountfathom, 'can you please keep a close watch on the goings-on at the Castle. We need to be warned in advance of any machinations that Major Fortflay is setting in motion.'

'You have some suspicions?' says Dorrick. 'Something in particular?'

'I do,' says Luke's mother. 'He talked of requiring additional powers. If he is going to enlist Magical help from elsewhere – beyond those of the Politomancer – we need to know.'

'I shall keep both eyes and ears wide open!' says Dorrick, and he too fades fast from his mirror.

Only two faces remain, and both Devine and Gorebooth ask, 'And us?'

Luke's mother says, 'I request that you both come to Mountfathom.'

Gorebooth looks relieved, excited! Devine looks not altogether agreeable, but he gives a grim nod.

'Lawrence, I know I am taking you away from your own family and your farm,' says Lady Mountfathom, 'but I believe we need more members of the Driochta here to help, should the need arise.'

'We would be glad to,' says Jack Gorebooth. 'By sunrise I shall be at Mountfathom.'

'And I too,' says Lawrence Devine.

'Thank you,' says Lady Mountfathom.

And Luke watches the final two faces disperse into darkness and instantly says, 'It was my fault. You and Father left me here in charge.'

'It was the fault of no one,' says his mother. She doesn't look at her son; stays focused on the mirrors. 'It is a great loss to us and of that there is no doubt. However we must remain strong – it is what Mrs Bogram would have wanted.'

Luke begins to say more but –

'Nothing else just now, Luke.' His mother looks at him, softens a little. Sees Luke's pale face, his eyes red with crying. 'Apologies, son, but I am afraid I am simply not in the mood for more discussion. Now, I believe your father requires your help – go to him, and do what you can to make Mountfathom safer.'

KILLIAN

Left alone in the library, Killian wanders restless. After their chat – Killian telling all he recalled about his journey from

Belfast, all that was said on the turf-barge and a little of what he managed to puzzle out about Mr Gassin – the posh fella told him not to make a nuisance of himself. Said to sit and wait and behave and someone would come and see to him. But Killian is incapable of sitting and doing nothing.

He climbs one of the tall stepladders to the top shelf and pushes himself along, wheels sliding smooth across the wooden floor. He selects so many books – covers of velvet and lace and something that looks like human skin, spines sewn tight or neatly embossed or loosely woven or bound with brass – and reads the last page of each book, and understands none of it. Jams them back onto the shelves in the wrong place. And he decides to shout his name loud and enjoys the boom of his voice and the bounce of its echo . . . until the books begin to whisper back: *'Killian . . . Killian . . . Killian . . .'*

He swears loudly and leaps from the stepladder and lands on the floor with a violent thud.

'Enjoying yourself in here? Not a playground, you know.'

Killian turns and tucks his hands into his pockets and tries for innocence.

A tall man, skinny as a drainpipe, has appeared in the library. Balanced on one hand is a silver tray; he approaches, saying, 'I was told to provide you with some refreshment.'

Killian returns to the centre of the room – reclaims the leather seat behind the deal-topped desk, leans back and rests his feet on top. Has the desired effect – the manservant wrinkles his nose and rolls his eyes and says, 'Very amusing of you. And where do you suggest I put this tray?'

Killian thinks: *I know where he can put it!*

'I'll take it off your hands,' he decides to say, and hops to his feet and snatches the tray from the man. 'Cheers. Now, off you go!' And sits down with the tray on his lap and gets stuck into some tea with plenty of sugar and toast that he covers with a good slather of strawberry jam.

Mr Findlater says very slowly: 'Let me give you some advice, young sir – I would not get too comfortable here, if I were you.'

'Really?' says Killian, cheeks bulging with toast, lips dribbling tea. 'And why not?'

'Because we have long memories here at Mountfathom,' says the man. Killian pauses. 'There are a lot of people greatly upset by what has happened here tonight. I myself worked with Mrs Bogram for the past thirty-five years. It is therefore very upsetting.'

'Really?' says Killian again. He swallows. 'Because you don't look too upset to me, good sir.'

Findlater says nothing.

And Killian smiles and looks the manservant over and takes in so many little details: the heavy mauve bags under both eyes, so mustn't sleep much; the nails clipped so close to the quick, the tracks of a long-toothed comb in his slicked hair and the white scalp showing through.

'Going bald, Mister?' asks Killian.

Findlater shifts his weight and says, 'How very observant you are.'

'I am,' says Killian.

'And you seem very secure in yourself also,' says Findlater.

'I am,' Killian repeats. 'And I believe I have the measure of you, my man.'

The manservant flinches as though scalded. He nods, stiffly, and turns and walks all the way to the double doors, and on the threshold stops (as Killian knew he would) so he can have the last word. 'Be careful, young sir. Times are shifting, and very quickly. None of us should feel too secure in ourselves, even a Lagan Rat who thinks he has the whole world worked out.'

LUKE

'Tell me your theories, son – I very much wish to hear them.'

'I'm not certain of anything. I only have ideas.'

'Ideas are good. Ideas are always a profitable beginning.'

Luke and Lord Mountfathom walk the boundary, son in the shadow of the father. Both have a left hand held to the limestone wall, their free hands weaving and resetting Spells of Seclusion and Security; a mere whisper and waving of a hand entices trees to ease together as though for comfort, entwine, branches to embrace; hawthorn and bramble to sprout and thrive and form a thicket, and any shattered or cracked stone to heal itself like a mended seam. This Magic is a slow and precise and diligent business. And it helps Luke – requires such concentration and focus he slowly starts to feel a little usefulness once more.

He says, 'My understanding is that the Spells we set around the demesne will only hold true if everyone at Mountfathom is united in its protection, is that not so?'

'It is.'

'Then I believe the men who were able to enter the grounds were invited.'

194

'Interesting,' says Lord Mountfathom. He Works a hand – a patch of nettles rises from thigh-high to neck-high. 'By whom?'

'I don't know,' says Luke. 'I was thinking – perhaps we should speak to each of the staff? See if they know anything?' He sees his father pause so adds, 'It may not have been intentional on their part. They may have let slip some information that allowed the Spells to be compromised. That is my theory.'

Under moonlight, they stop and face one another.

Lord Mountfathom allows some moments, and Luke knows his father is showing (attempting?) due respect to his son's words; is doubtful of them, but giving them polite consideration. Now Lord Mountfathom says, 'Luke, I understand your concerns. I would say your assumptions are both logical and sound; however, if we start interrogating the staff, that may only worsen matters.'

'How?' asks Luke. 'How else can we get at the truth?'

'Things are in a sensitive state,' says Lord Mountfathom. 'Feelings are running high. Not just here but everywhere in this country. We do not wish to alienate the people we have come to see as family. We cannot risk making enemies of those within our protection.'

'I realise that,' says Luke, and some note of impatience rises in his voice, 'but Nanny Bogram was my family too and no one protected her. And now –' his voice breaks a little, '– she is dead.' He looks at the wall – they have reached the tunnel that leads to Loughreagh, the opening visible only to those within the protection of Mountfathom. But –

'This is how they got in,' says Luke suddenly.

'Yes,' says his father. 'I believe that is so.'

'It was the same man who was on the causeway that day,' says Luke now.

'You cannot be sure of that,' says his father. Lord Mountfathom raises his Needle in his right hand – a low, whining note, a slow Conducting and from the ground burst a row of saplings that sprout branches that knot and twist and bind together tight to cover the opening in the wall. Somehow, the sight saddens Luke – this recoiling from the world and further retreat, this necessary withdrawal. His father tells him, 'All we can be sure of is that we need to be vigilant. Now, tell me what else you think we need here?'

Luke senses, knows, there is something his father is not telling him. But – 'Messengers,' he says.

His father nods.

Luke raises his hands and speaks a Spell to Summon a pair of tall, indistinct female figures – almost invisible under moonlight, and Luke thinks them the most substantial he has yet managed.

Father thinks so too. 'Well done.'

Luke moves towards the Messengers and whispers the command to the women, a bidding they are Magically bound to act on. 'If these Spells of Security fade – should this tunnel be opened for any reason – find me and inform me.'

Both figures nod, and further fade. Luke doubts that even a member of the Driochta would be able to detect their presence.

'Now to other matters,' says Luke's father. He has his hands in his pockets and his gaze is fixed on the far-off. 'I have spoken to the boy called Killian, and he has told me what I believe is the truth: that he was picked up in Belfast and brought here because he is an expert in breaking-and-entering. Luke, I should tell you that it is my intention to keep him here.'

'Why? He helped those men. He was the one who –'

'There is no sense at all in sending him from us. He has seen too much; knows too much. We must be sensible. I believe it better that he stay here.'

'So we are to have an expert thief in the House?'

Lord Mountfathom looks at his son.

'He is also a child, Luke. Scarcely older than you. And just as you have known only the light and colour of Mountfathom, he has known only the darker places of the world.'

'Are you saying it is not his fault?'

Lord Mountfathom doesn't offer a reply.

And Luke understands his father's intention now –

'You want me to befriend this boy? Treat him like he belongs here?'

'Yes,' says Lord Mountfathom. 'As we would do with any other – we must show him understanding, and give him somewhere where he can feel safe. That is your task.'

'Why?' asks Luke. 'Is this instead of accompanying the Driochta on missions? To babysit?'

'It is my express wish.'

'But, Father – why take such a risk in keeping him? He might betray us.'

It feels to Luke a long time before his father replies, before the Lord of Mountfathom offers an answer that Luke feels is full of such wistful wishing: 'I have hope, son. I believe people can change. And I believe we need all the allies we can find.'

Luke's father moves on with a renewed vigour, casting Spells left and right that hover like a low haze in the air. He tells his son, 'Our priority now is one of survival, for us and for those we care about most! As you said yourself – if we within Mountfathom are divided, then like a poison it will wither our every Spell. And trust me now: if that day comes, there will be no Magic on this island that will be able to protect us.'

KILLIAN

A tap on the shoulder wakes him. Killian, snoozing, forgets where he is: shoots out of his seat like he's about to be stabbed, full of shouting. 'Get back! Leave me be or else!'

When he sees only the boy called Luke standing in front of him he calms a bit. Now feels suddenly vulnerable so attacks again. 'Could've given me a bit of warning before you woke me!'

Luke says, 'I am to look after you. I'll show you to one of our rooms.'

'Kind of you!' says Killian. 'Sleeping in a chair could destroy a good man's back!' He feels fully awake (too awake, if there's such a thing) – highly-strung and quick-tempered and on edge. He keeps talking, wants to keep attention away from himself, 'You must be wrecked, keeping yourself up so late.'

'Not at all,' says Luke. 'I don't sleep much even on normal nights. Especially not tonight.' Luke's mouth makes a shape like he might want to say more, but won't allow himself. Simmers with resentment, but refuses to show it.

So, thinks Killian, *not only obedient but polite to a fault too!*

He says to the boy, 'Well, then, lead on, good sir! Give me the guided tour.'

LUKE

And Killian exclaims at everything! Is full of questioning –

'What kinda corridor is this?'

'What's that a picture of? Is that in Ireland?'

'Which direction are we facing now?'

'That can't be a real creature!'

'How many rooms are there in this place?'

'Look at the size of that thing! What is it?'

And despite all, Luke likes to give answers. Slowly, he tells –

'It's called The Gallery of Learning.'

'That is a painting of an Irish elk.'

'We are heading now into the western wing of the House.'

'That Griffin was created by my mother – she enjoys strange taxidermy.'

'About one hundred and thirty rooms, but we haven't counted in a while.'

'That's a shell from a giant tortoise. Father found it on the beach when he was in the army and they went to the Galapagos.'

Into the Entrance Hall and –

'Jaysus! The size of them bloody stairs!'

Killian races to the staircase and starts climbing and shouting and enjoying the echo that bounces his words back and forth.

'It goes up and on forever (*ever-ever*)! Is that a big glass dome (*dome-dome*)?'

'It was designed by my great-great-grandfather Frederick,' says Luke. Finds himself following quickly after. 'Galway marble! Two hundred and fifty-two steps from top to bottom!'

Killian swears, loudly.

Luke stops mid-step.

They listen as the echo of Killian's word goes on and embarrassingly on.

Killian says, 'Sorry there. Is there more stuffed animals or things like that?'

Luke wonders how much he has given away of himself – is the boy playing him? He asks cautious, 'Are you at all interested in animals?'

'Course!' says Killian. 'Who wouldn't be – better than humans! I'd rather have a dog than my old da any day.'

Luke decides. 'In that case, I know the room you need to stay in.'

KILLIAN

He has discovered that people like to feel they know you. If they think they have you all worked out they relax a bit – they let you in. And this young fella, thinks Killian, needs to be won over. So he decides to tell his usual tale.

'To tell you the truth, Luke, I wasn't born in Belfast. Nope, wasn't always a townie. Was actually born in the countryside near Dublin. Reared in a field! Brought up in the backend of beyond! Not like this though – it was rough as hell. Mam died when I was one year old. No siblings. Me father was a clerk for a big tea-merchant in Belfast so we moved there. But he wasn't a wise man, my da. He was framed for stealing money even though he never would've stolen a sweet. But when the Peelers turned up it was his name all over the dockets! He got the boot from the company and he couldn't deal with the shame so he jumped in the Lagan and that was that.'

They stop on the first floor.

Luke watches him.

Killian has to suppress a shout of, *'It's the truth! Honest!'* He's told this story so many times and thinks he has it perfect – just enough detail of place and age, and he reckons the bit about his da being a tea-merchant a fine bit of invention. Good dollop of tragedy too to make it all sound like he's been a helpless 'victim of circumstance' (one of his father's favourite phrases). But this boy, he doesn't seem to be buying it.

Luke says, 'That is quite the story.'

'Tis and all,' says Killian. 'No harm to you but I'm wrecked! Now where's this room of mine?'

LUKE

An ivory disc on a door – *The Menagerie of the Dead*.

'Sounds a bit grim,' says Killian.

Luke pauses, fingers on the brass door handle shaped like a magpie with wings outstretched. Wonders, *Why do I even want to show this boy this room?*

201

But he has no time at all for pause.

'Well, come on then!' Killian pushes his way past. Some moments, and Luke hears him announce from inside, 'Christ, this is some bedroom!'

Luke follows.

Moonlight is enough to lay a pale gleam on glass and wood and bone – to show specimens displayed on pedestal and within cabinet and beneath bell jar. All neatly labelled with date and time and place of discovery, names inked in English and Latin and arranged by phylum, order, genus, species . . .

'How many here?' asks Killian. 'Where did you get them all? Who helped you? Is this even allowed?'

'Over five hundred specimens,' says Luke, 'mostly from the grounds but some were given to me – I keep separate the ones I get as gifts. I collected most of these myself.'

'Hold on,' says Killian, somewhere in the centre of the room. 'Let me get this right – this is a whole room just for you and for animal stuff you've collected!'

Luke nods.

Killian says, 'And your oul fella lets you do this?'

'Of course,' says Luke. Hasn't thought of this before – supposes there are some fathers who mightn't let their boy collect bones? 'I used to keep them in my room but the collection became too big, so Father gave me this room to display them in.'

Killian swears again. 'I could spend days in here having a look at all this! Did you use Magic to collect them?'

'No,' says Luke.

'But you can do Magic? The fella that brought me here – he said people in this House know Spells and things.'

'Yes,' says Luke. 'My mother and father are in the Droichta – it is an ancient Order that tries to help –' Luke pauses. How best to phrase things now for someone who doesn't know what is what? 'An Order that works with the Government in Dublin.'

'You do Magic?' asks Killian, still wandering, still asking his questions.

'I can, yes,' says Luke, still standing, and now not wanting so much to answer.

'Like the fella who brought me here from Belfast – he could do Spells too.'

Luke thinks on this – once more pictures the man with the faded hair standing in the stone corridor, pistol in hand. He decides to ask a question of his own. 'How did he allow himself into the grounds?'

'Had a letter,' says Killian. Half-shrugs and adds, 'Or some bit of paper that he burned after reading it – said something about it being an invitation.'

Luke nods. Thinks, *I was right*. Says nothing but is already making plans for the next day – investigations he can begin, Spells of Uncovering he may be able to Cast.

He tells the boy, 'Well, your bed is over there by the window.'

Killian looks at him.

'Seriously?' he says. 'You trust me to stay in here with all your stuff?'

Luke hasn't thought of this. But again the questions.

'These bird skeletons,' says Killian, palms pressed tight against one of the cabinets, 'how many of them do you have?'

Luke tells him.

'I like birds best,' says Killian, blast of his breath misting the glass. 'My mother was a professor of birds at Trinity in Dublin. She taught me all about them till she died.'

'Didn't she die when you were one year old?' says Luke.

Killian glances at him, and with hardly a pause says, 'Yeah – I can remember being nought years old, can't you?' Sound of springing bedsprings as Killian finds the bed and shouts, 'Night then!'

Luke says goodnight and walks to the door, mind whirling. He thinks, *Can I trust a thing he says? The boy is surely lying, but why?*

The dishonesty itself doesn't bother Luke though. What he wonders more about is this: why is Killian going to such trouble to make things up? Why so much energy into lies and untruth? What is it of himself that he wants so desperately to hide?

*It is true that to begin with there were not
Five Magical Principles, but Six.
(The Sixth being: On The
Inevitability of Death & Ending).
It is my humble belief that this
Sixth Principle was subsumed by the Fifth.
For is not death the ultimate unknown?
The final step into a necessary ignorance.*

On the Origins of the Five Principles of Magic
Lord William Mountfathom

LUKE

A dream: that his bedroom has been invaded. Perhaps a nightmare: that *The Amazon* has been overcome – the scene within the wallpaper has spilled forth, floor a tangle of root and vine writhing at his feet. He dreams great trunks have sprouted, split floor and walls to reach towards the ceiling and spread damp leaves that scatter noxious spores, the whole place poisoned with the stench of age and neglect. And some nastiness, some evil . . .

Now: a dream or not?

Luke surfaces suddenly from sleep. Sits upright to see his arms and legs and entire body submerged – struggling under the choke of ivy that has swamped his bed, he and Morrigan both trapped tight beneath it. He screams a Spell of Fleeing and Spell of Escape and the ivy is severed, split – loosened enough for him to scoop up Morrigan and leap from his bed and bolt from *The Amazon*.

KILLIAN

About the same time –

> *'Another child now – another witness to the faltering!'*
> *'Another spectator to the fracture and split!'*
> *'What Magic can save us now?'*
> *'What Magic? Soon no Magic! Magic leaves as love does –'*
> *'As blood does drain from a dying heart!'*
> *'As thoughts do from a dying mind!'*
> 'Would you ever shut the hell up?'

This last is Killian and he is up out of his bed, swinging fists – but they touch no flesh, only slice through the Traces who retreat to rise to the ceiling, still spilling their melancholia into the morning air. Though one swipe from Killian connects – strikes one of the pedestals . . . sets it tottering and toppling; the skeleton of a starling and the bell jar that shielded it both falling to shatter loud on the floor.

Killian stops. Breathes deep.

He struggles to remember where he is – sees more bones and broad cabinets, glass and polished wood, and slowly the memory of the night before returns in a sweep . . . He sinks back onto the bed.

No time for himself or his own thoughts – a sudden thud of feet and a hammering at the door and voice, 'Killian, are you awake? Can I come in?'

Before Killian can part his lips for yes or no the door is thrown wide and in bolts the boy called Luke. Red in the face and breathless, he stops in the centre of the room and says, 'Something has happened.'

'Yes,' says Killian, and he leans back and stretches full-length on the bed and tucks his hands behind his head. 'Something has happened – I've been very rudely woken up. And too early for my liking, mate! A man needs his sleep, you know.'

But Luke isn't listening – at least not to Killian. He has his head half-cocked and is approaching the window. Says in whisper to himself, 'I didn't draw the drapes last night. Nor did you. So why is it so dark . . . ?'

Killian lets out a sigh . . . but still and all, has to admit it is dark enough. If the clock in the corner is correct then should be a bit lighter by now. Curiosity makes him rise again and together they walk to the window.

'Time for a bit of detective work,' says Killian, cracking his fingers and unlatching the sash and heaving the window high as Luke tells him, 'Careful!' And in spills a swell of ivy they have to wrestle back – the reek of must and rot!

Kicking and extricating themselves (Killian doing plenty of swearing), the boys back away.

'What the feck is this?' asks Killian.

'Same in my room,' says Luke. 'I left my window open a bit and it got in and spread across the floor and my bed. If I'd slept in any longer it may have suffocated me.'

'Right,' says Killian, eyes on the ivy – on its slow inch and crawl across the floor. 'This happen often here, does it?'

'No,' says Luke. And he shuts his eyes for a moment. And says, 'Can't be the Spells Father and I set last night. They wouldn't overcome the House itself. Magic must be confused. Must be something not right.'

Luke continues on and Killian thinks to himself, *Mental – whole place is mental!*

'I need to find Mother and Father,' says Luke, opening his eyes. Though he doesn't move a single step.

From somewhere above, the Traces groan –

'Has its own ways and means, this House!'

'Has its own deep roots of Magic and Spell-Work!'

'No force can tame it! No hand can still the coming storm!'

'We must be cautious now! We must keep an eye on the shadows!'

'You think someone is doing this to the House?' asks Killian, not knowing what to say but not wanting to say nothing – especially not wanting to listen to those Traces.

'No,' says Luke. 'This House makes its own decisions – this much I have learned.' A pause. 'I think Mountfathom may be trying to protect itself.'

LUKE & KILLIAN

Not only *The Amazon* and *The Menagerie of the Dead* – Luke checks *Valhalla* and *Berlin* and the Seasonal Room and there too the ivy has found entry through window and skirting and floorboard and flue. And not only the ivy – that same stench, same signs of neglect . . .

Killian says, 'House looks like no one has lived in it for years! How long did we sleep for? Like some bad Faerie tale.'

Luke agrees with him, though he stays silent.

'Quickly,' is all he says. 'I must find my mother and father.'

Each step of the marble staircase harbours a murky puddle –

'You need to get the roof looked at,' says Killian.

Walls are displaying continents of yellowish mould –

'Don't let damp get a hold in a place or you'll never get rid!' suggests Killian.

Luke quickens his step and Killian follows.

As they reach the ground floor and the entrance hall with its chequered tiles (all suddenly unsteady underfoot) the front doors open – Lord and Lady Mountfathom and Mr Hooker step inside, all three deep in conversation.

'Father!' Luke calls and runs to them. Stumbles and almost falls. 'Mother! What's happening?'

'Nothing to worry about,' says Mr Hooker. 'Exact same thing happened with your grandfather about forty years ago! Place got broken into so he went and set Spells around the boundary, and the next day we all woke up and thought we'd fallen asleep out in the grounds! Ivy everywhere, great big rhododendron sprouting beside my bed! Was an awful panic at first, but we sorted it out. No need to worry, lads.'

Luke and Killian have the same thought: the gardener sounds too keen to quieten their worries, too determined to soothe. So Luke watches his father's face – knows that the man can never hide his feelings. And there is a definite darkness in his expression. A shadow that Killian notices too, and describes to himself as *shifty* . . . that Luke sees, and describes as *sadness*. Luke opens his mouth to say more, but his mother nods at him, gently.

'Luke,' says Lady Mountfathom, 'there is no cause for concern. And now, you need to get yourself smartened up and made presentable!'

'Why?' says Luke – in the same moment, remembering.

'The funeral,' says Luke's mother. 'We will be burying Nanny Bogram at midday. At the Temple of Ivory on the Rise.'

LUKE

'You need to get dressed, sir,' Findlater tells Luke.

'A moment – this is important.'

'Why now, sir? Why not afterwards?'

Good question, but Luke needs to know – if there is something else on the horizon, and he can interpret it, he needs to try. He applies another drop of ink to the mirror, weaves his hand low over the surface and waits. But he can bring only the same pattern as the previous evening – two small dark figures, standing hand in hand.

'What is it showing?' asks Findlater. 'Who are those two boys?'

'I don't know,' says Luke. 'Who would you say they are?'

'I am sure I do not know,' says Findlater, and he crosses to the wardrobe. Sounds despairing. 'Now, what on earth are you going to wear?' Luke can hear him muttering to himself about the difficulty of a funeral so soon, but this is the Mountfathom way –

Luke focuses again on the surface of the mirror – sees himself amidst so much spilt ink. Seems a mistake, a childish mess – no trace of Magic or chance to foresee anything. Morrigan leaps onto his lap and gives him an appreciative look.

'If I may be blunt,' says Mr Findlater, 'I believe Mrs Bogram would want you to look your best today. If she were here, she would be scrubbing and sewing and fussing to get you well-presented.'

Findlater is right. So Luke stands and says, 'I'm sorry. I should get ready.'

Side by side, they peer into the wardrobe but see very little – have had to light two lamps in his room to see by, ivy clustered so thick around the window.

Suddenly, Luke finds himself asking, 'Where were you last night?'

'Pardon me?' says Findlater.

'When they broke in, I banged on your door and you didn't answer.'

'I was asleep.'

Luke watches the manservant for a moment. Has more to ask but decides not to press Findlater further. Not yet. Says instead, 'I'll wear the blue suit. Mrs Bogram liked that colour best. She always said it was her favourite.'

KILLIAN

'You look very decent,' says Mr Hooker.

'I'd say I look a right fool!' says Killian.

'Nonsense. Come here till I have a good look at you.'

Killian steps into the kitchen, as close to sheepish as he's ever been in his life.

Couple of the Errander boys stand about, spit-polishing their boots and sizing him up through narrowed eyes – Killian gives looks as unforgiving as the ones he gets. Some of the maids too – heads down, wary, not wanting to meet his eye.

Killian has been well kitted out though – old tweed suit and white shirt found in an upstairs press, a navy tie loaned by Mr Hooker. Now: he doesn't know how he feels. Uncomfortable more than anything, and not a bit like himself. Killian is used to duping people, that bit doesn't bother him. But what does bother him – the very worst thing! – is when people see through him and he's caught out. So he is sure someone will soon point him out and say, *'No, no! Take that off! Who do you think you are? You're fooling no one!'*

Doesn't know if he can carry this off. Feels an idiot in these clothes. An intruder. What are they doing, taking him in like this?

Mr Hooker sips some tea and says, 'You'll be grand. Don't worry.'

Mrs Little is there too, finishing the last of the breakfast dishes, and she spares him a sideways glance. Tells him with a snap, 'Stand up straighter.' She is in a tidy dark dress – pale lace at the cuffs and a small black hat with a folded veil. She leaves the dishes and says, 'If you're going to stay here, you may as well look presentable.' She brings a damp cloth and gives him a once over – swipes the cloth over his shoulders, loosens and redoes his tie, starts rubbing at some muck on his chin. Killian knocks her hand away and recoils – swears at her.

'There's no need for that kind of language,' she says, looking not only annoyed but a touch afraid too. She goes back to her dishes. 'You'd think you would have some manners, after what happened.'

214

Killian doesn't say sorry. Says nothing. He is already thinking of escape. Thinks this funeral will be a good opportunity. Everyone elsewhere, distracted . . . so will be easy to slip away unseen. And maybe he can grab a few bits before he goes, for selling when he gets back to Belfast? Might make a few bob out of this after all.

Mr Hooker stands, wears a tweed suit the same colour so says, 'Sure we could be twins!'

'Don't think so,' says Killian. 'Sure you're ancient.'

'He's sulking,' says Mrs Little.

'Amn't,' says Killian. 'Just not comfortable in this bloody outfit!'

'No coarseness today,' says Mr Hooker. 'This is a solemn occasion. Ever been to a funeral before, lad?'

'Course,' says Killian. 'Loads of them! I've seen ten dead bodies.'

Mr Hooker and Mrs Little look at each other.

'Well, then,' says the gardener. 'You'll know how to behave.'

LUKE

Statues of the Veiled Ladies are in full mourning; low sound of weeping from their ivory lips, the mutter of prayers and supplication, spilling grief into the dark air.

Small gathering stands silent on the cold Rise. It is raining, the scene washed of all colour; Lady Mountfathom and Lord Mountfathom, the others from the House in dark coats with collars turned-up, and around their feet slips of ivory, gravestones like so many discarded letters, embedded in the ground unread.

Luke thinks, *Would Nanny Bogram have wanted this – so much seriousness on so many faces?*

Softness seems the only suitable mood. And sorrow and whispered solicitude. So many bowed heads and neatly clasped hands.

Luke wonders why death brings people into such silence. Like all fight has gone out of them. Where is the rage and shouting – why such easy acceptance?

'Luke,' says his mother. 'You are talking to yourself.'

Old habit, hadn't realised he was doing it.

Such a small gathering: handful of staff only, most asked to remain behind in the House because (though no one says it aloud) the Lord and Lady Mountfathom will not leave their House emptied. Only two of the Driochta are present – Lawrence Devine, wearing the same suit he always wears when the occasion calls for a suit, and Jack Gorebooth standing shivering, a small leather notebook clutched tight in his hands. He is going to lead the service, and Luke hopes that the poet hasn't written one of his interminable epics – an attempt to tie the death of one woman to the wider concerns of the country . . .

A slow shuffle, the gathering turning to see – up the slope come the two undertakers, carrying the coffin with the help of two Errander boys. Luke wanted to be a bearer, but his wish went nowhere. And as they approach, Lady Mountfathom performs a traditional rite. Works her right hand in the air and the rain that falls on the Rise is halted. Elsewhere and beyond it continues to fall, but where they stand each drop has been suspended – hangs in the air like beads of glass.

The coffin passes by.

The Temple of Ivory has no visible opening – pitched ivory roof held high by a ring of ivory statues. But as the coffin arrives Lord Mountfathom weaves a hand and two statues step aside, their heads bowed. The coffin is allowed entry. And slowly tugged along in its wake, Luke tucked between his parents, they pass into the coolness of the Temple.

But before Luke steps inside, he sees the boy – standing beside Mr Hooker, pair of them in smart matching tweed. Killian gives Luke a small smile. And somehow – suddenly, so unexpectedly – this simple thing makes Luke feel stronger.

KILLIAN

He was telling no lies about his experience of funerals – has been to so many it's become a bore! Da would drag him along always, saying on the way, 'We need to go and pay our respects. Scrub that dirt off your face! Just decent, so it is. And put some spit and shine on them shoes!' Killian knows this whole routine – the coffin, the sad looks, songs, sniffling.

But what he doesn't expect is the Magic – the rain and the way it slowed like time was being slowed down and then just stopped . . . He reaches out and sweeps a hand through the air, it comes back damp and dripping, and glistening. He thinks this is how funerals should be, how people should be given a send-off – the feeling that even things like rain should be made stop for a few minutes in respect. And as he stands alongside Mr Hooker in the circular Temple, Killian surprises himself when he starts to listen to the words of the wee bald man with the glasses –

'We have such a short time on this earth. And for some, it is true that there will no longer be any tomorrow. But for us – surely the blessed and the spared – we have today. We have this moment. Let us mourn, yes, but let us be happy too! Be glad for what we have! We should never get used to being in the world – it is a gift, and we should be aware every moment of the uniqueness of our lives and the newness of the now. For it is only a fleeting thing, this world. A rose blooms only to wither. A moon waxes only to wane.'

But what's this now? The boy of the Big House, Luke, suddenly darts out of the Temple and is away, leaving behind the sound of sob. Bit of an awkward pause, everyone looking at each other . . . but the bald fella goes on –

'We are so many stars blazing, but surrounded always by the cold dark of the Heavens. We can only wonder at what may await us all in the unknown – in that great dark between here and the elsewhere.'

LUKE

As he passes, the Veiled Ladies turn to follow – heads bowed, hands clasped, full of concern. But their weeping and lamentation leaves no mark on Luke; he has had enough of mourning.

Luke finds an ivory bench on which to settle. And he sees now an almost conquered Mountfathom – ivy cloaking windows and stonework, almost overcome; from the flowerbeds weeds spilling and swarming around the foundations of the House . . . the twist of corkscrew hazel and tangle of bramble, all in close conspiracy, all (he imagines) trying to obscure Mountfathom. And the sight of it all makes him wish suddenly for escape – imagines Mogrifying, lifting into the air and leaving, flying beyond the boundary wall and across Loughreagh and heading for the fringe of ashen Mourne Mountains and –

'I know what you're thinking – people dying is shite.'

Luke turns.

Killian stands with hands dug deep into his trouser pockets, scuffing his smart (borrowed) shoes on the grass. He walks slowly towards Luke saying, 'Let me guess something else – you're sitting there deciding it was all your fault and if you could go back you would do things different.'

'No,' says Luke. 'I was thinking I'd quite like to escape from here.'

This stops Killian short. The boy smiles a bit, now continues. 'Fair enough! But running away won't do any good, mate. Trust me, I know what I'm talking about.'

Luke can't quite get used to being called 'mate'.

Killian drops onto the seat beside him and says, 'Look, I know what you're going through. My mother died when I was only wee and I thought it was all my fault.'

'And what do you think now?' asks Luke.

'That things just happen,' says Killian. 'That it isn't your fault, that some things can't be stopped. And that you'll be alright.'

Luke opens his mouth to speak – to disagree, debate – but finds nothing to say. Rainfall is a sudden fresh sound – the Spell of Enclosing his mother set has faded. Things begin again, and Luke realises that the world is ready to continue.

'*Lord Mountfathom!*'

A cry from Mr Findlater, striding-running up the Rise.

Luke and Killian both stand and see in the manservant's grip a small fold of paper. Findlater goes straight to Luke's father and says, 'Urgent messages from the Gloaming – from Mr Dorrick in Dublin and the Halters on the Dragon Coast. You must contact them at once.' A moment, and in a small, fierce whisper Findlater tells Lord Mountfathom, 'They say the Ash-Dragons have awoken.'

KILLIAN & LUKE

Back in the bloody library again! Would be boring, except for the fact that three dark mirrors with the dimensions of doors have been wheeled in and each one holds at least one face that is floating and chatting.

'Jane, Joseph,' says Lady Mountfathom, 'tell us everything.'

'Dozens of Land Grabbers arrived today,' says Mrs Halter.

'Started to dig before dawn,' says Mr Halter. 'To smash rocks and break open the earth. 'We did all we could to stop them, but they have the assistance of the Cailleach – they are too powerful.'

Says Mrs Halter, 'Made pits and dropped in jars of Indigo Fire into the earth.'

Says Mr Halter, 'Wasn't long before we registered movement beneath us. Many of the Dragons have taken flight.'

'When was this?' asks Luke.

'Almost an hour ago,' says Jane Halter.

'Which direction?' asks Lord Mountfathom.

'Inland is all we can be sure of,' says Joseph Halter. 'To Dublin, most likely – but could be elsewhere too.'

'Fast?' asks Lady Mountfathom.

'Free of the ground and into the air and out of sight within less than a minute,' says Mrs Halter.

And the final question that needs to be asked is asked by Killian: 'How many of these Dragons?'

The two faces in the mirror shiver, and together say, 'Almost two hundred.'

Killian swears and no one says anything. Luke doesn't blame them – the boy is only voicing how they all feel.

'What of your negotiations with the Boreen Men?' Lord Mountfathom asks the Halters. 'We need as many allies as we can get.' Luke turns to his father – this is the first he has heard of any 'negotiations'.

'Stubborn as anything,' says Jane Halter.

'We've tried to work our way in with them,' says Joseph Halter. 'Given them help building a small colony within the old Faerie Rath, but they still have so little trust of anyone.'

'Especially anyone associated with Magic,' says Mrs Halter.

'I don't blame them,' says Lady Mountfathom, and looks at her son. Luke remembers their trip to the Dragon Coast – recalls too well the merciless sweep of Spell-Work that reduced the men, shrunk and twisted and transformed them . . .

'I appreciate your efforts,' Lord Mountfathom tells the Halters. 'Please do keep trying.'

The Halters nod, and within moments their faces fade from their mirror.

Soon as they go, the face in the second mirror that has been so impatiently waiting begins.

'He knows,' says Flann Dorrick. 'He knows everything. Knows that Mountfathom has been compromised and therefore its Spells weakened. He knows that there were intruders and that one of your staff was killed.'

'Who told him?' asks Luke.

'We do not yet know,' says Lord Mountfathom. 'The fact is this – Major Fortflay knows, and he will want to take action. Is that correct, Flann?'

'Yes,' says Dorrick. 'He has already made a speech to the Castle, saying that this intrusion is yet another ruthless act by the Land Grabbers. Says we must act quickly and decisively if we are to put a stop to them and their rebellion.'

'We know what is next,' says Lady Mountfathom. 'He intends now to request more Magical powers from Westminster? From the Politomancer?'

'Not without a vote,' says Lord Mountfathom. 'And not without the consent of the religious Orders on the Aran Islands and Skellig.'

Flann Dorrick tells them, 'A vote which is to be held this very evening. And to which no member of the Driochta is to be invited or admitted.'

Luke and Lord and Lady Mountfathom look at one another.

'Let us hope our discussions with the monks will stand us in good stead,' says Lord Mountfathom.

'They did seem sincere when they promised to stand up to any more Magical interference from across the water,' says Lady Mountfathom.

'Never trust anyone from the church,' says Killian. Everyone looks at him. 'That's what my da used to say – sure they're only out for themselves!'

Luke asks a question. 'Has anyone heard from Lady Vane-Tempest?'

'I received a message from Helena last night,' says Dorrick. 'She said she had traced the Cailleach who has been aiding the Land Grabbers – to the tenements in Dublin. Said she was going to make a discreet trip there to investigate. But since then, I have had no word of her. And I cannot reach her through the Gloaming.'

'*Discreet*,' repeats Lady Mountfathom, with a small shake of the head.

'I know,' says Dorrick. 'That woman couldn't be discreet if she tried!'

'Flann,' says Lord Mountfathom, 'do we know what type of powers are being proposed by Fortflay?'

'Rumours only,' says Dorrick. 'One in particular that I believe is a great worry – that the Politomancer from Whitehall intends to come here personally to oversee his Magic. That he is determined to keep the peace in Ireland using any Spell he deems necessary.'

More silence; much more thought.

Luke watches his parents and wonders what decision they will make. And isn't surprised when his mother says, 'We shall travel to Dublin. Flann, please continue to investigate. Find out what you can and we shall meet you at the Castle gates in time for this vote.'

Wordlessly and with only a nod, the face of Flann Dorrick vanishes from the mirror.

'Go to Dublin?' says Luke. 'Is that wise?'

'Not wise at all,' says his mother, and already she has turned and is moving towards the door of the library. 'But it is what we must do.'

'I wish to go too,' says Luke.

Lady Mountfathom looks at him.

'I am sorry, son,' she says. 'This is simply too dangerous for –'

'I am a member of the Driochta,' says Luke. 'I can't just stay here in this House any more – it is no more safe here than anywhere else, that is what we've learned. Please – I can be of help.'

'Well,' says Killian, feeling he too should offer his services, 'if he's gonna go then so should I. I don't know much about Magic or Spells, but I can turn my hand to most things.'

Lord and Lady Mountfathom look at one another; their resolve softens, relents. And Luke's mother says, 'Come along then! Quickly now! And let us hope that we make it to Dublin before the Ash-Dragons do.'

*Know this: the Ruling State and the
state of Magic never meet neatly.
No politician on this good earth has
(good) enough sense to use a Spell.
A truism: those who seek power are
those most ill suited to having it.*

Magical Misdeeds
Flann Dorrick

LUKE

'And where will you go, Father?' asks Luke.

They stop at the bottom of the staircase leading to the second floor. Lord Mountfathom lays a hand on Killian's shoulder and says, 'My companion and I shall find Lady Vane-Tempest. Now, Killian, last night when you related to me your life story, you told me that you were brought up in the tenements of Dublin, did you not?'

'I did and all,' says Killian.

Luke knows he could say, *That's not what you told me!* But doesn't see what purpose it would serve at this moment, so keeps quiet.

'Good,' says Lord Mountfathom. 'Then you shall be my guide.'

Killian looks more than a little stricken.

'Or was it not true?' Luke asks him. 'Were you not raised in the tenements?'

'I was!' shouts Killian. But Luke knows that aggression is no guarantee of sincerity. And Luke watches more but he cannot read this boy. Is he telling the truth now or not? A worse thought: has Killian told these lies so many times he's come to believe them himself?

'Decided then,' says Lord Mountfathom.

'We shall need to be appropriately attired,' says Lady Mountfathom, casting an eye over both boys.

'Quite true,' says Lord Mountfathom. 'First things first – clothes.'

'No,' says Killian, 'this is the first thing you should be thinking about: you haven't a hope of getting into Dublin today.' The Mountfathoms look at one another, and smile. 'Dunno what you're grinning about! You said this vote thing is at six o'clock this evening? You'll never make it in time. Not a chance in hell!'

KILLIAN

Fools, he thinks. *Bunch of fools! No idea what they're getting themselves into, especially going into the tenements!*

Up another flight of stairs and along a corridor with pale blue walls and tapestries showing ships riding high on the deep blue waves. And as they pass, Killian swears he sees the surface of the tapestries roll and ripple . . . Suddenly they stop before the only dark thing in sight: a wardrobe made of wood of blackest black.

'Stand aside,' says Lady Mountfathom. From her belt she takes the sharp pencil-length stick of metal that Killian has heard them call a 'Needle' and slips it into the small keyhole on the wardrobe . . . waits a moment . . . withdraws it. And the wardrobe doors ease open.

Lord and Lady Mountfathom and Luke step inside.

Killian watches the nearest tapestry: sees a whale breach the surface of the water and vanish with hardly a thread of a ripple. And he has to overcome all kinds of warning in his head – *Too weird, all this! Should just leave now. Take your chance and turn around and run while you can! NOW, you fool!*

This voice sounds very like his da. But somehow he ignores it – adventure trumps apprehension, does it not?

He steps inside.

Is suddenly inside a wardrobe, yes . . . but a wardrobe the size of a music hall! Rail after rail of coats, jackets, tailcoats, skirts, suits, dresses; steamer trunks spilling stilettos and boots and bags and scarves; vases stuffed with canes, umbrellas, parasols, all fashioned from ivory, mahogany, horn, paper . . . Killian walks on and sees crates of belts and braces, and hangers laden with hundreds of ties, and carved boxes containing cufflinks and bracelets and earrings . . .

He wonders, were these the things the man with the faded hair was thinking of robbing? Cos he would've found plenty of value to sell on in here!

'Over here, young man!'

Killian hears the voice of Lady Mountfathom, sees her large, rough hand waving to him. He passes seamstress dummies wearing strings of pearls and tangles of chain and scalps scattered with hatpins . . . lets his head fall back to stare – higher and higher climb shelves, hardly reachable, crammed with hundreds of hats on hats on hats: trilby and top and bowler amidst heaps and tangles of false hair . . . stumbles into Luke and almost swears. Swallows it back and says, 'Some place this!'

Lady Mountfathom is nearby, on her knees elbow-deep in a casket of Venetian masks. Lets out a sigh and says, 'My goodness, we really must stop collecting.'

'I agree,' says Lord Mountfathom, close by, searching through a box of battered brogues. 'I know our errands are oftentimes exotic but really' (holds up a pair of boots, grey-green and with a sickly glisten to them) 'when will circumstances ever call for thigh-high snakeskin boots?'

'You never know,' says his wife, standing up, smiling. 'No more shilly-shallying now – let's get ourselves kitted out!'

LUKE

'Mother – what if this vote does go through?'

'No sense fretting,' says his mother, hands busy assessing and dismissing one suit after another. 'Let us worry about changing ourselves into terribly impressive people!'

Luke asks, 'Why?'

'To intimidate,' says Lady Mountfathom. 'Show them we won't be quelled! Clothes can be great armour, Luke. We shall send a message when we enter that Castle – so something in scarlet, I think.'

Luke doesn't bother with protest. Feels funereal still, so would like to keep on the suit he has. But his mother –

'Here now! This'll do.'

Not scarlet but a dark crimson.

'Quickly now and try it on,' she says. 'We don't have much time. I shall find something to match – we shall look a mightily formidable pair!'

KILLIAN

Somewhere else in the vast wardrobe –

'Too bloody heavy for me this! I'll be sweltered!'

Lord Mountfathom says, 'Not the weight of the thing that matters, as such, but the look of it.'

'I'll look like an idiot, is that the idea?'

'No – you shall look as though you have the whole world on your shoulders, which is precisely what we want.'

So: Killian swamped by an army greatcoat. *Sleeves too long,* he thinks. *And how will I be able to fight if I need to? You can't throw a punch with so much stupid sleeve flopping around! And no one in the tenements even has a coat warm as this!*

He thinks about telling Lord Mountfathom, but the man looks to be enjoying himself too much.

'Oh, and this too – flat cap for you and one for me. We shall be well disguised, I believe. Very much incognito!'

Sad – this fella thinks this is all some jaunt. Some nice trip to the slums!

'Ready?' comes a call from Lady Mountfathom.

'My dear, we are very much ready!' Lord Mountfathom calls back.

No, thinks Killian, *we're not one bit ready! This fella doesn't have a clue what he's about to step into.*

LUKE & KILLIAN

'You know you look a right prat,' says Killian. 'A red suit and tie?'

'I shall take that as a compliment,' says Luke.

'You look like a rotten tomato,' says Killian.

'You just look as though you're rotting,' says Luke. 'And you smell like it too.'

'Now now, boys!' says Lady Mountfathom. 'You're beginning to sound like bickering brothers!'

LUKE

At the dark door, decisions.

'We should go first,' says Luke.

'Agreed,' says his mother, checking her watch. 'If this damnable vote is at six then we have only one hour and a half to reach the Castle.'

'I doubt the discussions will last long,' says Lord Mountfathom.

'Where will we enter?' asks Luke. 'Not somewhere close – don't think Major Fortflay or the Gards would like us just turning up on the doorstep.'

'Right again,' says his mother. 'But I know a place. Somewhere your father and I used to frequent. Should be quiet enough.'

She slots her crimson key into the lock. Holds it there. A few seconds, and the signalling sound: a high, squealing note. Key is withdrawn and Luke turns the handle shaped like a beckoning hand – somehow the Gloaming appears to him more forbidding than ever.

'You going to keep those seashell earrings in for occasion?' Lord Mountfathom asks his wife.

'I could not leave them behind,' says Lady Mountfathom. 'They are my own special talismans.'

'Good luck, my dear,' says Luke's father, and places a kiss on his wife's cheek. 'Be careful. I fear things will be much changed in Dublin.'

'Likewise to you,' she says, touching a hand to her husband's cheek. 'Safe journey and safe home.'

And Luke and his mother take two small steps into the Gloaming and vanish.

KILLIAN

'Where the – ?' (Can't help it – has to swear.)

'Ordinarily I would reprimand you for such language,' says Lord Mountfathom. 'However, seeing as this is your first time travelling through the Gloaming, I shall let it pass.'

'Where did they go?' asks Killian. 'Why was it so dark in there? How did they – ?'

'I shall explain a little on the way,' says Lord Mountfathom, adding his own emerald key to the lock. Moments before another loud note – only this one to Killian sounds sad, mournful – and the key is withdrawn and the door opens to the same brand of blackness.

'After you,' says Mountfathom.

Killian waits. Not out of fear – not a bit! – but because he has to script the situation for himself: *And so our courageous adventurer stands now on the brink of the unknown . . . What shall he do? Shall he retreat or shall he advance? And if he steps inside shall he survive?*

What he does is take a breath, and with the faintest faint smile –

He steps so bravely onwards into the dark!

LUKE

So many times now, but still hollowness in the stomach and head an unsteady weight – Luke concentrates on the only light, the crimson glow in his mother's hand. And always the sense of some other presence, same thing he felt at ten years old – something watching, awaiting . . .

His mother says faintly: Almost there.

Feels her hand take his.

And they arrive at their decided door and crimson light slots into dark – key unlocking a doorway far from Mountfathom as Luke and his mother step through.

His senses are too alert –

Smell: stench of stale alcohol.

Sound: scrape of his own footsoles and thump of his own blood.

Sight? So little to see. A darkness dispelled only in smudges – candles arranged on small circular tables casting globes of grubby light. Partitions of sepia-coloured glass, stools with cracked leather tops and brass studs.

A pub, Luke decides, that looks as though it hasn't seen a patron for an age.

He swallows and his first question is hoarse: 'Father and you used to come here?'

'We did indeed,' says Lady Mountfathom.

'Has it gone downhill a bit since your day?'

'Not at all – has the very same rustic charm as always!'

Summoned by the sound of voices, a small bald man appears behind the bar. He takes them in through a sharp squint, but it's not long before he shouts, 'Edith! How are you? God almighty, I haven't seen you in years! How're you? Is this the son? Grand-looking lad altogether! Now, what can I get for you? Drinks on the house!'

'No time for a tipple,' says Lady Mountfathom, trying a smile. 'More's the pity!' Luke sees her slip two silver coins onto the bar. She asks, 'How are things in Dublin these days, Ronnie? Any visits from the Gards?'

'Nah, very quiet,' says the barman. Some of his enthusiasm leaves him; folds his arms and leans against the bar. 'Quieter today than ever – it's that dark outside! Whole of Dublin shut down.'

Luke had taken it for dirt and grime – solitary window showing only a square of unforgiving black.

'Is that so?' says Luke's mother. She leans likewise against the bar, gives Luke a little nod so he goes to investigate. Looks to him like a storm cloud has descended on the street outside, some darkness swirling against the pane to stain it.

'How long has it been there?' asks Lady Mountfathom.

'Couple of hours,' says Ronnie. 'Some Spell or something?'

'Nothing the Driochta have set.'

'Are you heading to the Castle?' The barman starts to pull a pint. 'Not exactly the day for it! Sure why not stay till this all blows away or blows over?' Sips a bit of the pint himself with a smack of the lips. 'I was gonna do a roast. Boil a few spuds and carrots. How about it?'

'Another time,' says Lady Mountfathom. 'May we borrow one of your candles, Ronnie?'

'Surely,' says the barman with a small laugh. 'Doubt it'll get you far in that mess outside though!'

'We shall see.' Luke's mother lifts a candle from the nearest table and stands it upright on the palm of her hand. Luke is about to suggest another candle, maybe one with a longer-looking lifespan. But his mother twitches her Needle above the flame and teases it into tallness. 'Should be better than nothing,' she says. 'And we shall need a Spell of Enclosing for the journey too, I think?'

Luke nods, and starts to weave the Spell around them as his mother opens the door. The darkness stays outside, doesn't try to cross the threshold.

'*The Shade*,' says Lady Mountfathom. She calls back, 'All the best now, Ronnie! Look after yourself.'

And Luke and his mother leave the bar behind: step through another doorway, venture into another type of dark.

KILLIAN

Killian tries to describe the Gloaming to himself – imagines later telling somebody who will listen rapt. *It was worse than any dark night, I tell you! And I didn't know where I might end up. Just this posh fella and a key glowing green, that was all I had to go on . . . all I could see was –*

Some sense of something close makes Killian turn. Makes him stop and his heart shudder: he knows well the feeling of being followed and feels it now, as though he is being stalked.

You are doing very well, he hears Lord Mountfathom say. Keep going – concentrate only on the destination. I need you to lead me.

What? asks Killian, eyes still searching the dark. Why?

We need a safe place to enter the tenements, says Mountfathom. Somewhere deserted maybe. Any ideas?

Killian has only one: Aye, I know a place.

And suddenly – another emerald light, unfurling like a path from their feet.

Good, says Lord Mountfathom. Keep fixed now on where you want to go. That's all you need to do. And let us follow.

Soon, an outline of a small doorway appears –

At their approach it brightens and Lord Mountfathom slips the emerald key into the lock and the door eases open.

After you, says Lord Mountfathom.

But Killian is still concerned about the dark they've passed through – so featureless but feels teeming with so much. He cannot describe this to himself, only feel it – as though his whole life is hovering around him, as if he could pluck some memory from his mind and he'd be able to run out into the dark and meet it –

We must go, says Lord Mountfathom. You could waste a lifetime wandering in the Gloaming – could grow old on your own years.

Slowly, Killian steps through.

And where do they stand? In a small space holding hardly more light than the Gloaming. Some surroundings seep into view: tiny room with a battered table and a single toppled chair; empty dresser and a grey rectangle of window, the pitiful scratch of rats behind skirting and crackle of rain against the tin roof.

'Why this place?' asks Mountfathom.

So many lies race fast through Killian's head, but for some reason he decides on the truth. 'This is where I used to live. This is where my mother died.'

He takes a few steps in his tough new boots and warm coat and fancy flat cap, and thinks how far he's travelled, only to return to this same place. He stands on something and stops – crunch of glass, wooden frame splintered. Sees a soiled sepia photograph.

'Not easy to return to the place you came from,' says Lord Mountfathom.

'I hated it here.' Killian takes a breath. 'I think I have an idea about this creature you're looking for – the one you mentioned when we were walking through the Gloaming.'

'Oh yes?' says Lord Mountfathom. 'The Cailleach?'

'Yeah,' says Killian. 'When I lived here, there was an old woman who lived in the house at the end of the next street. We were all scared of her. People said she snatched children if they hung about too late on the street. Some people said as well that she could do Magic.'

'That sounds like a good place to start,' says Mountfathom. 'Through that door.'

And when Lord Mountfathom isn't looking, Killian ducks down and plucks the photograph from the floor and folds it into his coat pocket.

LUKE

Wandering the dark of Dublin – a cloud of coarse cinder and clinging ash. Suddenly Luke sees a face and stops.

'Keep going now,' his mother tells him. 'We cannot afford to pause.'

'What is this Spell?' Luke asks, moving on slow.

'The Shade,' says Lady Mountfathom. 'Soldiers. I have seen this Spell only once before – during the Lock Out it was used to drive the Boreen Men out of the city, and to keep everyone else indoors and afraid to step out. It is the work of the Politomancer. We need not be too wary of them. They are here to cause fear, nothing more.'

Luke discerns not just faces now but long limbs – bodies of roiling dark. Hundreds, he thinks. Or some countless amount! Whole legions Summoned to bring a halt to the City, to keep things darkly placid and peaceful. Luke knows this as a powerful type of Magic . . .

'You are doing well,' says Lady Mountfathom. The flame on her palm is a shrunken thing, clinging to the smallest pool of wax but still burning. 'Not much further now.'

And Luke is Working tirelessly – weaving the Spell of Enclosing, keeping the clog of ash and cinder a foot and a half at bay in all directions.

Their progress is slow, near silent.

Lady Mountfathom keeps checking her watch.

As they pass, Luke discerns subtle shades in the darkness; sees one of the Shade turn to face them, watch them as they go by.

Now a looming bridge – a skinny thing, extending over the Liffey like a pale arm reaching through the dark. They cross quickly, and on the other side Lady Mountfathom turns left, then right. They pass into a tangle of streets until they meet a high wall just visible on their left. And here the Working of the Politomancer is most potent – soldiers of the Shade standing in neat rows and so close together.

'You think Mr Dorrick was right?' Luke ventures to ask. 'The Politomancer is in Dublin?'

'Perhaps. And I have heard such rumours about him: that the Politomancer has experimented more deeply with Magic than any other. Has become less than human – more Spell than flesh now, and very powerful indeed.'

'More powerful than the Driochta?' asks Luke.

His mother says nothing more.

KILLIAN

'Jaysus – forgot the stink!'

Lord Mountfathom stays silent as they step out – matches the mood of the place – into a narrow, rain-washed street, signs of life scarce. Solitary cat on the pavement, its bones sticking out sharp; sheets flapping sodden on a line strung overhead;

narrow chimneys squeezing out threads of blue turf-smoke. A small window is elbowed open for only a moment, some dark water hurled out and the window slammed shut again.

A sign says –

FAITHFULL STREET

'Shall I show you where she lived?' asks Killian.

And Mountfathom still says nothing – a look on his face like he's suppressing shock that makes Killian want to say, *Well, what did you expect? Something more romantic maybe? Children playing jump-rope or marbles or kicking a ball about instead of being inside in their beds, slowly starving?*

'Yes,' says Lord Mountfathom. 'Yes, Killian, do lead on.'

So they start on their slow way.

Killian no longer knows how he existed here, how he didn't notice things so obvious to him now – houses all too tight-knit, as though daylight is a thing denied; gutters clogged and letting rainwater (and whatever other waters) pool and stew and steam. And cannot get reaccustomed to the reek . . . He sees some shifting behind dark curtains, dark faces watching, suspicious.

Keep walking, he tells himself. *Walk quicker.*

A sound stops them – high and clear and thin.

On a broken doorstep sits a small child, a young girl with eyes raw. One of her tiny hands clings to the hem of her stained dress. And that sound she makes, that low wail, draws Lord Mountfathom to her.

'Are you alright?' he asks. Stoops to say, 'Where is your mother or father?'

Girl doesn't react – doesn't appear to notice them.

'Do you have food, my dear?' asks Mountfathom. 'Something to eat?'

Killian sees more movement behind windows and he says, 'You can't help her. We can't hang about. We need to do what you came here for and then get out.'

Lord Mountfathom looks at him.

'She isn't the only one,' says Killian. 'There's too many more like her. You can't help them all.'

'Yes,' says Mountfathom. He straightens up. 'Yes, you are quite right. We must continue. We don't have much time.'

'No,' says Killian, eyes still on windows, on doors. 'No, we bloody well don't.'

LUKE

'You made it! Thank goodness!'

Flann Dorrick is heard before he is seen – hails them from beside a shut sweetshop, dressed in a long, dark coat with a fur collar, his own Spell of Enclosing keeping him clear of the Shade. Lady Mountfathom doesn't slow, so Dorrick has to fall into step beside, telling her, 'It is nearly six and I thought you would not be here in time!'

'How many delegates are present for the vote?' asks Luke's mother.

'Hardly any,' says Dorrick. 'All left for the day!'

'The monks?' asks Lady Mountfathom.

'Not yet arrived.'

'So our friend Major Fortflay will try to force a majority to devolve more Magic.'

'What is your plan, Mother?' asks Luke.

'To stop him,' she says. And says no more.

Now a pair of wrought-iron gates replaces the wall; they've been left open.

A sign on the wall says simply –

ENTER IF YOU CAN ENTER

'Come along now,' says Lady Mountfathom.

'We can just walk in?' asks Luke.

'Oh yes – the Driochta set the Spells of Security here, so I think I should be well capable of undoing them.'

Without pause Luke's mother passes through, Working her hand fast. And in her wake Luke feels the Spells protesting, straining to fight them back and deny entry . . . but his mother delicately dismantles the defences so she and her son and Flann Dorrick can pass through and out into a wide courtyard of clean flagstone and cleaner air.

Above them: a ceiling of Security Spells holds back the Spell that has been settled on the rest of the City. So dark though – lamps have been lit and settled on flagstones every few feet. Luke and his mother and Dorrick keep walking towards a tall brute of a building with a dull grey dome. Windows narrow and dark, few flags hanging limp. And the sight of the place unsettles Luke: such quiet, their footsteps as sharp against stone as eggs being cracked on the rim of a bowl.

'Any talking to do,' his mother whispers, 'let me do it.'

A pair of dark doors and a short flight of steps – Luke, his mother and Dorrick manage to mount only two before one of the doors opens and disgorges a disgruntled Gard. He is dressed in grey. Now Luke knows why his mother insisted on such adventurous colours for them both (shame about Dorrick, dressed in dark clothes and looking sheepish). The Gard has a large polished rifle in his hands.

'I am afraid you can't enter,' says the Gard in grey.

'Don't be ridiculous!' says Lady Mountfathom. 'Do you know who I am?'

'I know exactly who you are,' says the Gard. Not an Irish accent, thinks Luke – sounds English. He says dully, 'You're from that Big House near Belfast and that is your son and that other fella used to work here and as I said you are not allowed in here.'

'What do you mean "used to"?' says Dorrick.

'We don't like sneaks or turncoats here,' says the Gard. 'You've been given the boot – there's some nice news for you.'

'Well,' says Luke's mother, 'you are just a font of information, aren't you?'

'Ridiculous!' says Dorrick. 'How dare you!'

'Can I ask who gave these orders?' says Lady Mountfathom. 'Who sacked a well-respected member of this Castle's administration? And who has decided to deny entry to an Order that is centuries old, and as such has a democratic right to enter this building?'

'You can ask but you won't get an answer,' says the Gard.

'Well, really – now you are just being rude,' says Luke's mother. 'Naughty young man.' The Gard tries to stand taller, opens his mouth to say more but Luke's mother says, 'You also are no doubt aware that I could Work any number of Spells that would allow me to enter quite easily? If I so wish, I could get past you. With only a quick whirl of my hand!'

'You could try,' says the Gard, and he lifts his rifle a little. 'But I think a bullet might travel faster than your hand. Look – I'm going to assume you don't want to cause any trouble or hassle here.'

'You are quite wrong in both assumptions,' says Lady Mountfathom.

'Fair enough, then I'll make things clear: piss off.'

And the Gard turns and opens the door to step back inside and Luke knows they have only a moment, a blink before the door is shut –

A quick look between mother and son –

One moment they stand as themselves, and a shiver and shimmer of a moment later: panther and starling, one lifting lightly into the sky and slipping through the gap in the open door and the other leaping –

The Gard turns but only in time to be cuffed across the cheek by a graceful and powerful paw. He falls to the floor unconscious. Panther and starling land alongside one another, restored to the forms of Luke and Lady Mountfathom.

'Hate the need for violence,' says Luke's mother. She calls to Dorrick, still standing on the second-from-bottom step: 'Come along now, Flann – don't dawdle! We have got the fate of our country to decide.'

245

KILLIAN

'This is us,' he says.

Smallest house on the street – only a single storey, as though someone has swiped the top half. Lord Mountfathom takes the measure of the place before he says, 'We shall have to be both polite and cunning, crafty and courteous.'

'I can be whatever I need to be,' says Killian.

'Yes,' says Mountfathom. 'I believe you can.'

They start up the short path.

The door of the smallest house is blistered and weather-beaten and has a palm-sized panel of dark glass but no keyhole nor handle nor knocker. So Lord Mountfathom raises his left hand and gives the door three hard slaps. Some stirring inside? Something surely beyond the door starting to rouse – now certainly footsteps of someone starting towards them, a sound of locks being snapped and chains being raked across and the door opens. Killian has to look down.

'Here's visitors! Oh, indeed! How charming!'

Some small figure stands on the threshold. So small that Killian wonders if it (she?) is a child – dressed in an old grey shirt and skirt, a stained lace shawl low around her shoulders and gloves with the fingers snipped off raw. And bald and so wrinkled! The way she takes them both in is clear-eyed and keen . . . but does she look a little caught-out, a little nervous?

Lord Mountfathom says with good cheer, 'We meet again!'

The Cailleach speaks in a slow croak: 'Good evening to you both! I am glad you've come. Was expecting you!' She smiles a smile full of spittle and small brown teeth. Her fingertips rub

246

and rub against one another. She settles her eyes on Killian and he feels his thoughts stumble, as though someone has swept in and out of his mind and stolen something. And with her stolen knowledge the Cailleach says, 'And you brought one of the locals! Always a good idea to have a guide, or you never know what might happen in dark places such as these.'

'May we come in?' asks Lord Mountfathom.

A certain sense of pause – Killian can see the reluctance of the woman.

Lord Mountfathom says, 'I know you are surely being well paid by the Land Grabbers for your services, but I believe I could make it more than worth your while.' And from his inside pocket he produces a small drawstring bag and empties into his palm a clutch of gold coins.

Fool, thinks Killian. *Bloody fool! Showing so much gold in broad daylight in a street like this and for everyone to see!*

But the greed of the Cailleach has been captured.

'How could I refuse?' she says, smiling, standing on tiptoe to take one of the coins and inserting it between her tiny teeth for a testing chew. Lord Mountfathom says nothing. 'Come in, of course!' she tells them, and with small feet shuffling she heads off into the dark of the house. Shouts back, 'Quickly now! Don't want to hang about!'

Killian takes Lord Mountfathom's arm and says, 'She's right – we can't wait about here. But we should leave.'

'We cannot,' says Mountfathom. 'This is where Lady Vane-Tempest was last known to have gone. And I say with no attempt at modesty, I believe my Magic is much greater than anything this crone could possibly conjure.'

'Look, mate, it's not the old woman I'm worried about. People don't take kindly to strangers turning up here and I can tell you now, these dirty coats and flat caps aren't fooling anybody. Specially when you're flashing gold about.'

The Cailleach shouts from inside, 'Are you coming in or not? Don't stand there letting all the warmth out!'

'Please trust me,' says Lord Mountfathom. 'I need you to be my ally here, Killian.'

Slowly, and so reluctantly, Killian removes his hand.

Lord Mountfathom says nothing as together they step inside.

LUKE

'Left now,' Lady Mountfathom says, passing through yet another barrier of Spell-Work – a faint veil of vapour – and easily Dismissing it.

'Spells are very weak,' says Luke.

'Unravelling,' says Dorrick.

'Failing as the Castle further distances itself from the Driochta,' says Lady Mountfathom. 'Take a right now.'

Along another bland corridor that at intervals splits and sends identical copies off in different directions, as though contrived to confuse.

Dorrick and Lady Mountfathom say together, 'Left.'

Somewhere, a bell is being rung and rung –

All three break into a sprint –

'You wait outside the chamber,' Luke's mother tells Dorrick. 'Keep watch – we may need a quick getaway. Listen for a signal.'

'Yes indeed,' says Dorrick.

'Wait!' calls Lady Mountfathom, arriving at a pair of double doors about to be shut. 'Two more for the discussion, thank you kindly!'

And before the grey-uniformed Gards on duty can protest (or be anything other than surprised), Luke and his mother are in.

A round room beneath the cold, grey dome – tiered benches of dark wood; flags the only presence of colour, hung from the walls wherever possible. Luke is instantly colder – feels as though he has arrived somewhere buried deep beneath the surface of the city. And all his knowledge of Magic tells him instantly that he has stepped into some Spell – is in the midst of the Workings of the Politomancer.

'Follow,' says Lady Mountfathom, taking his sleeve.

She leads Luke up the steps and along a bench to sit.

Luke sees a raised platform with a table and one tall chair and two tall windows behind, both piled with sandbags. More Gards than delegates are present – only a dozen or so representatives from the counties, and all trembling and pale-faced and strained, their breath rising ragged.

'Even fewer than I thought,' says Lady Mountfathom, with a small shake of the head, a small shiver in her voice.

'Some Spell has been set in here,' says Luke, and hears in his own voice the same quiver. 'Something is infecting the atmosphere.'

'Well spotted,' his mother tells him. She swallows and says, 'No Spell can sow fear itself, but you can create the conditions for it. This is a Spell of Presentiment – a threat Worked into the air. It is already in our lungs; soon will be in our head and hearts too.'

A door opens behind the platform.

A long line of monks in dark robes file onto the stage.

Lady Mountfathom swears.

And Major Fortflay follows them – Luke notices the pistol at his belt and a single sheet of paper in his hand. Appears as uncomfortable as any with the Spell that has been set in the chamber, doesn't wish to linger. Doesn't sit but instead scans the room – he sees Luke and Lady Mountfathom, and his mouth at first makes a sour shape, but soon becomes more akin to a smirk.

A moment more, and Major Fortflay is joined on the platform by another figure.

Luke hears his mother breathe: 'The Politomancer.'

A man, but like no man Luke has ever seen – like the Spell he has set on Dublin, the Politomancer is composed of pale smoke and vapour. Like a Messenger, but more substantial. Like a Trace? More malign – eyes a cold blue-white, and as he drifts silently across the platform into position beside the Major, the Politomancer fixes his gaze on Luke and Lady Mountfathom. And Luke thinks to himself, *He knew we would come. We have been lured here. This is a trap.*

KILLIAN

When the room does show itself there isn't much to see – large table, battered but spotless; a chimneybreast harbouring no fire but with hundreds of books packed without benefit of shelves into two spaces on either side.

'Never thought I'd see the hour,' says the Cailleach, somewhere thereabouts in the dark, 'that the Lord of the Mountfathom, the head of the Driochta, would come to this lowly bit of the city!'

'Believe me,' answers Mountfathom, 'I would not be making such a trip if it were not necessary.'

'Oh, then how lucky I am!' says the woman, and shuffles into sight. 'Should praise dull stars and grey slop of sun in the sky!'

'Give over!' says Killian.

The Cailleach smiles, shows those small teeth.

'I do realise,' says Lord Mountfathom, 'that the relationship between the Driochta and those who practise other brands of Magic has not been the most harmonious.'

Laughter from the woman – a damp snort followed by, 'True enough! Harmony doesn't tend to follow capture and torture, does it, my good sir?'

'However,' says Mountfathom quickly, 'I wish to remedy this. I think we may now need to rely more on one another. That is part of my reason for coming to you today.'

'And the other?' asked the woman.

Many moments begrudgingly go by. Killian wonders when Mountfathom might mention the missing woman – Lady Vane-Tempest – but instead Lord Mountfathom says, 'We would like you to Uncover someone.'

The Cailleach finds a stool beneath the large table, drags it out with a squeal and scales it. When she is settled, hands over her potbelly, her smile still wide, she says, 'Why not yourself? No mirrors left for Predicting on? No ink left to spill and shape?'

'That is not the reason,' says Mountfathom.

'Then why?' demands the woman.

'I cannot,' says Lord Mountfathom. 'The House is too open now – the Spells around the demesne are failing. We are too vulnerable, and such a Spell may as much draw others to us as much as we would seek to Uncover them.'

Killian feels he should speak, thinks Mountfathom is stupidly saying too much truth to this woman. But when he steps forward and opens his mouth, the Cailleach tells him, 'Oh, calm yourself, boy! I have no wish to steal one of the Big Houses and set myself up with the family silver and finery! I place no value in fine furnishings.'

'I can see that,' says Killian.

'So those in the Castle no longer trust their most faithful servants?' says the Cailleach, turning back to Lord Mountfathom. 'How the upstanding are beginning to crumble. That foolish Major must be running rightly scared.'

She laughs.

But Lord Mountfathom stands taller and says, 'You may gloat at what is happening, but I assure you now it is no cause for mirth. If the Major has his way, these tenements would be the first things to go. He has no conscience for the poor or ill-fated.'

'And you do?' says the Cailleach. Her eyes shiver a little, resettling on Killian. 'Oh, but the answer is here with us – taking in strays now in order to ease your own guilt?'

Killian swears at the woman. This amuses her muchly.

'Oh, yes! A true child of the tenements he is, with a mouth like that!'

Killian silenced. It bothers him, being seen so clearly by this creature. He struggles to say, 'She can't help us. Let's go. This was a stupid idea.'

'Oh, I can help,' whispers the Cailleach. 'I think perhaps I am your only help now.'

Killian doesn't speak.

Suddenly her slack old face finds a tautness and she says, 'I will need your blood, Mountfathom. A drop is all. As you would use ink, so I will need blood for this Uncovering.'

And Lord Mountfathom says without a pause, 'Agreed. Let us begin.'

LUKE

The Major begins to speak.

'We have never known such dark times! Never experienced such unrest and dissent! Never known such evil as now. Houses are being burned, families massacred, lives wiped out!' Major Fortflay stops, turns over the page and continues in a stilted, stumbling fashion. 'This country is slowly being dismantled and its Union and bonds of friendship fractured. This is something, regretfully, that it is not within my power to repair. However, I will not see out the remainder of my long service on this island as a mere overseer of civil war and ruin.'

'He didn't write this,' Lady Mountfathom whispers.

'How do you know?' says Luke.

'I have, unfortunately, known the Major for years. He is not an unintelligent man, but this polite turn of phrase is not his. The sentiment belongs to him, no doubt about it. Our Major Fortflay has become a mouthpiece – a ventriloquist's dummy sitting on the knee of the state, with the hand of Westminster up his backside.'

'The time has come for action,' says the Major. 'I believe we can only bring this country under control by force! I have the consent and agreement of the oldest of Orders in this country.' He looks to the line of monks on stage – hands tucked into their sleeves, heads lowered. They say nothing. 'And we have agreed on a way forward. We have tried to reason and debate with these Land Grabbers, but the time has come for more aggressive powers. For a more merciless form of Magic.'

Major Fortflay looks now to the Politomancer – the pale and silent figure that Luke realises is the one now in control of matters within the Castle. Realises something else too –

'There isn't going to be any vote.'

'No,' says his mother. 'There never was.'

The Politomancer raises one near-transparent hand and Luke feels a sudden stab at his heart – an arrow of pure cold. And on the platform the monks shudder and one by one sink to their knees. Around the room all delegates shiver and slump in their seats at the intensity of the Spell.

'Mother,' is all Luke manages to say. He feels her taking his hand.

'Be ready,' she says. Squeezes his hand tighter. 'Be ready to fight.'

The door behind the platform opens: a fresh Spell enters the chamber –

Luke hears his mother swear once more –

In a slow, silent prowl onto the platform, creatures composed of the same smoke and vapour as the Politomancer – not wolves nor dogs nor hounds, but something close. Claws sharp and eyes blue-white, the pack stops silent on the brink of the platform.

'The Pall,' says Major Fortflay, and in his voice Luke detects some thread of fear. 'They shall go into the countryside and track down each and every person who opposes the rule of the Crown, and they shall destroy them. They do not tire or need sleep, and shall be our best weapons against any resistance. From this moment on, the Politomancer will oversee all brands of Magic in Ireland. Anyone who is caught performing any Spell or Enchantment will be arrested, and will be executed. Consequently, the Order known as the Driochta is therefore disbanded, and its members now considered enemies of the Crown.'

Once more Lady Mountfathom tells Luke, 'Be ready.'

And all eyes – delegates, Gards, Major, the Politomancer and creatures of the Pall – settle on Luke and his mother.

Fortflay cannot suppress a smirk as he says, 'Gards, arrest them.'

KILLIAN

The Cailleach raises a long silver needle and tells Lord Mountfathom, 'Your wrist.'

'Why there?' asks Lord Mountfathom, with more curiosity than concern.

'It is where the blood is bluest,' says the Cailleach.

Mountfathom unbuttons and peels back his sleeve and the Cailleach pierces the needle deep. Killian wants to shout out or snatch Mountfathom's wrist away but forces himself to wait. When the needle is coated in blood, the Cailleach takes from beneath the table a small rectangle of mirror. She holds the needle above.

'Not unlike your Mirror-Predicting,' says the old woman.

Mountfathom doesn't reply – he and Killian watch the dark beads of blood tremble on the tip of the needle . . . and still they do not fall.

'Are you prepared for what you might see?' asks the Cailleach.

Lord Mountfathom waits. Nods.

And finally blood leaves the needle to fall and blot the mirror.

Instantly: surface is swept with dark, with an unknown not unlike the Gloaming. Killian watches the last scrap of reflection vanish. And Lord Mountfathom tells him, 'Killian: I want you to describe the man who brought you to Mountfathom.'

Killian looks at him. Confused. Opens his mouth to speak, but –

'Please,' says Mountfathom. 'Do as I wish.'

Killian says, 'He had all this white hair. He had dark eyes. He –'

Stops. Already the Gloaming is trying to Uncover someone – already a small storm at its heart, a pale swirling like so many hands delving, seeking . . . Uncovering . . .

'Keep describing!' croaks the Cailleach.

'Please keep going,' says Lord Mountfathom.

Killian wets his lips and says, 'He was skinny.'

'What did he say to you?' says the witch. 'No one can be Uncovered merely through sight – what did this man say to you, what words?'

Killian says, 'He told me he was someone who could've been someone. Said he had the chance once but it was taken away from him. He –'

Falters at the sight – the Gloaming has something and is trying to show it but the thing is struggling. Like something hooked in the deep that doesn't want to be reeled in . . .

'Don't stop!' cries the Cailleach. 'We're going to lose him!'

'Killian, you have imagination,' Mountfathom tells him. 'Use it – what do you think he meant by his words?'

Killian shouts, 'I don't bloody know! I think he must be linked to someone at the House.'

And then the mirror clears – for only a moment they see the man called Mr Gassin.

'Where is this man now?' asks Mountfathom.

The picture widens: they see the man with faded hair in a field, and beside and around him are a whole battalion of soldiers.

'Gards,' says Lord Mountfathom.

But Killian has his own question to ask.

'Who does he know at Mountfathom? Who gave him that sheet that invited him into the grounds?'

Another figure surfaces in the mirror: hand in hand, the man with faded hair stands beside a tall adolescent, someone skinny and dark-haired and looking a lot like that manservant Findlater –

'No more!' says Lord Mountfathom, and Works a quick hand in the air and the mirror cracks as though struck by a hammer. 'We have seen enough.'

LUKE

'Now, Luke!'

Lady Mountfathom stands and whips her Needle from her belt and whirls it in the air –

A roar as a rush of amber fire surrounds the platform –

Delegates fall to the ground to cower, monks still on their knees and praying ardent prayers –

Gards hurry towards Luke and his mother with rifles raised and aimed –

Luke weaves a complicated Spell of Inertia. The approaching Gards are swept into the air as though by an invisible tide and in an instant are drifting, helpless as slumbering infants –

'Go,' says his mother, and pushes him on towards the door.

Cry of the Major, 'Get them!'

More Gards lift their weapons –

Doors of the chamber are thrown open and into the room springs a cheetah that pounces on the Gards and swipes the rifles from their hands –

Luke sees Fortflay take the pistol from his belt and aim at them but his mother is alert to all – another whirl of her Needle and a torrent of water crashes through the tall windows behind the platform and knocks Fortflay from his feet.

But the Politomancer and the creatures of the Pall do nothing – do not move or act or try to pursue.

His mother pushes him on – 'Keep going!' – and with the cheetah beside them they leave the chamber and bolt down corridor after corridor and out into the courtyard –

Air polluted with dark –

Spells of Security are crumbling; so much cinder and ash finding its way through in sliver and fleck, like dark snowfall sifting through the air and settling on flagstones.

'My Lady,' says Dorrick, 'look!'

He is pointing his Needle towards the sky. And at first Luke does not see . . . now suddenly, shockingly, a glimpse: the blackness parts and for a heart-chilling moment he makes out the sleek body of a flying Ash-Dragon.

KILLIAN

Another smash of glass –

By the window – men from the tenements trying to force their way in –

Killian sees a rifle in the hands of one of the men so shouts, 'Get down!'

Window shattered by gunshots as Killian falls to the floor –

But Lord Mountfathom doesn't shift – in a moment he has his Needle whipped from his belt and whirls it through the air to divert bullets, sending them into wall and floor and ceiling.

And the Cailleach is screeching and crawling towards the fireplace –

'Don't let her leave!' shouts Mountfathom. 'We must find Helena!'

Killian has been waiting for this moment; takes so much relish as he grabs the old woman by the throat and shouts, 'A woman came to see you – where is she? We know she's here! Tell me or I'll bloody strangle you!'

A slash of silver –

Needle wielded by the Cailleach swipes across his cheek and he releases her. She crawls fast into the fireplace and is swallowed.

Ringing silence: some pause as the men outside reload –

Killian stands beside Lord Mountfathom and tells him, 'She didn't tell me anything.'

'No matter,' says Mountfathom. 'I told you my Magic is more powerful than any Cailleach.' And he lifts the hand not holding the Needle and commands, *'Foilsigh!'*

Killian feels the whole room – whole house – vibrate; tremble as though it is being squeezed for its secrets. Shaken and shaken until behind them the Spell Mountfathom has shouted springs a concealed panel. Killian sees inside an animal: blue-green and faintly iridescent, bound by the legs and around the wings. A peacock.

'Free her,' says Mountfathom. 'Quickly!'

Killian snatches up a shard of mirror they used for the Uncovering and kneels to carefully saw through the ropes knotted around the peacock. His fingers touch feather, feel the stickiness of blood – the bird looks on with small and near-lightless eyes. But as soon as the bonds fall free the peacock is on its feet and extending its wings, testing and flexing them.

Lord Mountfathom shouts, 'Be ready now!' And to Killian he hands the emerald key and says, 'Stay close to us. We need a door, and quickly.'

And as the men of the tenements raise their guns, Mountfathom Mogrifies into the Irish elk – a towering form! All heaving flank and dark eyes and antlers so vast they touch the walls on either side –

Moments of surprise amongst the men outside –

Enough for the elk to charge and the peacock to take flight and crash through the remains of the window with Killian following in a leap –

Onto the cobbled street where the dozen tenement men are falling back. But Killian knows any confusion or fear won't last long in them.

A door, he thinks. *A door!* So simple a thing but now he is so desperate he can't see one! Most are open or have other men at them, watching.

He shouts to the elk and the peacock, 'This way! Follow me!'

It has taken less time than he thought for the men to regroup –

Gunfire resumes –

Elk charges into the men, scattering them –

Peacock lifting into the air and plunging, diving with such violence downward to rake shoulders and arms and scalps –

Killian rounds the corner and is back onto the street where he used to live shouting, 'Here! Here!' Stops and stands on the doorstep of his old home. 'And here goes.'

He jams the emerald key into the lock and turns it. Waits and hardly a moment later arrives the long, loud note; opens the door onto the Gloaming.

Killian turns –

Peacock sails past him through the doorway but –

A gunshot strikes the elk on the hind leg and Mountfathom falls.

'For fecksake,' says Killian. He runs to the animal and meets the man Lord Mountfathom instead. 'You couldn't just use your antlers and injure them a bit?' says Killian, taking the Lord under the arms and lifting. 'Had to be charitable to the end, eh?'

Mountfathom is saying, 'Leave me. Go now.'

'Oh, shut up,' says Killian, little bother to him dragging a fully-grown man – has done it enough when his father is found half-dead on the streets of Belfast.

Mountfathom tells him, 'You must not tell my son what we saw in the mirror. You must not tell Luke. He won't understand. Promise me.'

Killian says nothing. Sees a gunshot strike the doorframe and feels another clip the ground at his heels as he and Lord Mountfathom tumble through the doorway and one of the tenement men is almost on them with rifle raised –

Killian gives him the finger and kicks shut the door.

LUKE

Lady Mountfathom takes Luke's hand. They run free of the Castle grounds with Dorrick beside them, back into the Shaded street. Luke raises his hand to weave another Spell of Enclosure but his mother says, 'No – you need to concentrate on finding a door.'

And she pushes the crimson key into his hand.

'Why are you giving this to me?' asks Luke. 'We go back together or not at all.'

'Do not be disagreeable,' his mother tells him. 'Quick now – stay with Flann.'

Dorrick puts a hand around Luke's shoulders to lead him, Lady Mountfathom a few steps behind, Needle in hand. Only moments and Luke feels beneath his feet a tremble.

'Faster!' is all his mother says.

Left and back the way they came – towards the riverside, into narrow streets, Luke's eyes so desperate for the sight of some door.

'Stop now,' says his mother, in only a whisper.

'Be ready to run,' says Dorrick. 'You must keep your reflexes sharp, otherwise these creatures will –'

He has no chance to say more.

Lady Mountfathom pulls her son aside as the ground beneath Flann Dorrick is broken open and something swallows him, pulls him screaming down into the dark.

'Run!' shouts Luke's mother.

But Luke sees now: worming free of the ground in front of them, a creature long-necked and dark-bodied. Recognises the Ash-Dragon in an instant from books and tapestries. But things unlearned from pages or portraits – the heat and sense of power, serpentine shape sliding smooth across stone, tasting the dark air with a fine, forked tongue.

He and his mother stop.

And the Ash-Dragon stops, makes a soft hiss. A twitch of its small legs; shakes itself and opens a pair of papery wings to fill the air with a fresh choking of ash. Creature turns its narrow head towards them and opens a pair of milky eyes.

'Find a door,' shouts Luke's mother as she pushes her son aside.

The Dragon springs towards them –

Lady Mountfathom swings her Needle high and from the Liffey surges a hand of water that storms through the narrow street and sweeps the Ash-Dragon out of their path.

Luke's mother takes his hand and they run and Luke cannot see but can feel so certainly the presence of more Dragons rising from the ground.

And then at last –

'A door!' Points ahead – the shut sweetshop.

'Go,' his mother tells him, tearing her hand from his.

'Not without you,' says Luke.

'I am just behind you, my love!'

Too long a pause. A Dragon falls from above and pins Lady Mountfathom to the ground as another explodes from below –

Luke Works the first Spell that comes to hand and encases the Dragon in ice. His mother drives her Needle into the skull of the Dragon on top of her –

With ear-shredding screech it leaps away, taking the Needle with it –

'Please go!' she shouts to her son, still on the ground, now sobbing. 'Please, son!'

Luke turns and screws the crimson key into the lock –

Second Dragon shakes itself free of the Spell, sheds the shell of ice and moves towards Luke –

Still on the ground Lady Mountfathom plucks a knife from her boot and hurls it and strikes the Dragon in the heart but still it slithers on –

Panicked note as the door connects with the Gloaming –

And a last look between mother and son –

Luke opens the door and steps through as his mother shouts, 'Do not look back, son! Do not look back!'

Feels the heat of the Ash-Dragon at his neck –

And his mother is suddenly seized by the ankles by another Ash-Dragon and dragged into the ground, a final scream leaving her. *'Go!'*

Luke slams shut the door and hopes and hopes for home.

PART FOUR

THE RISING

For too long Magic has been only for one type of man.
Only the privileged have been allowed it,
Spells and the like.
But by God no more!

Magic & The Decent Everyman
Anonymous

LUKE

Who is it?
Someone there?
Can you hear me?
Can you see?

Luke alone.

Killian with Lord Mountfathom and Lady Vane-Tempest beside and both injured . . .

Someone bloody help if there's anyone there!
Killian! Is that you? I'm here. I'll find you!
I'm going to find you . . .

Crimson light and emerald reach for one another. Luke runs through the Gloaming with one hand outstretched until it meets another: both grab and hold tight and throw questions at one another.

What happened to Father?

Where's your mother?

Ash-Dragons in Dublin . . . I didn't know what to do.

Which bloody way do we go now?

Back to Mountfathom.

No. Lord Mountfathom speaks. He is leaning heavily, injured, on Lady Vane-Tempest. Reaches out to Luke, seizes his hand. Says again, No. We cannot go back, not yet. It is not safe.

Luke says, Why not?

It takes a long time for his father to speak. He seems unable to look at Luke. Finally, he asks, What happened in Dublin? What was the result of the vote?

There was no vote, says Luke. The decision was made and we had no say.

Two-faced bastard, says Lady Vane-Tempest, faintly.

Luke goes on. Fortflay made an announcement too – says there are to be no more Spells Worked in Ireland other than Magic approved by the Castle. The Politomancer is in charge of Magic now – and the Driochta are enemies of the Crown.

We must find the Halters, says his father. We must get to them before Major Fortflay does.

Go to the Dragon Coast? asks Luke.

Yes, says Lord Mountfathom.

And as soon as the decision is made the way becomes clear. In Luke's hand the crimson key brightens, to show them the way ahead.

Luke speaks to his father. I left Mother behind in Dublin. And Mr Dorrick too. I don't know what happened to them but I think –

Do not speak of it now, says his father. Please, Luke – your mother can look after herself. Do not worry yourself.

So they walk.

And like a picture frame hung askew, a lopsided doorway is their destination. Luke slots the crimson key into the lock and when the door opens it is a threshold onto more dark. Reminds Luke so much of Dublin he worries that he has led them there, back into danger.

Go through, says Killian. He has the emerald key in his hand. He says, I won't let anyone get the better of us!

All four step through.

KILLIAN

Killian has heard tell of this Dragon Coast and always quite fancied paying a visit. Now? Wishes he could turn back and take his chances anywhere but here.

Air all about is streaked with trails of ash. Ground coated with a layer of warm and still smouldering cinder. Around them, shattered columns of basalt like broken chimneystacks – the places where the Ash-Dragons must have been slumbering. Sea must be somewhere close; Killian can only hear it, a faint rush of unseen waves against unseen shore.

'How will we find anyone in all this?' he asks Luke.

Luke says nothing for a moment, then whispers, 'We need a Messenger.'

Luke stoops and from dark ground teases a pale figure into existence – a woman. He whispers to it the message, 'Find the Halters. Tell them we are here and to find us at once. Tell them they are in danger and to trust no one but the other members of the Driochta.' A wave of the hand and Luke sends the Messenger on its errand – it takes to the air and is swallowed soon by the darkness.

'We cannot stay in the open,' says Lady Vane-Tempest. Her face is heavily bruised, dried blood staining one side of it. But she is stern of voice when she says, 'We must find some cover at once.'

'Aye,' says Killian. 'I don't like hanging about like this.'

'Luke, I believe the abandoned Rath is somewhere close by,' says Lord Mountfathom.

'Yes,' says Luke, recalling his previous trip here with his mother. He weaves his hand in the air and a breeze rises, parting a portion of the dark. They see a forest climbing a steep hillside. 'That way,' says Luke. 'Through the trees.'

'Onward then,' says Lady Vane-Tempest, and she supports Lord Mountfathom. Luke and Killian follow close behind.

Soft crunch of cinder like shattered bone underfoot, acrid taste of smoke on their tongues. Suddenly –

Cry of Lady Vane-Tempest: 'Luke! Seems we are about to have some company!'

LUKE

Through unravelling smoke he sees an oncoming rush, a wave of grey-black leaving the shelter of the forest and storming down the slope.

Killian asks, 'What the hell are those things?'

Luke doesn't speak until he knows for sure.

'A pack of Irish wolfhounds.'

'What're those things on their backs?' asks Killian.

But no more time for guesswork; suddenly they are surrounded and are being shouted at.

'What do you want here?'

'Come to destroy more of us?'

'Was it not enough that those bloody Dragons have now woken?'

Wolfhounds encircle; seated on each is a figure the size of a small child. Earthen bodies, human eyes, primitive weapons tight in earthen hands – blades rusted and bitten and bent but directed at Luke and Killian and Lord Mountfathom and Lady Vane-Tempest with an unequivocal aggression.

And Luke remembers who these men are – recalls the horror of the underground, the wicked Magic spilling into the chamber and transforming.

Though it is Killian who says, 'The Boreen Men? I heard tell of them from one of Da's mates! But I thought they'd all been tracked down and killed. Everyone in Belfast always said –'

'You think we give two frigs what anyone in Belfast says!' A shout from the nearest Boreen Man and he takes a swipe at Killian's arm with his blade – breaks the skin.

When Killian sees the blood he swears and shouts, 'You're gonna get a good kicking in a minute, wee man!'

The other Boreen Men threaten attack –

'You'll do nothing of the sort if you wanna stay breathing!'

'Who do you think you are coming and setting foot so close to our Rath!'

'You're lucky we haven't slit your damnable throats already!'

And Luke can see this too swiftly escalating. He shouts, 'We are not here to fight! We're here to see some of our Order – the Halters. Do you know where they are?'

Things quieten a little.

'I know you,' says the nearest Boreen Man suddenly, staring at Luke. And Luke knows the Boreen Man: recognises the eyes of Malone. 'You were there that day, when it all happened. You came into our Rath and tried to get us to discuss matters, and then the Magic came and transformed us all. You tricked us!'

Uproar from the other Boreen Men and Luke opens his mouth to reply, but it is Lord Mountfathom who speaks. In a voice low and halting and full of sincerity he says, 'We can offer no apology for what befell you that day, and I would not wish to – it would be an insult to your integrity. But I can assure you that my son would have been acting only to help. The Driochta have tried to stay impartial in this conflict, but I fear we cannot do so any longer. We have tried in the recent past to negotiate with you; if you could see fit to help us now, we would be very grateful indeed.'

Lady Vane-Tempest says, 'We have been betrayed by the Castle in Dublin, the very same as you.'

Grumbles of disagreement from the Boreen Men – plenty of doubt and disbelief, though Luke notices that Malone is saying nothing. So it is to him that Luke speaks. 'The Politomancer has come to Ireland. Before that, he Cast his Spells from across the water, but now he is in the Castle in Dublin. He has brought something with him – my mother called it the Pall.'

It is the first time Luke has made mention of this and the reaction is immediate – Lady Vane-Tempest turns to him and mouths the word *No* faintly. His father closes his eyes and shakes his head. And the Boreen Men look to one another, their wolfhounds shifting restless.

Malone tells Luke, 'You best not be lying to us. We're small but by God we aren't simple-minded!'

'It is the truth,' says Luke. 'I promise you.'

Malone looks to the other Boreen Men. A moment, and he turns back to face Luke. He says, 'Follow us so and we'll take you somewhere safe, if there is such a thing as "safe" now in this Godforsaken island.'

KILLIAN

'I don't trust these wee fellas.'

'Killian, why does that not surprise me?'

'Give me the bloody creeps.'

The two boys are walking now a narrow path through the forest, following the Boreen Men on their wolfhounds.

Luke says, 'It is not their fault they are as they are. They cannot help it any more than we can help our own nature.'

Killian says, 'Very grand statement there – well done. You sound just like your father.'

Both boys stop and face one another.

'My father took you into Mountfathom,' says Luke. 'Kept you safe.'

'I didn't ask him to,' replies Killian, and means it. 'Look, all I'm saying is, your father went casually as anything into the tenements, and sent you and your ma to the Castle, and he didn't think about what might happen.' He waits for these words to hit . . . but Luke says nothing, only stares at the ground and doesn't disagree, and this only angers Killian more. 'You need to stand up for yourself! You all need to take the bloody blinkers off and see that when it comes down to it, no one gives a damn about anyone else. Not in this country and maybe not in any!'

'Now you are the one making grand statements,' says Luke, in only a whisper.

'Because I know things,' says Killian, and starts to point a finger – at himself, at Luke. 'I've been places. You think I need you and your da and that House of yours to keep me? Wrong. I can go anywhere and do what I like. I don't need anyone's help.' A pause. 'And I definitely don't need you.'

And he turns and walks, shoulders hunched and hands deep in his pockets. Keeps walking until he has walked away but –

LUKE

'Please!' Luke's voice comes out in a shout and this is what stops Killian. 'Please – you may not need Mountfathom, but Mountfathom needs you.'

He watches Killian's back.

Stands and waits, and is rewarded with only a few harsh words.

'You're too weak, Luke. You shouldn't beg to people.'

And Luke says, 'You're right – I know nothing outside Mountfathom. I'm not like you. I haven't been in the world to learn how to be sly or tell stories or lie.'

Killian turns to face him – not in confrontation, but with perhaps a little more respect.

Luke says, 'The truth is I need you to help me.' And adds, deeply desiring of an answer, 'Will you?'

And this boy from Belfast – this person he has known for so short a time yet it feels somehow longer – answers him. 'Okay, I'll help. Sure I've got nothing much else planned for today.'

'Stop hanging about there!' calls Malone. 'All chat and no action, that's your problem!'

'I think he might have a point,' says Luke.

'Ah, stop feeling sorry for yourself,' says Killian, and walks to Luke and slaps a hand on his back. Keeps it resting there as he says, 'Could be worse – you could be like one of these fellas, three feet high and made of dirt!'

KILLIAN

Forest thins, trees go no further – cease at the point the ground starts to rise in a smooth slope of dark earth and wild heather to meet a vast and rounded mound.

'What is this?' asks Killian.

'Never seen a Faerie Rath?' says Luke.

'Not many of them about in Belfast,' says Killian.

Up the slope, Lady Vane-Tempest still helping Lord Mountfathom, Killian and Luke step over and around a scattering of shattered limestone.

'Sorry remains of the wall that used to keep the Rath protected,' says Luke.

'Couldn't have been much of a wall even when it was standing,' says Killian.

'Would have had Faerie Enchantments on it – they were powerful Workers of Magic. No wonder the Major wanted rid of them.'

On the mound itself, maybe a dozen more Boreen Men stand guard. When they see the approach of the group, some hurry down to meet Malone. Killian watches – sees an agitation of earthen limbs, a narrowing of eyes, words passing in fierce whisper and hiss . . .

Killian asks, 'What's up?' Walks up to Malone. 'What's the trouble?'

'Trouble,' says Malone. He slips from the back of his wolfhound. 'Some of our scouts sent word that Gards from the Castle have been seen within a mile of here.'

'Looking for the Land Grabbers maybe?' says Luke. 'The ones who woke the Ash-Dragons?'

'Wouldn't be so sure of that,' says Malone, and spits onto the heather. 'We need to be ready to fight – we should trust no one. No one is on the side of the Boreen Men.'

'Maybe you should stop feeling so sorry for yourself,' says Killian.

'And what do you know about it?' says Malone. 'What do you know about what we went through with the Lock Out?'

'Oh, give over,' says Killian. 'Are you just gonna keep harping on about history from now till forever? What good's that gonna do anyone?'

'And you'd be happy to just forget! Exactly what those bastards in the Castle want – Fortflay would love us to lie down like dumb dogs and do as he says. Well, I won't! Not for him nor anybody else.'

'You'd happy die for this mound of earth?' says Killian.

'I would,' says Malone.

'Then you're a fool.'

LUKE

Lord Mountfathom whispers to his son, 'We need to stop this. Need to show them we can help.'

'How?' asks Luke.

'They distrust us because we know Magic,' says his father. 'So show them that Spells can be Worked for good. Show them, son. I am too weak.'

And Lord Mountfathom offers his Needle to Luke.

'No,' says Luke. 'I can't use this yet. I'm not ready to.'

'You must be ready now,' says his father. 'You are a member of the Driochta. We have no more time for doubt. I have faith in you, son.'

And so Luke closes his fingers around the Needle.

First thing he feels is how light it is, and how frail. But how potent – tarnished and careworn, a thing imbued with such history, and power. Luke whirls the Needle in the air and instantly a broken slab of stone rises . . . Brings gasps from the Boreen Men. Most surprising thing for Luke: it is easier than he thought. He knows on instinct how to move and manipulate the Needle and within moments is Conducting not just one stone but many, stacking them and reforming the wall in a circle around the

Rath as the Boreen Men point their blunt weapons at the air, as though the stones might turn on them and attack . . .

Only Malone is untroubled: simply watches.

And within a minute, the five-foot wall around the Rath is rebuilt.

Luke lowers his arm. Feels nauseous – muscles in his arm strained and aching as though he has been holding one of the stones and only now settles it on the ground.

Lord Mountfathom says, 'Well done, Luke.'

Lady Vane-Tempest says, 'I am very impressed, young man!'

Luke returns the Needle to his father with, 'I think that is enough for the moment.'

'Well, now,' says Malone, slow-clapping his small, earthen hands. 'Maybe the young Lord of Mountfathom isn't the weakling I thought.'

'Look!' shouts Lady-Vane Tempest.

A pair of swans crosses the sky – one white and one black. And descend in a slow circle and when they are feet from the ground Mogrify into Mr and Mrs Halter; as soon as they can speak they say together, 'Gards from the Castle are on their way. They shall be here in less than an hour. Major Fortflay has given them strict orders: destroy this Rath, and capture all members of the Driochta.'

KILLIAN

Inside the Rath, stooped in a low chamber dominated by corkscrew roots. Lord Mountfathom lies on a blanket, being ministered to by one of the Boreen Men and Mr Halter.

Killian paces as much as the space permits him to pace, asking his questions. 'How did you know what plants to put on the gunshot wound? How do you know it'll help?'

'Because I have studied such things,' says Mr Halter. He slowly wraps a linen bandage around the thigh of Lord Mountfathom. 'Though I would say such a wound would be better tended in Mountfathom, and not beneath a Faerie Rath. Tell me, why did you not return to the House directly?'

'I can't tell you,' says Killian.

'Oh?' says Mr Halter. He stands. 'And why is that?'

'Things aren't safe enough at Mountfathom – that's all I can say.'

'Things are never safe at Mountfathom.' And Mr Halter chuckles to himself. 'Always some mishap or other around the corner at that House!'

'This is different,' says Killian. 'This is –'

Lord Mountfathom shifts, groans. And Killian remembers the promise he made not to divulge what (or whom) he saw in the mirror. So he settles for saying, 'Tell me what plants you used – I like to know things, might be useful some day.'

LUKE

'There is something Father is not telling me.'

Luke and Lady Vane-Tempest and Mrs Halter outside the Rath, close to the resurrected wall. The two women say nothing.

'I know he is trying to protect me,' says Luke. 'I wish he would not.'

'One thing I know for certain,' says Mrs Halter, 'is that your father always knows best.'

'Believe in his judgement,' says Lady Vane-Tempest. 'For if we cannot trust your father in all this, then I do not know who we can trust.'

Around them hurry Boreen Men, organising themselves for the impending attack – attempting to fashion new weapons from sticks of wood and twine and sharpened rock. Luke hears Malone shout, 'If we die then we'll die defending our honour and ourselves! We'll not be walked over! We'll not be slaughtered without taking a good few of them with us!'

'Not the most hopeful rallying cry I have heard,' says Lady Vane-Tempest.

'Why are men so hell-bent on an honourable death?' asks Mrs Halter.

'Something to put on a grand gravestone?' ventures Vane-Tempest. '*Here Lies One Who Put Stupidity And Chivalry Before Sense.*'

The two women laugh and get a filthy look from a nearby knot of Boreen Men.

'Keeping things from one's children,' Mrs Halter says to Luke, 'is the prerogative of any parent.'

'Even when I am the one who will have to one day look after Mountfathom?'

'Your father has a great many burdens,' says Lady Vane-Tempest. 'When the time is right, he will tell you what he feels you need to hear.'

'What if we have no time left?' asks Luke. 'My mother – what if she . . .'

Says no more; is unable to voice that worst fear.

'Your mother can take better care of herself than anyone I have ever known,' says Mrs Halter. 'She will return to Mountfathom, I promise you that. The question may become – will anyone be there to meet her?'

'Are you three going to just sit there?' shouts Malone, loping past on his wolfhound. 'Cos we could do with a bit more of that Magic, if you have any going spare?'

'I thought you were not a particular advocate of Magic!' called Lady Vane-Tempest.

Malone gives her a sour look.

Now a call from the top of the wall –

'I see them! A hundred or more Gards on the approach!'

Luke and Lady Vane-Tempest and Mrs Halter stand.

Luke says, 'We shall return to Mountfathom, but not before we show Major Fortflay that the Magic of the Driochta is not yet dead.'

LUKE & KILLIAN

Standing together on the rounded summit of the Rath they see: Gards surrounding, splitting into smaller battalions and stationing themselves at intervals around the wall, all armed with rifles and pistols, as well prepared for besieging a city as anything else. And dragging with them three gun carriages on dark iron wheels.

'Bit over the top,' says Killian. 'Have they seen the size of these Boreen fellas?'

'No Magic though,' says Luke. 'No sign of the Politomancer.'

'Oh good,' says Killian. 'So just a couple of hundred guns and God-knows how many bullets to deal with – easy!'

'Yes,' says Luke. He is watching Mr and Mrs Halter and Lady Vane-Tempest – they stand by the entrance to the Rath, Lord Mountfathom still inside. Lady Vane-Tempest gives Luke a nod. 'Yes,' he says, 'should be easy enough.'

And he raises his hands and beings to Work a Spell of Elements.

The Halters and Lady Vane-Tempest do the same.

And above begins the storm: grey coil of cloud swirling tight and tighter, darkening at its heart, throwing all into shadow. Killian swears loudly at the first explosion of thunder.

Luke is pleased to see the Gards cower.

'Are we gonna be able to beat them by using a bit of bad weather?' asks Killian.

Luke doesn't answer, is too focused on the Storm-Breaching; feels the force of it between his hands as though holding something unaccountably heavy.

Cry from one of the Gards: 'Fire!'

Cry from Lady Vane-Tempest: 'Now!'

Luke falls to his knees and slams both hands into dark earth.

A series of blue lightning-strokes snap out of the sky and strike the ground around the wall and the Gards are thrown backwards.

A moment and Lady Vane-Tempest and the Halters whirl their Needles in the air and a squeal of notes brings a squall; a gale spiked with sleet and rain whips around the high wall of the Rath and snatches the Gards from their feet, plucks rifles from hands and topples two of the gun carriages.

Another explosion of thunder.

Malone rides his wolfhound up the slope of the Rath and shouts to Luke, 'When can me and my men go out and fight?'

'You don't need to!' Luke calls back. 'You do not need to sacrifice yourself!'

'I'll not stay safe in here and not face these Gards!'

'We can Work any number of Spells that will –'

Killian interrupts, 'The gun!'

Luke sees: remaining gun carriage has been loaded by the Gards, is being aimed as Luke raises his hand to Summon another lightning-strike but –

The blast from the gun blows a hole in the wall –

Limestone showers the area around the Rath –

Shock roots the Boreen Men to the spot –

Gards rally themselves and rush forward and pour through the opening in the wall –

The Halters and Lady Vane-Tempest Work more Spells, use their Needles to Conduct the earth into rising figures ten feet tall that throw themselves on the Gards to battle hand to hand.

Malone tells Luke, 'You have done your best, boy of Mountfathom. But now you need to take your father and get out of here – you might be the best hope for this country. Go while you still have legs to carry you!'

And with a roar Malone digs his wolfhound with his heels and races down the Rath to join his fellows and face the army of Gards.

'He's right,' says Killian. 'We need to go. Is there any way else out of this mound?'

'Yes,' says Luke, 'I know a way.'

Down the slope of the Rath, both boys together. They join the Halters and Lady Vane-Tempest who are stirring the earth into shapes not just human but animal now, bear and lion and Griffin and wild boar, and setting them on the Gards.

'We cannot win this,' says Lady Vane-Tempest.

'What you need is a door,' says Mrs Halter. 'A way back to Mountfathom – it is the safest place now, and you must defend it.'

'Take Lord Mountfathom,' says Mr Halter. 'We shall stay and hold the Gards off as long as we can. Go!'

Luke wants to disagree, Killian too; neither wants to abandon the Halters and Boreen Men and save themselves . . .

'Do not look so saddened,' says Mrs Halter, stirring her Needle in the air and sending a volley of stone at a line of approaching Gards. 'We are made of stern enough stuff, Luke.'

'Indeed,' says Mr Halter, doing the same as his wife with an almost casual ease. 'Do not give up on us just yet!'

And Luke and Killian and Lady Vane-Tempest turn and run into the Rath – down a damp, dark tunnel, with the sounds of the battle receding but feeling every blast beneath their feet and in the shiver of the walls.

One Boreen Man is in the central chamber and he tells them, 'Mister Mountfathom is too weak. The gunshot wound is severe.'

'Thank you for both that diagnosis and your help,' says Lady Vane-Tempest, 'but we need to take our leave.' And she and Killian lift Lord Mountfathom from the ground. Luke sees his father clinging to consciousness and wonders aloud for the first time. 'Is he going to make it?'

The Boreen Man cries, 'Behind you!'

A Gard has followed them, enters the chamber with rifle raised.

Luke Works a Spell and the roots of the tree snap out to take hold of the Gard around the neck but a gunshot is still managed and strikes the wall beside them.

'Run now!' shouts the Boreen Man who has attended to Lord Mountfathom, and he snatches his own small weapon, only a sharpened stick of oak, and drives it into the leg of the Gard.

'This way,' says Luke. He leads Killian and Lady Vane-Tempest and his father into the same tunnel he walked two years before. And still the shocks of the battle; sections of the ceiling fall in response as they move faster, meeting the slope that takes them to the Quicken Tree where Luke whirls his hand (muttering a small apology to the memory of the Faerie Folk) to blast the trunk to splinters.

Out they climb and straight away a shout from someone close –

'There they are, like the Major said! Shoot them!'

He and Killian and Lord Mountfathom are pushed to the ground as Lady Vane-Tempest whirls her Needle in the air and the notes it sounds are sharp enough to explode bullets before they reach further than the barrels of the rifle.

Another call from one of the Gards. 'Bring down those birds!'

Luke and Killian raise their heads: a rush of wings, white and black, two swans transforming into the Halters who join Lady Vane-Tempest and command the roots of surrounding trees to erupt from the ground and lash and swipe at the Gards.

'On your feet, Luke,' says Mr Halter. 'You need to –'

Stops – Mr Halter is struck by a single gunshot.

And for a moment stands.

'Joseph!' cries his wife.

And the Needle slips from the hand of Mr Halter. He falls.

Disbelief on the face of his wife, and then bitter resolve; she Works such Spells to explode the guns of every Gard.

Killian takes hold of Luke and says, 'Where is this bloody door you came through last time? We can't just lie here and wait to be killed!'

'Keep moving!' shouts Jane Halter. 'I can hold them here!'

'Follow me,' says Luke.

They stumble on through the trees, Lady Vane-Tempest and Lord Mountfathom following. And leaving Mrs Halter behind.

Gards still in pursuit –

When they reach the edge of the forest Luke sees on the hillside the cottage he and his mother entered through on their previous trip.

'Quickly,' he tells them.

They climb the slope with gunfire following.

Lady Vane-Tempest spares whatever moment she can to destroy the bullets but only feet from the door of the cottage she suddenly stops – turns to face the Gards following them from the forest.

'What are you doing?' shouts Killian.

'Only my duty,' says Lady Vane-Tempest. 'I shall stay and hold them back!'

'Why is everyone determined to be a martyr?' Killian asks Luke.

But Luke has already slotted the crimson key into the lock, has heard the note to tell him to open the door of the cottage and faces the Gloaming.

'Go!' shouts Lady Vane-Tempest. 'I shall see you again! I shall walk again in the grand gardens of Mountfathom and there is no Gard in all of Ireland who will stop me!'

But before they flee, both boys catch sight of someone on the fringe of the forest: standing unconcerned, watching all as though overseeing, is the man with faded hair. Their gaze meets his. And both Luke and Killian long to rush at the man and demand the truth of things but –

'Now let us go home.'

Lord Mountfathom commands them – pushes both boys through and slams the door shut on any answers.

To Uncover or Reveal is a problematic business.
Who likes to be perceived (or to perceive) so clearly?
It is a matter of good manners perhaps,
but also a matter for fear –
We do not often deal well with what we see.

The Philosophy of Magic
Lady Edith Mountfathom

LUKE

Luke: 'Tell me – how much damage?'

Findlater: 'Ivy has invaded most of the rooms, sir.'

Mr Hooker: 'And is decomposing. Trees in both the Upstairs and Downstairs Orchards withering.'

Findlater: 'Smell everywhere is extraordinary.'

Killian: 'I think we noticed that.'

Luke says nothing.

Rain is impatient against the window.

By Lord Mountfathom's bedside: Luke, holding his father's hand tight, and Killian and two members of the Driochta – Lawrence Devine and Jack Gorebooth. Mr Findlater and Mr Hooker and Mrs Little also, giving their reports. And Luke tries to listen: to Mr Hooker's opinion of the bullet wound in the leg of Lord Mountfathom, about the loss of so much blood; to Findlater's account of how the House is beginning to crumble; to Clodagh's assurances that she will keep things going and not let a single maid or Errander boy rest whilst there's work to be done!

'And my mother?' asks Luke, venturing the question he so feared to ask.

'No word yet from Dublin,' says Mr Gorebooth. 'We know that the Ash-Dragons have moved on, but that is all.'

'Any word from anyone else?' asks Luke.

'No messages are making it through the Gloaming,' says Lawrence Devine. 'I'll keep trying though, don't worry about that.'

A bright fire burns in the grate – firewood snaps like stiff knuckles.

'I'll be heading back to the kitchens now so,' says Clodagh.

'Yes,' says Luke. 'Thank you.'

'I should get back to work too,' says Mr Hooker. 'I'll see straight away to getting some timber supports for the east wing, sir. Shouldn't be too difficult to bolster.'

'What do you mean?' says Killian. 'The place is falling apart! A bit of timber isn't going to help anything!'

'Doesn't mean we shouldn't try, lad,' says Mr Hooker. 'And maybe you should come and help me; let a father and son have some time together.'

'I'm staying here,' says Killian, and folds his arms.

Luke feels he should give some command. 'Mr Findlater, please instruct the maids to light all the fireplaces in the House.'

'We have very little turf left,' says Findlater.

'Coal, then,' says Luke. 'I want every fire in the House going. I feel it'll help.'

Findlater waits a moment, then says, 'I am sorry, sir, but I think that what your father and your mother would want now is for you to –'

'Please don't tell me what they would want,' says Luke. 'I need to make these decisions.'

'I understand that,' says Findlater. 'However I do believe that –'

'Listen,' says Killian. 'You're a servant, right?'

Findlater looks at him, doesn't speak.

Killian says, 'I'll take that as a yes. So, you're the servant here and he's the man in charge, so if he says light the fires then light the bloody fires. Got it?'

'Luke.'

Lowest voice in the room – enough to bring silence (and perhaps some sense).

Luke leans close to ask, 'Yes, Father? What is it?'

'I need to speak to you,' says Lord Mountfathom. 'Alone. There are things we must discuss, whilst we still have time.'

KILLIAN

'No – I'm waiting right here!'

Will not be shifted from outside the bedroom door. Promises not to listen but won't budge.

Mr Hooker sighs. 'I've no energy for arguing. Not tonight.'

Lawrence Devine and Jack Gorebooth talk of setting more Spells around the demesne, attempting to send more messages through the Gloaming. And the grumble of their conversation fades as they make their slow way off down the hallway. *Too slow*, thinks Killian. *Everyone too slow to take action! Not ready or prepared for this!*

'I should make my rounds,' says Findlater. 'I would think it more useful than simply standing in a hallway sulking.'

'Aye,' says Killian. 'Off you go then.' Thinks, suddenly, of events in the tenements: the Uncovering in the shard of mirror. The tall, skinny boy, who looked so much like the manservant standing before him now. He has a sudden urge to run to find Luke – to tell him – but knows he cannot. Thinks: he must find Lord Mountfathom, to speak to him again about this.

'You know,' says Findlater, 'we are not so different.'

Killian laughs – loud!

'Not as odd as you think,' says Findlater. Attempts to straighten a portrait on the damp-stained wall, without success. 'I was just like you. Ended up here by chance. Brought here by my father because he was so much in debt he had to offer his own son up for service.'

'Good for you,' says Killian. He sinks to the floor, pulls his knees tight to his chest.

'You have a father too, I'm sure,' says Findlater.

Killian looks at him.

'I made a few calls whilst you were away,' says the manservant. He smiles. 'You think you can leave all that colourful past behind – thieving and such?'

'You don't know me,' says Killian.

'Oh, I do, and better than you may wish to believe.'

'You're right enough,' Killian tells Findlater. 'Maybe we aren't so different. And if that's true then maybe you should watch yourself – cos maybe I know you better than you would want to believe.'

A look; something passes between them. Killian feels suddenly afraid – though refuses to show it. Findlater nods curtly, moves to the door; Killian is left alone, a rapid thudding in his chest.

LUKE

'There are things you must know,' says Lord Mountfathom.

'It can wait,' says Luke.

'It cannot,' says his father. 'I need you to listen.' He swallows, winces with pain. Continues. 'Go to my desk – you shall find in the drawer details concerning a little project I have been working on.'

Luke does as he is told.

He tugs the warped, wood-bloated desk drawer open and inside finds a small, fat notebook with a marbled cover. The flyleaf bears an inscription in his father's hand – *A Quest to Reclaim Imagination!*

Luke leafs through, sees diagrams, scraps of map, Faerie song, drawings of Lough Gyants . . .

'What is this?' he asks, returning to his father. 'Research?'

'More akin to a record,' says Lord Mountfathom. He does not take the notebook from Luke. 'It is all I have been able to discover about the Gyants and the Good Folk – the races Major Fortflay made it his business to destroy.'

Luke continues to examine the notebook – arrives at the centre pages and unfolds a map of Ireland with many areas circled with purple in.

'These are Faerie Raths,' he says. 'And the places where the Gyant colonies used to live.'

'Indeed,' says his father. 'They are the places that one could, if they so wished, begin to seek out and rediscover these lost races.'

Luke raises his eyes from the notebook.

Lord Mountfathom tells him, 'Luke, there are many important things which are lost, and many things of no significance which survive. The loss of the Good Folk and the Gyants – and many other Magical creatures – has been, I believe, the greatest tragedy of our time. It was the end of imagination itself. To lose so much . . . I believe it was the opening of a dark chapter in a dark and terrible story. A story we are still living within.'

'What can we do with all this?' asks Luke. 'If the Gyants and Faerie colonies are gone, then what use is this?'

'Nothing is truly lost,' says his father. He shifts himself, painfully. 'I wish you to keep this notebook – keep it close to you at all times. Now: I told you once that the dark door leads to many places. There are many things to be learned from the Gloaming, Luke. Do you remember the story told to you by Mr Gorebooth?'

'Yes – about the lonely Magician of Fermanagh.'

'Do you remember what he learned to do? Something no one else had managed?'

'To travel into the past, and the future – to revisit certain parts of his own life. But it was only a story.'

'And why should that matter!' says his father with sudden passion. 'Why can we not believe, for example, that we could return to our past? Do we not do it all the time? Do we not at times become utterly lost in memory?'

Luke lowers his head.

'Father,' he says, rising from his seat, 'I shall leave you now to rest.'

'You must face the Monster,' says Lord Mountfathom. 'You must know the Unknown.'

Luke remains.

'How?' he says. 'I will be alone.'

'No,' says his father. 'You are so very far from being alone.' Takes a breath, goes on. 'I want you to think of this: time can be likened to a well-thumbed book, can it not? It could feel akin to a familiar and much-read story?'

Luke is unwilling to think, doesn't wish to theorise. But he nods.

His father says, 'So, does it not then stand to reason that with a careful diligence and understanding of the story, you may learn to flick ahead or browse backwards? Does that not strike you as simply logical?'

'I suppose,' says the son. 'If I knew the story well enough?'

'Indeed!' says his father with sudden passion. 'This is the possibility! But as you say so rightly, if you do not know well the story, you risk losing your place. But more than this, you may risk losing your own self . . .'

Lord Mountfathom settles back into bed.

Luke sits silent beside.

He says, 'Everything is failing now. So how can I know where to begin? If I have no destination, how can I be sure where the door will lead?'

'You cannot,' says his father, in a keen whisper. And manages to smile. 'You cannot know for certain what awaits in the dark. And is that not a great excitement? As with an unknown story on the shelf – where will you be taken? My advice is this: simply open the book, and trust. Turn the page, and so begin . . .'

KILLIAN & LUKE

'Will all these Spells do any good?' asks Killian.

'Can't hurt,' says Luke. 'We need as many defences as possible.' His father's words echo in his head: '*You must know the Unknown.*' Yet Luke can only think of one thing now: to try to save Mountfathom.

They stand before the house under bright moonlight. Luke stoops to the shingle drive and teases from the surface a pale Messenger. Thinks of his discussion with his father and teases it taller, gives it the fiercest form he can conceive of – a Vale Gyant, muscular and snout-nosed, a heavy shelf for a brow.

'Nice,' says Killian.

Luke moves two paces to the left and again brings another into being – and continues until a row of Gyant Messengers stands in front of the House. And to the nearest whispers his command: 'If anyone enters the grounds, find me and give me the warning.' And the Messenger whispers this message to its neighbour who in turn passes it on, and so it is communicated to all who will stand watch over the grounds. Something in their whispering makes Killian shiver.

'I wouldn't fancy being woken up by one of these things,' he says.

'Young sir!' Lawrence Devine crosses the shingle from the direction of the lagoon. 'I have set some Spells – anything that tries to enter will have a hard time getting through and more than they bargained for!'

'Thank you,' says Luke.

They are joined by Jack Gorebooth – appears from the forest that leads to the front gates to report, 'I have given the command to the limestone lions along the drive – attack if anything tries to enter. Stubborn creatures, but they appeared to understand.'

Luke again gives his thanks. The air around him feels primed with such Magic – so ready to protect them he wonders how can they be taken by surprise.

'This is all great,' says Killian, 'but what about the House itself? All the rot inside – what can be done there?'

Lawrence Devine says, 'I have to be truthful here – I'm well used to Working Agrarian Spells and seeing them go a bit wrong, but I've never seen any go as bad as what is happening in Mountfathom.'

'Can you fix it?' asks Killian.

'You can't "fix" Magic,' says Devine. 'Don't work like that. Setting these Spells around the grounds can be like scattering seed – they can fail to take, or they can grow wild. Either way, we can't undo them.'

They turn back towards the House, mount the front steps towards the front doors as Luke wonders aloud, 'I don't understand what is causing them to turn on Mountfathom.

Why would the Spells turn bad? Turn inwards and try and ruin the House?'

And Killian thinks to himself: *Cos maybe someone in this House wants to see it fail.*

KILLIAN

'Feckin useless.'

Sits on the floor in *The Menagerie of the Dead*, trying to reunite all elements of the starling skeleton he has shattered. He would rather fix things than have to lie/invent/make an excuse, so he has set to work – discovered a pot of glue in a drawer, has even dug a book out from one of the cabinets and is using it for a guide. But things aren't working as they usually do for him – simple luck isn't enough with this, and it angers him.

'Bloody hell!'

He abandons the effort and already his mind is concocting the story he'll tell, when someone knocks on the door.

'What?' Killian calls.

The door opens a little and the pale face of Mr Findlater comes into view.

'What do you want?' Killian asks.

'Sorry to disturb you,' says Findlater. His voice is shaking. 'But I did not know who best to approach. I though it best to come directly to you . . .'

Killian stands.

'What is it? What's wrong?'

'I think,' says Findlater, 'it would be better to show you. If you would follow me?'

Killian moves fast to the door– what has the manservant worried? Some new threat appeared? Anyway, can't be good news, he thinks. Definitely can't be good news!

He steps into the hallway and sees: two young boys, both red headed – two familiar faces.

'What the hell is – ?'

Killian manages a half-turn and sees Mr Findlater raise a candlestick –

Is struck hard on the forehead and falls insensible to the floor.

LUKE

I have heard it tell that the Magic that was used to raise the Faerie Raths of Ireland was of the most enduring kind. I have to wonder: enduring, or everlasting? Can this Magic still exist in the very soil of this island? And so (does it not stand to reason) that this Magic could be resurrected, and with it the lost wonders of an entire species?

Luke as sleepless as ever – sits cross-legged on his bed with his father's notebook on his lap, reading. Morrigan is close beside – restless and half-rising at times as though she detects something, suspects the shadows. Luke stops reading for a moment, but the room offers no opportunity for thoughtfulness; too much distraction, rainforest wallpaper leaving the walls in great damp sheets, puddles spreading dark across the floor. And all around *The Amazon* made hollow by the distracting *drip-drip-dripping* into pots and trays, all settled on the floor to catch moisture leaving the ceiling like slow rainfall.

Luke turns the page of the notebook and continues.

Such things we could learn from the Good Folk! Such knowledge from the Gyants! How best to serve the island of Ireland, for one thing. And for another, the truth of existence, the true joys of the world as experienced by two species that routinely enjoy life-spans extending far beyond any human being! So much we could know, if we could only –

Morrigan stands and hisses, spine stiff.

Luke sees: a Messenger – not a Gyant but a woman – has appeared in front of him. She informs him without waiting to be asked, 'The Spells around the entrance to Loughreagh have failed.'

Luke settles his father's notebook on the bedside.

'Someone trying to get into Mountfathom?' he asks.

'No,' says the Messenger. 'Someone is trying to get out.'

KILLIAN

'Keep going! Do not stop or these Spells will try to get the better of you!'

First thing he is aware of is Findlater shouting.

Second thing: only pain, then dampness on his face he takes for blood.

Killian starts to struggle. Something soft has been crammed between his jaws to stop him shouting out. He feels the rub of rope around his ankles and wrists . . . but to his amazement he squirms and almost frees himself of whoever is holding him until Findlater shouts, 'Keep a good grip on the Lagan Rat! We cannot let him escape or the game is up!'

The two red-haired boys – one holding him near the head, the other at the feet – strengthen their grip.

'Quickly,' says Findlater. 'Almost there.'

They move on though Killian feels all the while a gentle series of tugs – like small and determined hands grabbing and grabbing at him, not wanting him to move any further. He knows what this is: has learned and seen and gleaned enough of Spell-Work to recognise it.

'Almost there!' shouts Findlater – though sounding distant, as though from the farthest side of a forest, his voice strained.

And suddenly a release as though Killian has resurfaced: free of the webs of Spell-Work, they emerge from the tunnel onto the shore of Loughreagh. Surface of the water bright with moon, and from somewhere a low grumble . . . a sound Killian recognises as the engine of a turf-barge.

'Where is it?' asks Findlater.

'By the wee island,' says one of the red-headed fellas.

'Along the causeway then,' says Findlater.

Killian starts again to squirm but the boys keep him fast in their arms, Findlater still telling them, 'Quickly! We only need him on the barge and then when we get closer to Belfast we can dump him overboard.'

'Why not here?' asks the boy at Killian's feet.

'Too close to Mountfathom,' says Findlater. 'They shall suspect something.' And as they move along the strip of dark rock towards the Isle of Solitude, Findlater lowers his gaze to Killian and explains, 'I know you like your stories, Lagan Rat. Rest assured, I shall see to it that all loose ends are tied up – some significant objects shall go missing from Mountfathom tonight, and when you also are seen to be missing, the connection shall be made. I shall ensure that your last story is a very convincing one.'

And Killian struggles hardest as they reach the isle and the tor and the turf-barge moored alongside – kicks and tries to twist out of the grasp of the boys as they mount a gangway and take him aboard, manages to spit out whatever rag has been pushed into his mouth to shout, 'Help! Help me!'

'No one to hear,' says Findlater calmly. 'No one to care.'

'I would not be so certain of yourself.'

LUKE

He and Morrigan stand on the isle.

'Let him go,' says Luke. 'Let him go and I shall let you go unharmed, Mr Findlater.'

Killian is dropped to the deck of the turf-barge and the two red-haired boys find two spades and lumber towards Luke.

But he is quicker. Works a swift hand through the air, bids a spout of silver water leap from Loughreagh to enclose the boys and drag them from the barge and out of sight.

'You have grown so much,' says Mr Findlater calmly, standing on the deck beside Killian. 'Learned so much in the way of Magic.'

'I asked that you release him,' says Luke. 'I shall not ask again.'

Morrigan sits by Luke's ankles, unconcerned.

'Now,' says Luke.

'Your mother and father have taught you so much,' says Findlater, and his tone is losing any coolness, 'but you know nothing of the world. They told you so little, and kept so much from you.'

'I know enough,' says Luke. 'I understand now: you betrayed us. You have compromised the security of Mountfathom. You wrote an invitation and gave it to the man with the faded hair.'

'Indeed,' says Findlater. 'The ubiquitous man with faded hair – otherwise known as my father.'

Luke's hand falls.

'It's true!' Killian shouts now. 'I saw the two of them together in the mirror in the Cailleach's house!'

'Just one of the things your mother and father kept from you,' says Findlater, 'was that my father was a member of the Driochta. And very powerful he was too. He took it rather hard when my mother passed away and he was left to raise me on his own. So hard did he find it, in fact, he decided to pass me over into the service of Mountfathom. And your father – so charitable, so understanding – both took me in and, perhaps seeing some potential in my father, offered him a place in the Driochta. The arrangement didn't last long. My father was rather too indecently keen on the power he was gaining, on the Spells he could Work. He is rather lethal with a Needle, as you and your cousin discovered.'

Luke sees again cousin Rose on the causeway – motionless, not breathing. Sees his Aunt Nancy distraught. Sees the man with faded hair working a Needle to make the waters of Loughreagh rise and consume them – to try to destroy them.

'Your father and my own came to blows by all accounts,' says Findlater to Luke, 'and his place in the Driochta was given to that other noble commoner – the farmer, Lawrence Devine. I think a little annoyance on my father's part was rather justified.'

Coldest breeze rushes across the water, across the isle.

'You let your father into Mountfathom,' says Luke. 'You are making excuses. You have betrayed us. It is your fault that Nanny Bogram was killed.'

'My fault,' says Findlater, softly. 'But also no doubt your father's fault. He knew what my father was and he chose to ignore it – he wanted to believe the best of people.'

'He didn't want anyone killed!' cries Luke.

'Indeed,' says Findlater, as calm as ever. 'And what did your father do afterwards? What ends did he go to when he knew who had broken into his House and murdered Mrs Bogram?'

'He did what he thought was right,' says Luke.

'And now who is making excuses for the behaviour of their father?' says Findlater. He looks to Killian, still lying bound on the deck. 'I think we all do that at times, do we not?'

Clouds converge on the moon, cloak it.

'You are banished from Mountfathom,' says Luke. Wishes so badly to make a decision and Work a Spell that will have some permanency so can think only of this: 'You shall not ever set foot again in the grounds!' Attempts for the first time in his life a Spell of Expulsion: mutters the required words and weaves his hand in the air but –

'That Spell will not take,' says Findlater. 'Or it will not last. All Magic is leaving Mountfathom – soon there shall be nothing left, not a single defence against what is coming.'

'Don't listen to him,' says Killian. 'He's only looking after himself! Doesn't care a damn about anyone!'

'Not entirely true,' says Findlater. 'Although I very much do not give a damn about a Lagan Rat.'

And he kicks Killian from the barge –

Splash of dark water –

Findlater grabs the wheel of the barge and turns it from the isle –

A roar from the engine, a cloud of turf-smoke –

And Luke has no choice; abandons Magic and throws himself into the water –

Breath-stealing cold, no brightness to see by; thrashes through a distanceless dark, pointing himself downward to kick and reach . . . and feels as though he is fighting his way through the Gloaming, trying to find the way home. A sudden flare! Emerald light blazing in the murk and Luke battles his way towards it and finds Killian's bound hands with the emerald key of Lord Mountfathom clasped between them. They take each other's hands and kick for the surface – struggle together up and out and free of the dark.

LUKE & KILLIAN

'Jaysus – the state of this place!'

'Oh, be quiet – you are still shivering.'

In *The Amazon*, Luke adds his coat to the stack of blankets covering Killian – hands him a mug of tea he made in the kitchen.

'No tea,' says Killian. 'I'm grand. Just gimme a minute to recover.'

He tries to sit up but fails – falls back on the pillows of Luke's bed.

'You need to try to sleep a bit,' Luke tells him.

'Nah,' says Killian. 'Something about the idea of those Gards from Dublin arriving, or maybe some Land Grabbers coming to burn the place down – isn't the best when you're trying to nod off.'

'True enough,' says Luke, thinking he might never find sleep again. But he tries: lies down on the bed beside Killian.

Only sound is the same *drip-drip-drip* from the ceiling.

'None of those Traces about?' asks Killian. 'A lot quieter without their moaning!'

And only then does Luke wonder about this, and wonder why he hadn't noticed. Only now remembers their warning: *'It is when we, the past keepers and custodians of this ancient House, decide to leave it that you will begin to worry. When the past has no place in the world, that is when things begin to burn.'*

Luke says, 'They are gone. They have left Mountfathom.'

'Just like that?' asks Killian.

'Yes,' says Luke. 'That is the way with Magic. They were the oldest ancestors of Mountfathom, experimented with Spells of Lasting and Transcendence, and so left some Trace of themselves behind. But if every Spell here is failing – if nothing new is going to take – then Mr Findlater was right, there is no hope.'

'Enough of that,' says Killian. 'I don't wanna hear about what that Findlater fella thinks about anything. Hopefully we've seen the last of him!'

Luke only feels uneasy. Thinks but doesn't say, *I would place a bet he'll be back.*

Killian hitches himself up on a pillow and says, 'Cheer up! What I've learned: Magic is fair enough, but it looks to me to cause as much problems as cures them! And anyway – I prefer things solid. Wanna see something that lasted a long time without any Spell?'

And from his pocket he takes a sepia photograph.

'Found this in my old house in the tenements,' says Killian. Lays it on the bedspread, flattens it with his fingers. Morrigan goes close to investigate.

'What is it?' asks Luke. Picks it up, brings it close: two girls caught on a lane, trees on either side dark and robbed of their leaves. A moment in late autumn, he would guess. And in the distance a ghost of a large House – distant, faintly present.

'It's my mother,' says Killian. 'Would you believe my da told me she grew up in the grounds of a place like this, but I never believed him. Must've been one of the few times he was being honest enough!'

Luke thinks of his own mother – wonders where she is, whether she is on her way back to Mountfathom. Stops himself wondering whether she is still alive.

He returns the photo to Killian.

'You should treasure it,' he says. 'You need to keep it safe.'

'Will do,' says Killian, and he tucks it into his shirt and shuts his eyes. 'Don't mind if I stay in this bed tonight, do you?'

'No,' says Luke. He closes his eyes, and finds to his surprise that he is ready to rest. 'No – not at all.'

A minute passes, and before Killian allows himself to be tugged away by sleep, he whispers: 'Don't you worry. I'll be here and waiting. I'm ready to fight if anything comes looking for trouble. I'm going nowhere.'

All Spells end – this is the inevitable thing.
Though, like all things given life, they do long to survive.
They will rarely be Dismissed without a fight.

The Power of Spell-Work
Joseph & Jane Halter

LUKE & KILLIAN

'They are here. Mountfathom is being invaded.'

Luke half wakes.

He sees one of the Gyant Messengers looming by the bed: their expression is calm, melancholy.

And Luke does not move, not yet.

Only when Morrigan swipes a claw at his hand and starts to cry does Luke Dismiss the Messenger with a wave of his hand. Only now does he begin to fully wake, to worry – his heart starts its panic.

Drapes never drawn, moonlight is allowed to lie long on the carpet – Morrigan leaps onto its silver and follows it like a path, padding fast to the window and up onto the sill.

Killian is snoring – mouth open and arms outflung.

Luke kicks back the covers, pulls on his coat. Pauses – takes his father's notebook from the nightstand and tucks it into his inside pocket. Moves fast on tiptoe to the window.

Below on the shingle drive, he sees the half-circle of Messengers. Looks closer and sees the gap where one departed

317

to come and warn him. Luke waits, and finally sees: Gards are approaching the House, too many to make out but enough to be a threat. They reach the Gyant Messengers and stop, wary until one looks brave enough (or perhaps has been told that the Messengers can cause no harm) to charge through onto the broken shell and shingle of the drive. The Gard stops, swearing at the noise it makes. And now turns his gaze to Mountfathom and sees Luke watching him from the window.

'Get down!'

Killian drags Luke to the ground – is awake, already so alert. In whispers to one another –

Luke: 'Gards from the Castle. We need to wake the others. We need to get my father to safety.'

A voice from outside commands: 'Break the front door down.'

Luke says, 'That's Major Fortflay.'

And another voice, a Gard, asks, 'What if we can't, sir? Might have Spells on it.'

And the Major replies easily, 'Then we'll have that Cailleach creature burn the place to the ground.'

Luke scoops Morrigan into his arms and tells Killian, 'We need to go. Now!'

And together they run from *The Amazon*.

Along the first floor and up the staircase to the second and along, meeting nothing but shadows and marble statues, and they burst into Lord and Lady Mountfathom's bedroom.

'Father, wake up,' says Luke. Lord Mountfathom does not stir. 'Please wake up!'

'We have to just lift him,' says Killian, dragging back the bedcovers.

And now sudden sounds below: door slamming, or being booted open; shatter of broken glass –

Morrigan leaps free of Luke's arms and onto the chest of Lord Mountfathom and swipes at his cheek.

'Stop!' says Luke, dragging the cat away.

'Did the trick – look,' whispers Killian.

Lord Mountfathom has awoken.

'What is it, Luke?' he asks. But he knows – hand is reaching for the Needle at his bedside. 'Tell me.'

'Gards,' says Luke.

'Where?' asks his father, swinging his legs out from beneath the covers, feet finding the floor. 'How close? In the grounds?'

'Yes,' says Luke. 'And maybe now in the House too.'

Moments pass as Lord Mountfathom gazes into the darkness – to the near distance, to the open doorway, to the window. And Luke sees such tiredness in his father and would like nothing more than to tell the man to ease back into bed, to sleep: only to dream.

Lord Mountfathom looks at his son. 'We must leave. It is not safe here now.'

'Give up Mountfathom?' says Luke.

'We must,' says Lord Mountfathom, perches on the edge of the bed. 'It is for the best.'

'Father,' says Luke suddenly. 'Let me try something. A Reclamation.'

Father and son watch one another.

'I know I failed before,' Luke tells him, 'but let me try. We must give the House one more chance.'

A pause; Lord Mountfathom nods. 'The library,' he says. 'Let us go.'

Killian and Luke take an arm each and heave Mountfathom
to his feet.

'Morrigan!' calls Luke, but the cat with its own contrary
mind slips away through the open door.

'My Needle,' says Lord Mountfathom. Luke takes it from
the bedside and places it into the hand of his father – it hangs
limp, and this sight makes Luke doubt just about everything.
His father tells him, 'We need to inform the others.'

Luke nods. Works a hand in the air and once more Summons a
twist of vapour and shapes it, unthinkingly, into the appearance
of a woman. He leans towards this new Messenger and whispers
the words that he needs delivered: 'We are under attack. Meet
us in the library.' Now whirls his hand once more and sends the
Messenger off into the House to rouse the remaining members
of the Driochta.

Out into the dark hallway and they encounter sure sounds
of intrusion – wood splintering, raised voices and orders being
thrown from one Gard to another. But quickly down the stairs
to the first floor and then down again into the cold and moulder
and damp of the entrance hall, and it is Killian who sees first
the shadows at the front doors. The hall reverberates with the
sounds of rifle butts beating at the doors.

'Some of the Spells are holding up,' says Lord Mountfathom.
'Those oldest Spells set by my great-great-grandfather are
keeping them out for now. Not for long though . . . hurry . . .'

Down cold marble stairs and into the shadows of the Gallery
of Learning. Almost at the library – a single Gard stationed
outside the doors. He turns and sees them standing in the
shadows and raises his rifle and no Spell comes to Luke's mind

and his father cannot lift his Needle to act. Killian thinks: *For feck sake!* Leaves Lord Mountfathom's side and charges at the Gard and knocks him off his feet – punches him hard in the face and snatches his rifle and uses the butt to strike him unconscious. Stands up and says, 'Now look – we've a proper weapon!'

'Do you even know how to fire that?' asks Luke, supporting his father as they arrive at the door to the library.

'No,' says Killian. 'But can't be that difficult.'

Sound of front doors falling, Spells failing –

Killian says, 'And maybe there's a book in here about guns – quick!'

They hurry inside and Killian shuts and bolts the doors.

Storm of boots in the hallway and shouts from Major Fortflay.

'Search the place! I want everyone caught and brought into custody! Any who fights back, you have my permission to show no mercy!'

Killian points the rifle at the double doors, like he's seen in the films.

'Draw the Reclamation,' Lord Mountfathom tells his son. 'Try to assert control over the House and grounds. It is the only way, son.'

Luke leaves his father with Killian and races along one of the wooden paths to his father's desk – finds a pen loaded with ink, a clean sheet of paper – and brings all back with him.

'Slowly,' says his father, 'and decisively.'

Luke kneels. He settles the page on the ground and crouches over it and tries to concentrate. Presses the nib to paper to see the slow bleed of black onto white, and starts to draw – small curl and down-stroke, blotting and retracing where needed and all the while muttering the names of Mountfathom's long line of custodians and when he arrives at his own name . . . pauses, starts once more. And is there the tell-tale tremble beneath his feet? Shake of shelves as ancient volumes slip from their place and fall to the floor and Luke wonders, *Could this work? Will the Spell actually take?*

'Keep going,' says Lord Mountfathom. 'Don't stop, son.'

Once more Luke recites the names and the page is almost covered and the shape that has been sketched (almost without his conceiving of it) is of Mountfathom itself.

Tall window behind them is smashed in and Gards are pouring over the sill; at the same time the library doors explode and the page bearing the Reclamation is whipped from under Luke's hands by the blast.

But not soldiers who enter. A chimpanzee and peacock and owl surge-speed-sweep into the room and attack the Gards at the window, driving them back. The peacock lands beside Luke and in a whirl becomes Helena Vane-Tempest.

Luke is wordless with relief.

Killian says, 'Survived, then?'

'Of course!' says Lady Vane-Tempest. 'I do hope you didn't doubt my word, young man?' A Gard sprints towards them and she slashes her Needle through the air and a sudden blast of wind kicks him backwards against a bookcase.

The chimpanzee transforms into Lawrence Devine and he grunts, 'Any plan here?'

'There is a passageway at the centre of the labyrinth,' says Lord Mountfathom. 'Beneath the statue of Cuchulain – we can make an escape that way.'

The eagle owl arrives beside them and in a moment Mogrifies into Jack Gorebooth. 'Leave?' he says. 'Surely we cannot abandon the House to them?'

'We are under siege,' says Luke's father. 'We must. Our attempts at Reclamation have failed.'

A fresh brigade of Gards arrives at the doors to raise their rifles.

And Lady Vane-Tempest Works a Spell with such speed that Luke is left breathless: all splinters and shards of the doors are called from wherever they were flung during the explosion and in an instant gather and reconstitute and rush to cover the doorway as they once did.

'That was unbelievable!' says Killian.

'Such a show-off,' says Gorebooth, smiling.

'Jealous much?' says Vane-Tempest.

But a fresh battery of noise at the doors –

'Window is the best way out now, I'd say,' suggests Devine.

'Let us go,' says Lord Mountfathom.

Across the library and Killian and Luke climb up onto the windowsill and together lift Lord Mountfathom through as the other members of the Driochta keep their eyes on the doors of the library.

'Grounds looks quiet here,' says Lady Vane-Tempest. 'But we need to know how things appear from above. Jack?'

'I shall take a look,' says Gorebooth, and with a shiver Mogrifies back into an owl and leaves them in favour of the night sky. Mere seconds later –

'More soldiers!' Gorebooth alights beside them and becomes human again to report. 'More coming from the western side, through the forest and down the driveway. And there are others approaching from Loughreagh. But not Gards.'

'Land Grabbers,' says Devine.

'Yes,' says Gorebooth, 'I believe so.'

'Everyone is bound for Mountfathom tonight,' says Vane-Tempest. 'Like one of the Midsummer parties from the old days!'

'Could work to our advantage,' says Devine. 'They'll be too busy fighting each other to bother with us!'

'The passageway in the labyrinth will bring us out a mile away from the House,' says Lord Mountfathom. 'But we need to get the staff out too.'

'I can do that,' says Devine, and in a blink he retakes his chimpanzee form and is gone, bolting off into the dark.

'We shall stay here,' says Helena. 'We shall hold off the Gards and give the three of you time to escape.'

Luke and Killian protest, but –

'Luke,' says Lord Mountfathom, with sudden passion. 'Please – your mother would want you safe and that is my priority. No book nor brick nor piece of mortar is more precious to me than your life.'

They stand together in the dark grounds, uneasy.

But Luke knows he can offer no more protest. And no time for more debate.

Gunfire from the western side of the House.

'Go now,' says Lady Vane-Tempest.

'We shall keep them at bay as long as it takes to get the staff out,' says Gorebooth. Both Mogrify and take to the sky as Luke and Killian support Lord Mountfathom past stagnant pond and rotting flowerbed and the pillars holding high the statues of the animal forms of the Driochta. And on: past walled garden whose walls have begun to crumble, and on into the labyrinth.

As they walk-run Luke keeps one hand poised in readiness to Cast whatever Spell he needs: expects with each moment and each turn to be shown someone waiting. And in his worry he must slow his step a little because Killian tells him, 'Keep going, Luke! Faster!' and his father says, 'The Driochta will protect the rest of our family as best they can. We have to trust them.'

Into the heart of the labyrinth – familiar statue of the warrior Cuchulain.

'Touch a hand to his hand,' says Lord Mountfathom.

Luke hurries to the statue and for a moment peers into the ferocious and impassioned face. Now he and the statue touch, palm to palm. And at the feet of Cuchulain the earth groans and falls away to show a stone staircase descending into dark.

'Easy enough,' says Killian, supporting Lord Mountfathom, bringing him to the opening. 'Now what are you waiting for?'

Luke hasn't moved. Soon as he sees this escape route – soon as he knows they could so simply leave – he knows he cannot. He opens his mouth to tell his father but when he turns he sees two figures entering the centre of the labyrinth. From their dress he knows them as Land Grabbers, pistols raised.

Lord Mountfathom slumps against the statue as Killian swings the rifle from his shoulder but fumbles it –

Luke hurls a Spell –

Land Grabbers dodge it –

'Go!' Killian tells Luke. 'Leave!' And forgets the rifle and throws himself, fist and foot, into a fight with one of the Grabbers –

The other runs at Luke who flicks his hand at the final moment and mutters a Spell of Escape – Spell shifts him five feet to the left and the Grabber crashes into the wall. The other Grabber has his hands around Killian's throat –

Lord Mountfathom presses the tip of his Needle to the statue –

A screaming note –

Cuchulain springs to life and takes two massive steps and swings one stone fist and sends the Grabber on top of Killian flying far into the dark.

Killian gets to his feet, massaging his throat and saying, 'Now can we just bloody go?'

'Impressive.'

A final shadow steps into the centre of the labyrinth. But not mere shadow – in the moonlight Luke sees faded hair and pale face and darkest eyes.

'Stay back!' says Killian, and he brandishes the rifle.

'Look at you now,' says the man they now know as Findlater Senior. 'Look how far the Lagan Rat has come! Trying to play with the people in the Big House, that it? Look what it did for my son – got turfed out on his ear and for what? For having me as a father. Hardly his fault, is it? Hardly fair.'

'Why don't you just feck off and die!' says Killian.

'No chance,' is all Findlater Senior says. Raises his pistol and points it at Killian's head.

A sudden blow from behind fells him.

There stands Mr Hooker, rusty spade in hand.

'Bartemius,' says Lord Mountfathom.

'Where are you heading to?' asks Mr Hooker.

'Escaping,' says Killian, and immediately wishes he hadn't said it.

'I see,' says the gardener. 'Sounds sensible enough – you best get going.' He pushes at Findlater's insensible body with his foot – no sign of consciousness.

'What about you, Mr Hooker?' asks Luke.

'Me,' says the gardener. A grim smile arrives on his mouth. 'I have been at Mountfathom for most of my life. I have been happy here – it is home. And with all due respect, I will not abandon it when it needs me most.'

From the House rises a sudden plume of fire; explosions of glass and stone and such screaming.

Luke turns to his father.

'I cannot leave either,' he says. 'I'm sorry – I cannot abandon Mountfathom.'

'No,' says his father. 'It does not seem as though we can.'

Mr Hooker takes the weight of Lord Mountfathom and leads him out of the centre of the labyrinth. There, they see the gardens at the back of Mountfathom become a battlefield: Land Grabbers fighting Gards, gunfire and fists, broken bottles holding Indigo Fire being hurled at the House. Luke spies the Cailleach, directing things from a distance. Scene reminds Killian of the riots in Belfast – blood and breaking bone as the Gards charge at the Grabbers, smell of smoke and burning harsh against his nostrils . . .

'This way,' says Mr Hooker, wielding his shovel with the fervour of any solider and Luke sees in the gardener such a will – a loyalty to this place that he has helped create and shape as much as any Lord or Lady of Mountfathom.

Now almost at the outside steps that lead to *The World*.

Screams from somewhere near the Temple of the Elements –

'Stay sharp!'

Helena Vane-Tempest is back beside them, flicking and twitching her Needle, and Lawrence Devine, who seems less bothered with Spell-Work, thumping and pummelling anybody who approaches.

Luke feels a sudden squirm beneath his feet. He knows. 'Ash-Dragons.'

Steps that lead to *The World* split and explode open.

Three Dragons burst through, spewing cinder and polluting the air so completely with ash that Luke and Killian lose sight of each other and the remaining Driochta. They cling to what they can – each other. And Luke remembers his mother's inspired Conducting on their flight from the Castle: raises his hand and commands the water in the nearest pond to rise.

Sees through the dark an Ash-Dragon rear, and a serpent of water drowns the creature, sweeps it from sight.

Mr Gorebooth runs out of the dark and says, 'Good idea – need to keep the fires doused!' And uses his Needle to Conduct more water from the ponds, directs it to the fires of Mountfathom, to the sound of hiss and sight of steam.

Killian hears Mr Hooker shout, 'Look out! Coming out of the ground!'

The two boys stand hand in hand, Luke Working to produce a gust to clear the atmosphere of dark. When they emerge from the cloud of cinder, when sight is returned, they see: on the borders of the gardens are more arriving Dragons, squirming dark from the earth with wings tucked tight and then twitching free to billow cinder whichever way they wish.

Killian says, 'I thought they were shy enough creatures? Someone must be angering them – making them do this!'

'Yes,' says Luke.

He hears the cackle and cry of the Cailleach, sees her standing by the Temple of the Elements commanding, 'Destroy them! Destroy the Driochta!'

'And I think we can guess who is responsible,' says Luke.

'What Magic works against that old crone?' asks Killian.

'Well, I've no Magic of any kind, but I can wield a shovel well enough!'

Mr Hooker gives them a wink, then rushes forward with shovel in hand and swings it at the Cailleach.

'Luke,' says Lord Mountfathom. 'We have only one plan left we can make use of. We must Raise Mountfathom.'

Helena Vane-Tempest is close enough to overhear. 'You sure, William? Just as we talked about one night when we were so very drunk?'

'Yes,' says Lord Mountfathom. 'Just as we discussed – not a bad plan, as I recall. Might be the only way to save the House.'

Helena smiles, then shouts. 'Driochta! Prepare to Raise Mountfathom!'

Some looks from Devine and Gorebooth – sceptical would be to understate it. They look aghast! And then slowly, appear thrilled with the prospect. Luke wonders at the audacity of this plan; has heard of a Raising, but never thought that it could be possible.

'I need to stand on my own,' Luke's father tells him.

So Killian and Luke stand back.

'Ready?' calls Helena.

Luke sees that she and the others have spaced themselves in a perfect semi-circle.

'*Now!*' cries Lord Mountfathom.

And Lord Mountfathom and the Driochta drive their Needles into the ground.

For some seconds, nothing – only sounds of continuing battle and the hiss and snarl of the Dragons. And then so many things – from each embedded Needle races a crack to split and topple and open a dark wound and all zigzagging towards Mountfathom –

Silence . . .

Moments of exquisite anticipation –

And now explosion!

Luke and Killian and all assembled – Driochta, Dragons, Land Grabbers and Gards – are thrown from their feet. And Luke watches: a fresh forest is sprouting fast beneath the foundations of the House, tearing it free. At first only saplings, then seconds later towering adults, a mass of boughs all straining to lift the House aloft – impaling it and ensnaring it as branches snake through walls and smash-erupt through roof and window –

The House of Mountfathom is leaving the ground and being raised skyward.

Devine is beside Luke suddenly and pulling him to his feet and shouting to everyone, 'Don't forget what all this spectacle is in aid of! Grab hold of something or it'll go without us!'

'This was worth leaving Belfast for,' says Killian, smiling at Luke.

'Quickly!' shouts Helena.

'Jump and grab hold!' calls Gorebooth.

Needles retrieved from the ground, and Luke and Killian and Lord Mountfathom – who has discovered fresh energy, as though energised by the sight so no longer needs to be supported – and the other Driochta mount broken steps and leap and grab hold of whatever bough comes into their hands and hold tight.

The rising continues – accelerates! New trees burst from the earth and add themselves to the effort, straining and shielding the House too with knot and tangle and thicket. And Luke sees beyond now – further than forest and shore road, to Loughreagh and the Mountains of Mourne and a sky alive with so many stars!

He hears someone call, 'Climb up!'

'Follow me!' says Killian.

Together they climb, have to squeeze through the lattice of branches but before long discover the glass doors of *The World*. Killian takes a handful of his shirt and smashes, reaches in and unlatches the door and they pull themselves inside, reaching out to help Lord Mountfathom. And once the rest of the Driochta joins them inside, Luke is the first to turn. First to see –

They are not the only people in *The World*.

Smoke, mist, pale vapour – a Magic brought from across the water, sanctioned by the Castle and taking the shape of hounds. A dozen pairs of blue-white eyes glittering and Luke has time only to shout, '*No!*'

But too late.

One of the Pall leaps at Helena Vane-Tempest and sinks teeth into her neck before she can cry out or scream. She drops, does not get up. Jack Gorebooth and Lawrence Devine are both caught too, consumed by the Pall, and for a moment stand only shivering, as though plunged into bitter cold, their faces drawn, eyes draining of colour and clothes withering on their bodies. Hair fading to white, skin as delicate as paper as they both fall soundlessly to the floor.

Lord Mountfathom backs away, Needle still in his hand – is forced to the glass doors by one of the Pall.

Killian forces Luke back into a corner and stands in front of him.

And the walls of *The World* are in turmoil – not static but storming, oceans rising to swallow continents, mountain ranges crumbling –

The creature before Lord Mountfathom prepares to pounce –

'Enough now,' comes a voice.

The Pall demurs – obediently retreats.

'Slaughter is always a shame, though almost always a necessary thing.' Major Fortflay steps free from the shadows. 'And great shame and a loss and so on and so forth.' Stops with his hands tucked behind his back.

'You bastard!' shouts Luke, and he moves towards the Major but Killian holds him back.

'Not the kind of language I would expect from a boy of the Big House.' Not the Major speaking now but another – Findlater Senior appears, bleeding from the blow Mr Hooker dealt him. 'But as I see, you've been hanging about with some lower sorts, so it is only to be expected!'

Luke says nothing, is struggling to understand.

'Strange alliances can be made,' Fortflay explains. 'Don't worry yourself about the ways of the world, lad. Let me state things simply, as your mother once did for me: we cannot allow Magic to continue in this country. We cannot allow renegade Magicians any more than we can allow renegade Irishmen! We need to bring it all under control. We need to eliminate. Understand?'

'Don't forget the keys,' says Findlater Senior. 'I want those keys. The crimson and the emerald. That's all I asked for in exchange, remember?'

'Don't give me orders,' says Fortflay. 'You do well to remember your place or I shall have you –'

Killian chooses this time to act; rushes forward but is stopped, held by a Spell of Inertia Cast from the hand of Findlater Senior.

'Filthy Lagan Rat,' says the Major. He approaches Killian, strikes him. Spits on him. 'Not one on the face of this earth that will miss you, is there? However, these blue bloods here, these people of the Big House – we need to account for their deaths.' He comes within feet of Luke. 'Would it not be a shame if one of the servants turned on their master?'

A final figure appears beside Lord Mountfathom – the manservant, Findlater Junior. He snatches the Needle from the hand of Luke's father and pushes him to the ground. Luke moves forward once more but the Pall closes in – forms a transparent barrier. And Luke is weeping now – with betrayal and grief and confusion. And Killian is weeping too, silently – in anguish and frustration but still unable to move, still held fast by the Spell.

'Do it now!' Findlater Senior tells his son.

Findlater Junior crouches by Lord Mountfathom, the Needle loose in his hand. Luke's father does not move, does not raise a hand or protest at all. Though Luke knows his father could so easily Work a Spell to save himself – to save them all. And Luke sees that the manservant is weeping too – sobbing as he says, 'I am sorry.'

'Do it now, you fool!' shouts Findlater Senior.

The manservant shuts his eyes and stabs the Needle into Lord Mountfathom's throat.

Luke's mouth opens with a scream that doesn't come out.

But an unexpected attack –

Morrigan reappears, and leaps at Findlater Senior and tears at his face –

Killian is released and with a roar swings a powerful punch at the Major and knocks him off his feet. And the whole of Mountfathom lurches! Forest that lifted the House free of the battle is buckling, all Spells failing –

And Luke remains, cannot take his eyes from his father. Knows that if the Spells of the House are no more, then his father too must be –

'We have to go!' Killian grabs his hand – shouts the only place he can think of that might give them escape. 'To the dark door and the Gloaming! We have to run!'

Luke knows they have only moments, and somehow he manages to uproot himself.

'Stop them!' shouts Fortflay as they reach the doors of *The World*.

But they are out into the corridor and running, Luke blinded by tears but Killian leading him on.

Everywhere Mountfathom crumbling –

Walls splitting and folding –

Ceilings caving –

Down the Gallery of Learning –

Into the hexagonal entrance hall and up the marble steps –

A fissure follows them, races alongside to rend the staircase, and as Luke and Killian reach the first floor, the house lurches once more, is being split down its middle, the eastern wing sliding away from them.

They grab hold and pull themselves towards the next staircase.

'Where do we go to when we get through the dark door?' shouts Killian. 'Where are we aiming for?'

'Nowhere,' is all Luke can say, remembering his father's words. 'Nowhere.'

To the second floor –

Furniture careening towards them –

A head-splitting crack as the green glass dome above is riven in two, shattering and sending myriad shards cascading into the stairwell. And still the two boys fight-climb-struggle.

Luke chances a glance behind – sees blue-white eyes, a gathering of pale smoke and shouts to Killian, 'Quickly!'

Onto the third floor. Corridor that leads to the dark door is almost vertical and with hands on whatever doorjamb or pillar they can discover, the two boys have to climb towards it.

Portraits of the Driochta are leaving their frames in a dark tide.

Luke reaches the door first, crimson key already in hand and he forces it into the lock and twists it. Will it work now? Will this Magic hold if all else has fallen away?

A single, low note, hardly above hearing –

Luke snatches the key from the lock, turns the silver hand and it falls open like a hatch and he pulls himself inside, reaching back for Killian –

But jaws of the Pall close around Killian's feet.

He cries out, 'Go on!'

And a sudden and bone-freezing cold consumes Luke; feels his heart shiver and almost stop as the Pall moves over him, imagines his hair turning to white, the same as Mr Gorebooth and Mr Devine.

Killian cries, 'Go! Leave me!'

But Luke will not abandon him; instead Works a Spell of Enclosing that tears the jaws of the Pall from Killian and almost tears Killian's leg with it as Luke drags him through, and the door slams shut by itself to seal them in darkness.

PART FIVE

THE MONSTER

In the Unknown,
In this deep darkness –
Two figures.
In the Gloaming, two boys wander hand in hand.

Where now?
   Which direction to go?
   What did Father say?
   What will become of Mountfathom?
Luke thinks these questions. Or perhaps speaks them because
Killian offers an answer.

We're here – that'll have to do for a minute. We're standing
here together.

Luke thinks/says: Can you walk?

Killian: Dunno about walk but I can limp. Why?

Luke: We need to start searching.

Killian: What for?

Luke: For the Monster – for the way to save Mountfathom.

Luke, your hair is white.

I know. We need to keep moving.

Luke walks and Killian limps, but still only through darkness. No light from the crimson key, it won't lead them – lays no ready path.

Killian says, Here – let me try this one.

And soon as the emerald key is in his hand a light stretches ahead from their feet and off into an Unknown.

You're more certain of yourself, says Luke. You know where you want to go.

Don't know about that, says Killian. When do you think we'll come across this Monster?

Luke says, I think that will be up to the Monster.

Killian asks, So where will we go till then?

And Luke knows; feels as though he has always known.

He says, I was told a story once about a Magician. He could travel into his own past, or his future. I think that is what we need to do – and we might find some clue or some way to save Mountfathom.

Is this only imagined? Something created?

I have no memory of this memory.

Luke and Killian stand in the stone passageway beneath Mountfathom. It has the feel of a winter evening – darkness finding a foothold at an early hour, fires kept alive until late, yet everyone safe and content indoors.

Killian asks, How can you be so sure?

Once again Luke discovers he has been saying all things aloud – any barrier between thought and utterance has melted away.

Luke answers, Because I am. This way.

They walk the corridor and take only a few steps before someone races ahead of them on tiptoe. A child of two or two and a half – races so quick to the kitchen where a fire is still warming the walls, and Luke hears a voice say, What are you still doing up? Do you know how late it is? Do you never sleep, child?

Luke walks faster and Killian follows.

They hear a voice of a woman half-scolding, And not a slipper or a dressing gown on you or nothing! You're going to get me into some trouble, you wee rascal!

Luke knows this voice – these words harsh but said in a tone soft.

They reach the window that gives a view onto the kitchen and, inside, Luke sees a woman settling a saucepan of milk on the range. Now unscrewing the lid on a large brown jar and spooning dark chocolate powder into a mug.

Thank you.

These words from a child who sits cross-legged on a rug by the fire. He is looking around the room with such curiosity and in his hands he is holding (perhaps too tightly) a disgruntled cat the colour of smoke and with turquoise eyes. Now the child is prodding the tiles on the hearth, counting them. Now is asking, How do you know when the milk is hot enough for making the hot chocolate, Nanny Bogram?

Oh, I know, she tells him. I've done it enough times for you!

Can I have some sugar in it? asks the boy.

Now now, says Bogram, you're sweet enough!

The child on the rug laughs.

Killian whispers, This is you?

341

Luke nods.

There we are, says Nanny Bogram. She hands the mug to the child and enfolds him in a blanket and the child goes sip, sip, sip . . . *sigh*.

The Nanny and the child sit and chat companionably. Laugh and disagree and wonder and –

She was so good to me, says Luke. She was so good.

But we have to keep going, says Killian. This doesn't help us save Mountfathom.

He is right, of course.

And Luke realises there are so many ways to become lost in the Gloaming – not only by slipping into the wrong part of the story, but lingering there and never allowing yourself to turn the page. So he allows Killian to take his hand, to lead him away from himself and back into the dark.

Hear that? Hear that whispering?

What is it? ask Killian.

It is the Monster, says Luke. It is the thing we must face.

And in the most distant of whispers: *You have more to see before you can be prepared to face the truth of things. You must face both past and future before the end.*

Yes, says Luke.

And the crimson key blazes bright – urgently leads them on, and suddenly they are back again in Mountfathom.

A party.

What sort of party?

I do not know.

342

They stand in a gallery looking down – a crowd of exotic colour below, so many people all crammed close to the double doors of *The World*. The sense of waiting is palpable, and the excitement of the assembly makes both boys smile.

Killian says, Lot of people here – wonder why?

And somehow Luke knows. They are here for me.

Killian asks, What for?

Luke says, For my Naming.

And they stand and watch as a voice makes an announcement and the smoky curtain rises and doors of *The World* open and the guests move in – such an excited tide. And Luke feels as though he has been living always in the world like this – both within it and at the same time hovering above, always observing-exploring-asking.

Killian asks, Can we do something here that might help save the House?

Luke says, Perhaps.

When?

When they will least expect it.

Do not ruin such a night as this – it will solve nothing.

Leave. Be sensible now about this. Depart while you still have some chance!

It is snowing and Luke sees the anguish in the eyes of his mother and father – the knowledge. They knew: they knew everything, always.

But still Luke longs for them to recognise and acknowledge him so says, Listen to me now – none of this will last. There is no safe place, not even at Mountfathom. Remember these things!

But he knows the past takes no heed of the future. He is neither a ghost nor a Trace but only a threat. No one wants to know – no one wishes to be forewarned. Luke doesn't blame them.

Let's go, says Killian, taking Luke's hand.

And it is the fear Luke sees in the eyes of those around that makes him flee – makes him run and become lost once more in the dark.

Keep going! We need to keep searching!

The Gloaming teems with memory of Mountfathom now, and the boys arrive in so many scenes. See Luke at so many ages.

The Amazon: As a three year old with stuffed toys in hand – tapir and capybara. Beside, a smoke-coloured cat lounging in a patch of bright sun.

Berlin: A little older, opening the doors of a large wardrobe to hear bursts of Bach – a blaring that ceases when he shuts the doors. Laughing and laughing with the joy of it all . . . and opening the doors again . . .

Atlantis: On his belly on an aquamarine carpet, maybe seven or eight years old now and pretending to swim, arms thrashing and bare feet kicking. Morrigan lies beside as though drowning – on her back, tail doing a lazy flick.

The World: Seated at a table with so many people – cousins and Aunt and Uncle and the Driochta, and a group of soldiers. Aunt Nancy suddenly rises, announces she has had enough and moves fast to the door. The soldier asks is the son of Mountfathom mute. Luke thinks, Yes. I am now. I can do nothing.

Killian whispers, It's pointless – we can't change anything here. We can't do a thing! Where do we go?

And before Luke can speak he hears a whisper –

Now you must face me – now you must see the truth.

Yes – we must face this Monster.

And as soon as the decision is made, a new way opens – like the burrow for some massive animal. The boys step into it together, hand in hand. Crimson light and emerald falls on walls that churn and squirm with so much sickly iridescence.

Killian falters but Luke says, Don't be afraid of it – that's what it wants.

And on and further in, and finally they feel more than see; they hear –

You have at last come to face me – to know the truth.

Yes, says Luke. I need to know how to save Mountfathom.

The darkness boils, trembles and groans, and there is the sense of something now, a creature of immense size and strength. Size of a mountain, deep as an ocean, fathomless and cold as space . . .

The Monster says, *You think that is what awaits you? You believe that is the answer and the end of things?*

Yes, says Luke. I believe it.

Silence.

And suddenly not a single word but all words – the beginning and end of all language! All Tragedy

Worry

Hope

Fear

Joy

Heartache

Wondering

Pain

Loss

Love

all pours from some void.

Luke feels as though his skin is being slowly stripped, thoughts plundered, jaw bolted shut, his only role to listen and learn and listen more. Only to obey; to hope to understand the truth of human feeling.

We have to get away from it, says Killian. Let's go!

But Luke will not move – he knows that the fear of this thing will only increase its power. He must withstand it, will not give it more to feast on. And the longer he stands and refuses, the more he sees – there is light beyond the dark. Behind the monster, there is truth. And he knows it is where he must go.

I do not fear it, Luke tells the monster. I will face whatever is ahead, whatever you are guarding. I need to see it. I am not afraid.

You are such frail beings – standing lost between one great dark and the next. Such threadbare souls!

Yes, says Luke. Now, please – give me what I want. Show me what I need to see!

And like a Spell Dismissed, the Monster steps aside. Shrinks and cringes as though Luke is brandishing a weapon, which perhaps he is.

And he and Killian are allowed to step forward and into the light.

We have arrived. This is what we need to see.

They stand in the gardens of Mountfathom at night. Stars prick the sky, cold and numerous.

Killian asks, Is this the past or the future or what?

Luke says nothing. He sees the Rise and the Temple of Ivory, and whispers, I do not know when we are, not yet, but I know where we need to go.

They start up the slope. Ground is brittle with cold.

Killian asks: How did you know what to do with that creature?

It wants to show us the truth, says Luke. And I want to see it, no matter what it is.

What if we don't get shown how to save Mountfathom?

Luke does not reply.

They gain the top of the Rise. And they see now how far they have travelled.

Mountfathom is no more. They see from their height only two walls still standing. Archway where the front door once stood – how many years ago? – is managing to stand too, a feeble testament. All else is overgrown and dark and broken. A place abandoned; appears unreal, like a House a child might make, or imagine.

Killian says: It doesn't survive.

Luke says: No. But nothing does. He understands now.

Luke's gaze drops to the ivory gravestones – slim as fingernails now, and planted at dejected angles. Shrunken but sending long shadows. And one of these draws Luke attention.

Killian sees first and says, No. Don't look!

I must, says Luke. I cannot be afraid. I've lost almost everything already.

He stoops, places his fingers in the grooves and feels –

LUKE MOUNTFATHOM

Dates engraved too, a line of poetry below. But these details don't matter; it is the fact of his death that strikes Luke. That makes him lie down on the cold earth beside his own grave and say, Mountfathom is finished. Everything ends.

There can be more, says Killian. He lies down beside Luke. He says, It is not just being born and dying.

Luke begins to weep. Feels as though his skin is shrinking, bones splintering, blood in his veins molten but slowing, slowing; taking its time to enter and depart his heart.

He says, I need to rest now.

Killian puts an arm around him and says, And I'll stay with you.

Luke dreams.

Imagines lying on the ground with Killian and the world hurrying through season after season with such speed, laying them with winter frost and spring and summer sunshine; bedding them in the fallen leaves of autumn, and once more the snow of winters . . . and all the while the stars overhead whirl too fast, become only white scars on the dark.

Luke dreams that he stands, shakes off the cold. He sees that the Temple of Ivory is not ivory now but bones. An old habit, he names each, seeing femur and rib and wing and beak and collarbone and skull . . . The doors open silently. He steps inside.

Within is a towering tree – bark of cracked silver, trunk wide and branches sprawling. Roots ancient and bold beneath his feet, breaking ground. And on each bough rests a burden of heavy darkness – a black bud, tender when Luke reaches out and touches.

A sudden crack and he steps away.

One of the buds sheds a soft shell in two clean halves. Reveals a papery carapace that unpeels, and tucked inside like tender fruit – a wrinkled coil of flesh. Silent thing . . . and then such a wail! Such a scream! It is an infant shaking its fists and crying, craving attention.

Luke watches. Knows what is next.

Takes only a minute. The wailing child on the tree grows quickly older, becomes bearded like a vegetable left too long in the ground, darkening and rotting on the vine until only a cold husk is left. It drops and strikes the ground, and softly disperses on the air like pale spore.

Like dust.

Like only dust.

Take me to the water.

Luke wakes from his dream and speaks before thinking.

It is morning. There is colour, and sunlight, and birdsong.

Killian sits up and asks, Where are we now?

Luke knows where he is; feels that they are no longer in the future, but the past. And knows what he must do next.

He asks Killian, Please. Take me to the water.

Asks because he feels so tired, so wearied.

Luke says, I cannot make it by myself.

Alright, says Killian. He looks so tired as well, but summons enough energy to stoop and lifts Luke into his arms.

Please, says Luke. Down to the lagoon.

Why there? asks Killian.

And if Luke knows anything now he knows this.

Because there are two people I need to see.

So much sound! As they make their way down the slope of the Rise, Luke feels so aware of everything – brightness of the blossom and heart-stopping swiftness of each bird and the careful industry of every insect. Everything fizzes and shivers in glory and blaze.

Luke thinks, Perhaps this is something. Perhaps this is something that never ends.

And almost too soon, Luke sees.

By the blue-green water, beside the statue of the Faerie King, they are waiting.

I can walk now, Luke tells Killian. Thank you. I would like to walk to them.

Killian settles Luke on his feet and steps back.

I am here, says Luke. I am here.

Already his parents are smiling at him. Are weeping for him. Are happy and heartbroken – burdened with such knowledge because they know, have always known, that Mountfathom will fail. And when Luke arrives by the water, he says, I fought my way here. I was trying to find a way to save Mountfathom, but I have failed.

Perhaps not, says his father. Do not be so hard on yourself, my son.

Did you meet what was in the dark? asks his mother. The Monster?

I did, says Luke. What is it exactly?

You tell us your ideas, says his father.

Is it death? asks Luke.

Perhaps, says his mother.

Or perhaps life? says his father. Perhaps the thing we must all face when we leave behind the familiar?

Perhaps, says Luke, it doesn't matter what name I put on it. What mattered more was how I looked at it.

And both his parents smile with such pride.

You have come so far, says his mother. You have learned so much.

Now a sudden pain claws at Luke's insides – now an ache, now a tearing at his skin as though something wants to snatch him from where he stands.

You cannot stay here, his father tells him. You cannot forever wander.

I must go back? asks Luke.

As if you did not already know, says his mother with a smile.

Another attack of pain and Luke almost folds –

What is happening to me?

His mother says simply: It is not so easy to return to the place you began.

But I haven't done enough, says Luke. He is weeping, has to fight his own sorrow to say, breathless: Nothing is saved. Mountfathom has fallen. Everything is lost. Everything dies.

And yet, said his mother, here we are. Here we are reunited. Take solace from that, my love. There are no certain answers in this world. No final thing to be learned. There are only the days, and how you best live them.

There must be something else, says Luke.

That's our boy, says his father. Always questioning!

They stand in silence and Luke knows that time is short; sees the clouds darkening, knows that soon will come the storm.

He asks, How can I go on now? How can I keep going without you?

You will find your way, says his mother. And you are not alone now.

Her eyes leave Luke for the first time and wander to Killian, standing so many feet behind but yet still so close.

Is there no answer? Luke asks his father. You always had some answer.

As I recall, says his father, I usually only have questions, do I not?

Then the break of thunder.

A scream and Luke turns and looks across the lagoon, sees himself standing at the far side, watching. Sees his cousin Rose run free of the patch of rhubarb to embrace her cousin.

It starts to rain.

His mother and father take each other's hands.

And his father says to him softly, My son, perhaps we can say this: that the brightness of this afternoon may pass, but it will not die. Perhaps a person's happiness can outlive them. Perhaps, in some way, we shall always stand here together in the sun.

So much dark, two boys standing at the heart of it –
There is nothing more to see.
The Gloaming has given up its secrets!
And yet . . .
So much more to come.

I cannot go back.

What? asks Killian. Where will you go?

I must do what my father wanted, says Luke and from his pocket takes his father's notebook. He says, I shall restore wonder and imagination to Ireland. I have a feeling that, in the future, we are going to need as much of it as possible.

They stand in silence.

Luke asks, Come with me?

Why? asks Killian, and already is half-turning away. What for?

The adventure! says Luke.

My place for belonging is not the same as yours, says Killian.

It can be, says Luke.

I don't want to keep wandering, says Killian, and keeps his face turned away because he is crying now. Tries to keep it from his voice when he says, I should find my father, find my own way in the world.

And at their feet, two paths are beginning to creep in two different directions – one crimson and one emerald.

Luke: Take my father's key. Keep it. It will lead you back.

Killian: Where to now?

Luke: Home.

I have no home, says Killian. He closes his eyes.

And already – so very slowly – he feels Luke's hand leaving his. Hears a whisper, You will find home. Just hope for it. And when you're ready, you will.

And when Killian opens his eyes once more, he is alone.

Sees only this final thing: a single starling flying fast, following the light of the crimson path, vanishing into the dark.

PART SIX

THE GHOST

Goreland Hall
Co Wexford
15th June 1926

Dear Luke,

I'm being followed. They're looking for me.

*Looks like I'm still on the run. Maybe always
will be!*

I'll tell how it happened.

*I was standing in the breakfast room when the bell
went and one of the maids went to the front door. I was
all for earwigging but one of the gentleman guests (he's
no gentleman though, only a mean old bastard who
seems to have taken a bit of a shine to me) called me
over asking for more coffee. Drinks gallons of the bloody
stuff! (I can't stomach the taste of coffee no matter how
many times I try it.) Anyway, he calls me over saying,
'Here, boy!' And I went and I was pouring the man's
coffee when I heard someone in the hall saying, 'I'd like*

to speak to the head of the hotel, if I may. Right away.
It's very urgent.'

And I was as sure as anything soon as I heard him
that it was a Peeler.

I heard the maid who answered the door saying, 'I'll
go get her. Want to wait here or what?'

I tell you, this used to be a big grand place (but
not as grand or big as your place was), but the staff
here are not a bit like they were at Mountfathom. The
maids are cheeky as hell and they like nothing more
than sitting skiving or when new guests arrive they
always make sure they're about so they can have a
good gawk at any fellas. They all have dreams of getting
married and getting out and going to America. That's
the big dream for most of them – America! I remember
this movie star came two weeks back to stay and you
should've seen them all drooling and falling over each
other to take his breakfast up! First time I've seen them
all so keen to work. I didn't recognise the fella. He had
a driver and two people to look after him and a big red
car like a cherry on wheels. I used to be fierce into films
but not any more. I don't like spending so much time
sitting in the dark watching things happen that don't
really exist.

Anyway, Clodagh (she's the one in charge here)
went to the front door and I heard her chatting to the
Peeler and she told him to come in and she took him
into her wee office to chat. They were in there a long
time. I still had to keep going around pouring coffee

*like normal and collecting plates with the hands on me
shaking like leaves!*

*Eventually Clodagh and this Peeler came out of her
office behind the front desk and she was saying, 'Yes,
Detective. I will certainly, Detective. Absolutely. If I
hear anything I shall let you know.'*

This detective tipped his hat and left.

*When Clodagh checked the breakfast room to make
sure everything was ship-shape she gave me a bit of
a funny look. She always gives funny looks though
so it could be nothing. I can't ever tell what she's
thinking. She said, 'Alright there?' I said, 'Yes, madam,
everything is in order.' And she said, 'I should hope so.'*

She's a sharp one.

*I'll keep my head down now, I think, and just keep
working away and hopefully it'll all be grand.*

*I hope you get to read this. I know you probably
don't have much time. You're probably very busy but if
you could maybe send a letter back, I would like that.*

Your friend,

Killian

Goreland Hall
Co Wexford
17th June 1926

Dear Luke,

A new fella started here today called Johnny. He'll be a waiter like me but a barman too because he has some experience of that. He used to work in The Belvedere in Dublin so he's used to hard work, he says. He's sharing my room but has a fierce amount of stuff with him – he likes reading and must have about two dozen different books with him. He says I can borrow them if I'm careful and don't break the spines. Your father would've liked him – he was into his books in a big way, I remember.

Johnny tells me he's trying to get himself educated and reading is the best way there is. Says he'll hopefully go on and do something with his life. He has it down to go to London because he says there's more to do and see

and that's where it's all happening now. He says there
are all sorts in London and it isn't as straight-laced
and uptight as Ireland. He doesn't want to be a servant
forever, he says. I said to him, 'You're only arrived and
you want to go already!' He says to me, 'You always
need to have a plan! Nothing lasts forever so you need
to be ready to know where you want to go next. Life's
too short for messing.'

Well, he's right there. He seems decent enough.

The detective hasn't come back so that's good news.
When the phone rings at reception I'm always keeping
an ear out to hear what's being said but I don't think
he's phoned either.

I've been at Goreland Hall a month now and I feel
well settled in. It's better than the last place I worked
in Belfast. It was a pub and there used to be awful
fights in it especially at shutting-up time. It's mad up
North now – all the hassle over the Union and people
disagreeing, I can't see it calming down anytime soon.
I left there because I didn't like it. I also left because
someone was pinching money out of the till and
drinking between times and they started pointing the
finger so I says to them, 'To hell with this! I'm away!'

Best get out before the arguments start. I couldn't be
bothered with it.

I only stayed one more night in Belfast after that.
Thumbed my way to Dublin and then Enniscorthy
and I heard they were looking for people with
experience of serving customers so I came here and got

*a job just like that! Always with Lady Luck on my
side, you know me.*

I'd like to get a bit more educated too.

*Been five years since, but I still remember well
the animals you showed me when I first got to
Mountfathom. Remember you had them all labelled
and all? I asked Johnny if he had any animal books
and he says all he has are* Moby Dick *and* The Jungle
Book *so he'll lend me them to read.*

I'll leave it at that for now. Write if you get a minute.

Your good friend,

Killian

Dear Luke,

You'll not believe this but I found out today I'm
working with someone from Mountfathom! She's called
Clodagh and I think I mentioned her before? She was
the one interviewed me for the position so I met her the
first day I started but didn't know her background till
now. What kind of luck would you call that? She's a
sharp thing, but I don't mind that. She's fair enough, if
you do as she says. Plenty don't though and you should
hear her shouting! Sometimes she swears like a trooper,
and I said to her today, 'I bet they didn't let you talk
like that at Mountfathom!'

She gave me a look and didn't say anything.

She says she remembers when you were born. She
told me about the biggest, strangest party ever at

*Mountfathom! (I didn't tell her I had seen some of it –
how could I go about explaining that to her or anyone!)
She said they were cleaning the whole place for days
and even your mother mucked in but your father just
sat in his library like always, reading. She says she
never saw the like of it then or ever since. She says she
still has wild dreams about it. Then she says to me
suddenly that she thinks she recognises me. And when
I ask her where from she says, 'You were there at the
party. That night, I remember you.' Then she looked to
shake herself a bit and said, 'But of course you couldn't
have been. You would've been hardly even born!'*

*I said, 'I know, aye. That would be a strange thing,
wouldn't it?'*

*She says to me, 'It would be strange indeed. But it
was a strange place, Mountfathom.'*

*I don't say much. I don't want to let on how much
time I spent there. I tell her I just visited once because
my father was a tea-merchant in Belfast and he had
some dealings with Lord Mountfathom. I says to her, 'I
was only there the once and a good few years ago but I
got a powerful impression of the place!'*

*She says, 'It's a very different place now of course.
Like most of the Big Houses it was destroyed. Like this
one was, once upon a time. It'd be very different now.'*

*I says, 'Maybe it'll be a hotel like this one. Would
you go back to work there if it was?'*

*I don't think she liked that idea. She got up right
quick then and said she better get back to doing the*

rounds else the maids will be sitting having a gossip and the rooms won't be done properly. I said, 'Aye, probably best.' And she gives me a long look.

On second thoughts, maybe I'll keep my distance from her. Wouldn't want the poor woman to think she's losing her mind!

Johnny says he doesn't like her. He calls her a 'job's worth'. Says she isn't educated and shouldn't be put in charge of people just because she's spent her life at places being a servant. I said to him, 'She's good at what she does. She has experience.' He didn't think much of that. He says being a good servant is about as worthwhile as being a good toilet brush. I think that was a bit harsh of him but I didn't say anything. I don't want to start any arguments. Want to keep my head down, as I say.

But Johnny and me have great chats. We were awake the pair of us last night till after twelve talking about life and other things. All the mysteries of the universe! He likes talking about science and religion. He's reading a book at the moment that he just got delivered called On the Origin of Species. Have you read it? It's about animals too so I might read it after him. (I'm struggling with Moby Dick – there's a fierce amount of water in it and not enough of the whale. I told Johnny and he says to me, 'That's the whole point! Tension!'). He says he's agnostic (I got him to write it down for me I can get the spelling right). He says this means he does not believe in no God or yes definitely there is a God. I told him my problem wasn't God because it makes no odds to me whether God exists or not – each to their own. I says to him, 'My problem is all the other stuff. The Church and all the money they make!'

I said to him I just cannot be believing in Heaven or Hell.

I tell you why I can't – because it doesn't let people change. Some ones I've known have been real wicked but then when you don't expect it they do something nice, so where do they go? Heaven or Hell? Where will I go? I thieved a lot before Mountfathom but haven't since. Or not much anyway – I took a few coins from the collection box when I left the chapel after speaking to that priest, but he deserved it. It's not even his money anyway! I know you're reading this thinking I'm very stupid but I look at my life like this – I was born in the tenements and I got out, so that's things changing. But if you die and end up down below in Hell you're going nowhere, are you? Doesn't say anywhere in the Bible that you can be put there but maybe if you do some good work or help people, you can work your way up and have a shot at getting into Heaven, does it? There's no early release for good behaviour when you go to Hell, is there? You're feckin stuck.

Makes me feel trapped just thinking about it.

Anyway, I better go. Johnny just knocked on the door and said Clodagh is looking for me. You'd like him. He's interested in lots of things. To be honest with you,

he's helping me get through the days. I look forward to
the nights when we can sit and have a smoke and chat.
He's a bit interested in what I have to say. We get on
well together and I can talk to him very easy.

   I'll say goodbye for now.

Still your best mate,

Killian

Dear Luke,

*I nearly choked when I saw the headline on the front
of the* Enquirer *today! Usually just all that boring
political stuff but here was something that I knew
about! I wanted to shout when I saw it. Instead I just
kept it all in. I tore out the headline and enclose it
with this letter.*

GYANTS SIGHTED NEAR KILARNEY:
SPECIES REAPPEARS AFTER
FIFTY-YEAR ABSENCE!

*It's you, isn't it? Like you said about restoring
imagination to Ireland – this is what your father
wanted to do and now you're doing it!*

*Will have to stop there. Clodagh wants a word
with me.*

*So I've decided – today is my last day here! I've had
enough. I know you're thinking – you can't just leave
a job just like that! But I can. I have to. I saw that
headline in the paper this morning and it inspired me!*

Also, I can't stand that Clodagh.

*She called me into her office this morning and was
being more stiff and sarcastic than usual. She sat me
down and says to me very serious, 'Now look. There's
been some whispers. Some hints of an impropriety and
we can't have that here. Not at Goreland Hall.'*

I says to her, 'Whispers about what? About me?'

*She says, 'I won't go into details but I think maybe
you should think about seeking another position.'*

*I says, 'Well, I would like you to tell me more about
what these whispers are, Missus!'*

*She said, 'Don't call me Missus. And please let's
not embarrass ourselves. Now. I'll write you a good
reference and you'll get your full pay up until the end
of the week. By the end of the day Friday you should
see that you've taken all your things from your room
and moved on.'*

*I sat there. I could've said a lot. I could've said
how no one works as hard as me – how the other
fellas spend most of their time necking with the maids
and swiping food from the breakfast trays. I could've
said how I know what she gets up to herself – I've*

seen her slipping pennies here and pennies there into her handbag. Or about how she always reeks of the drink. Tell you the truth, I could have called her a cow and spat in her eye, and still I'd have walked out with my head held high and more dignity than anybody else here!

But I didn't.

Times like this is when you realise you've changed. I'm not like I was. I don't know if I like it or if it's a good thing or not. I used to always say what I wanted (you'll remember that, I'm sure!) and to hell with what people thought. And now, well I don't know what I am.

I did say to Clodagh, 'I am more respectable than any of the rest of you put together.'

She looked at me and had a big smirk on her face when she said, 'Is that right? So tell me this – why is there a detective from the North down looking for you? Something about some thieving and someone being stabbed in Belfast at a bar you used to work at? What's that about, Mr High And Mighty And Respectable?'

I could've punched her but I didn't. I just left.

Mountfathom has done this to me. Has made me soft.

I feel like I'm somewhere between things all the time. You won't like me reminding you of Mr Findlater but I keep thinking about something he said to me. I think he might've been right about some things even though he was a real bastard too.

I think when you're young you can be whatever you like and no one bothers about it. They like it when you get new ideas about things you want to do. But when you get a bit older, people want you to know where you belong. They want you to be put in your place and stay there.

I won't say goodbye to Johnny. I'm still reading Moby Dick *so I'll take that with me. I'm sure he can afford another copy when he gets educated and goes to London and makes it big. It's a bit his fault anyway, all this.*

I'll pack my things up – there isn't much except Moby Dick *and some clothes and the photo of my mum when she was a girl and something I keep to myself and will never show anyone so I won't even mention it in this letter in case someone reads it.*

I will leave here but not because I've been told to. I'll leave on my own terms because I want to. And what I want is to go back to what I was before.

What I want is to come back to Mountfathom.

Best wishes,

Killian

Dear Luke,

*I write to wish you Happy Birthday! I don't know
how I remembered but I did! When I get myself
sorted for a job and I see you next I'll take you out
for a drink or whatever you like. I'm in Dublin for a
couple of days just till I can get the fare for the train
to Belfast.*

*I saw another exciting headline today. Posh fella
left it on the bench beside me in the Green. I enclose
it here.*

FAERIE RATH APPEARS IN TIPPERARY:
GARDS SAY "GOOD FOLK" HAVE
BEEN SIGHTED AT NIGHT.
IS ANCIENT MAGIC
RETURNING TO IRELAND?

*I can't tell you how exciting it is to see you doing this
work and having these adventures! I hope I can get
involved too?*

*I'll try to get some sleep now. I don't sleep much. I
have nightmares. I didn't even know until Johnny woke
me up one night because he said I was making such a
racket screaming. He said I was crying too and saying
someone's name over and over. He says to me, 'Who's
Luke?' I had to tell him something so I said, 'He's my
friend. He's a good friend of mine.' He sat up with me
after that and we chatted but I didn't tell him much
about Mountfathom.*

*I'm glad I'm not in Dublin for long. It's a right tip!
Fierce dirty and everyone malingering (do you like
that word? I read it in the paper this morning) about
everything to do with politics and money.*

*But I don't like the idea particularly of being back in
Belfast either.*

*I thought I was a city person but I'm not sure I am
now – there's another change, you see! Or maybe it's
not changing and it's just growing up a bit and realising
a few things. I'm not sure where I belong at all but I'll
know it when I get there.*

*Now I'm spending the night outside the station. It's
cold and raining a bit but I spent a few hours in the
pub this evening so I'm well warmed! I won't write
much because it might come out like bollocks because
of the drink. 'Tis only the drink talking!' My da used to
say that. He was usually talking about himself!*

It's half three now and it's cold as sin but I have a blanket so I better go to sleep. I keep writing because it gives me something to do and not sit here brooding. My train leaves first thing for the North tomorrow so I'll be home and dry! I'll be in Belfast by midday. And then with a bit of my usual Lady Luck I'll be in Mountfathom by tomorrow night.

So I'll say bye and goodnight for now. I am on my way.

Your friend,

Killian (the Lucky)

Dear Luke,

Mountfathom is not the same. I am glad you are not here because you wouldn't want to see it. I don't know where in the world you are but I am happy you haven't come back. I have written these letters this past couple of weeks but I haven't posted any of them and I'm glad I didn't.

I thumbed a lift from Belfast to Bangor and then got another lift down the road. And that's another thing – any Sean or Paddy can come here now, no bother! Whatever Spells were on the place have gone. I arrived and some wild-looking children were running about in the gardens and swimming in the lagoon. Swinging off the trees and playing catch in the walled garden, no one there to tell them any different!

Them they saw me and started screaming (probably scared at the state of me).

I felt like a ghost.

Then some farmer comes along and says, 'Can I help you?'

Apparently he is the owner of the land.

I asked him how he had come by Mountfathom and he said that when the Lady went missing and the Lord died and their son couldn't be found, they didn't know what to do with the place. Then a will turned up that said if no one in the family could inherit the House then it was the rightful property of the staff. And the staff decided to sell the House and split the money between them. He tells me he has bought the whole site and is going to be building houses on it. He says he might rent them to people. And sure enough his two strapping young blond sons were marking out the foundations with string and wooden stakes. The farmer says to me, 'Do you know the place?'

I said, 'No. I just came for a look to see what was left of it.'

Then the farmer said, 'Strange, you aren't the only one. Sometimes there's some woman who comes to have a look about, goes picking through the ruin, even if I tell her stay away. I do it more for her benefit than mine – could collapse on her and then I'd be in some bother!'

'Who is she?' I asked him.

'Dunno. Looks like one of these Travellers – hair a mess, long red skirt on her. Earrings like little seashells. Doesn't say a word though. Just wanders around. Sometimes sheds a tear or two, and then before I know

it she's gone. Who she is – your guess is as good as mine, lad.'

I don't know when I might see you, Luke, but I wish it'd be soon.

Your friend,

Killian

Dear Luke,

I don't why know I am still writing to you. It doesn't make me feel better or make me understand things more. So I have decided – this will be my last letter.

I haven't left Mountfathom. I managed to get inside and there is still a lot of it here. The staircases for one thing, and some of the rooms – The Amazon and Valhalla *and I think* The Menagerie of the Dead *– but I don't want to go in there. I haven't gone up to the third floor either. Not yet anyway. And there are lots of other things that remind me of how it used to be. Things no one else would know about.*

I found where the library was but there are no books in there, just the pages. Stories all scattered everywhere. If I gathered them up and put them all together it might make one book and one story, but it wouldn't make sense, would it?

I got a shock today – an old friend appeared. I was sitting in the library and the next thing I see a rush like smoke somewhere in the corner and it's a cat trying to get at a mouse. A battered and bow-legged big cat with turquoise eyes! I was so glad to see her. She's sitting beside me now as I write this and I'd say she misses you too.

I saw you today. Or I thought I did. I can't stop seeing ghosts. I can't stop myself waiting for someone to appear. I keep thinking I catch you out of the corner of my eye. But then I turn around and you've gone. You're away running into the dark like we did together. I can't catch you.

I know you aren't reading this but I know you'll return. I will stay here until you come.

How do I know you'll return? Because I need you.

Today I saw a rose. Don't get the wrong idea – it wasn't a big deal but there it was anyway. It was yellow and very clean and fierce delicate. Everything is growing whatever way it likes now in the grounds. (Mr Hooker would be annoyed if he could see it!) And then there was this flower. I daren't touch it. I looked at it and I decided something – I cannot live any longer like this. I would prefer the dark.

I've waited until night and I've opened my bag of things I brought and I tore up the photograph of my mother and found some matches to burn it. I tore up the clothes and burned those too. What do I need them for now? I left the copy of Moby Dick. *I didn't finish it. I have put it in the library for someone to find.*

I have my decision made.

But then a funny thing – I take out the last thing, the only thing I own now apart from the shirt on my back. It is the key your father gave me. It has been dark for years. I've tried lots of times, Luke – mightn't believe me but I did. I have spent so much time thinking of where home might be. But it never showed me.

Now it does. Now it is glowing.

Maybe it is because it knows it is back at Mountfathom. And I know now what I have to do.

Your best friend,

Killian

Outside the Dark Door
23rd June 1926

Dear Luke,

I don't know where you are. I don't have a clue where I'm heading to either. But that makes no change, does it? I never did know. But I am not afraid. I am excited. It is not such a bad thing to be lost for a while.

You said to me that one day I would find home. You said it would only happen when I was ready. Now I know where to look for it. I know that it isn't here or anywhere else – it isn't always a place.

What I believe is that when I step into that dark that you will be waiting for me. It has been dark for so long, and now I have this light to lead me.

I am going to bring Morrigan with me on this adventure – I wonder what she'll make of it.

I'll stop writing now. There's a time for words and a time for doing.

I have all I need in the world – a door and a key and the big Unknown!

And I know what I'll be looking for.

I only hope you'll be there – waiting for me in the dark.

Nigel McDowell

Nigel McDowell grew up in County Fermanagh, rural Northern Ireland, and as a child spent most of his time battling boredom, looking for adventure - crawling through ditches, climbing trees, devising games to play with his brother and sister, and reading. His favourite book as a child was The Witches by Roald Dahl.

After graduating with a degree in English he spent almost two years living and working in Australia and New Zealand with his long term partner, Chris. With him he took a small notebook containing notes about a boy called 'Bruno Atlas', and a seaside town called 'Pitch End'. When he returned to Ireland after his travels, one notebook had multiplied into many, and eventually his notes for Tall Tales from Pitch End filled a large cardboard box. TALL TALES FROM PITCH END was Nigel's first novel, followed by THE BLACK NORTH.

THE HOUSE OF MOUNTFATHOM was Nigel's final novel, before his death in early 2016 at the age of thirty-four.

HOT KEY BOOKS

Thank you for choosing a Hot Key book.

If you want to know more about our authors
and what we publish, you can find us online.

You can start at our website

www.hotkeybooks.com

And you can also find us on:

We hope to see you soon!